Praise for THE TI

“A delightful, cinematic read: A perfect [illegible] action, and drama. Charlie’s journey will make you laugh and cry, and you’ll welcome both.” — **Erica Arvold, Film Producer and Emmy®-Nominated Casting Director**

“*The Titanic Test* is a gripping adventure/love story, a page-turner that left me hoping for a sequel.” — **Anita Sharpe, Pulitzer Prize-Winning Journalist**

“A beautiful, inventive story woven into the *Titanic*’s inaugural voyage. The imaginative time travel created the opportunity to experience the journey of the *Titanic* in a new way, and I felt so many emotions along the way. [It] is a book worthy of expanding to other entertainment platforms, like TV and film.” — **Nancy Silberkleit, Co-CEO, Archie Comics**

“This is time travel done right: a new look at an iconic event in history, filled with plenty of heart, romance, and adventure. If you love strong female characters, fun historical details, and edge-of-your-seat action, then you won’t be able to put this down.” — **Rachel Carter, Author of the *So Close to You* Series**

“Simpson has done her research; she brings the *Titanic* to life with sumptuous, detailed descriptions of the ship’s décor, the fashions on display, the food, and many of its notable passengers and crew. In addition to being an action-packed adventure, the narrative raises a quintessential question of morality: Can Charlie, knowing that some 1,500 people will soon die in the frigid Atlantic, really refrain from trying to prevent the tragedy?” — ***Kirkus Reviews***

# THE TITANIC TEST

## A LOVE STORY

ANN K. SIMPSON

ISBNs: 979-8-9915402-0-9 (hardcover);
979-8-9915402-1-6 (paperback);
979-8-9915402-2-3 (Kindle e-book)

Library of Congress Control Number: 2024919685





Printed in the United States for the US market.



Framing Hill Media
Washington, DC

Visit the author at annksimpson.com.

For Mina

*When you and I behind the Veil are past,*
*Oh but the long long while the World shall last,*
*Which our Coming and Departure heeds*
*As much as Ocean of a pebble-cast.*

From the *Rubáiyát of Omar Khayyám*
Translated into English by Edward FitzGerald

An edition of which lies at the bottom of the
North Atlantic

# one
## present day

Bobbing at the edge of the surf zone off Oahu's Waimea Bay, I straddled my board and watched slate-gray storm clouds gather on the horizon. They were rolling toward me just like my dreaded junior year and its mysterious Junior Year Test. I closed my eyes for a moment, pushing aside thoughts of what was coming in the fall, concentrating instead on the summer days stretched out in front of me and the sensation of fading sunlight on my shoulders.

Then, hoping to catch a last ride of the afternoon, I spotted THE ONE as it sprang to life in a gathering wall of water. I pointed the nose of my board toward the shore and paddled hard, glancing back to make sure my tail was perpendicular to the wave. When I felt the surging Pacific gaining speed behind me, up I went. I popped into my stance with legs bent, more weight on my back foot than the front, arms out.

I found myself full-out frontside tube riding for the first time, the white-edged wave curling over my head like a giant hand made of liquid glass. Time stood still in an epic freeze-frame moment—at least until the hand closed over me and I wiped out, tumbling into the surf. I twisted and turned, forgetting which way was up in the swirling whitewater. Holding my breath until I thought my chest might explode, I spotted the sun and kicked, propelling myself up and out of the water. I pulled salty air into my lungs and coughed. Then I raked the hair out of my face, turning to see my wave receding from where it had washed up on the shore. My father stood knee deep in the ocean, leaning in with his hand shading his eyes. When he spotted me, he flashed a relieved smile and fist pumped like I'd just won the Hawaiian Pro.

Back in Malibu after that island vacation, the rest of my long, flip-flop summer had been perfect—bingeing sci-fi with Sammy, my chatty little brother; hanging out with my best friend, Tiana; and surfing along the Southern California coast until my fingers shriveled like prunes. Such a dreamy school break really should've ended slowly and casually, instead of with a jarring alarm at zero dark thirty and a bleary-eyed stumble through the closet. Wishing I was back in Hawaii, or anywhere else really, I stood in the bathroom with my hands on the cool stone counter, delaying the inevitable. Like a tsunami I knew was coming—but surprised me anyway—my junior year at Windline Academy had finally arrived. And I was a wreck.

In seventh grade, I got so nervous before going onstage in the school play that I threw up. Distant cousins of those nerves had shown up with their suitcases recently, ready to move in. Only this time, I'd be facing the Junior Year Test instead of a friendly audience with low expectations. The committee of teachers, shrinks, and "developmental coaches" at Windline could literally force me to spend the better part of the year surviving eighteenth-century Siberia. Maybe I'd find my true calling on the Russian tundra, huddled by a fire with frostbitten toes.

I wondered if my genes, including the "lucky" genetic variations that allowed me to time travel, contained my whole life story before I even started living it. Mom and Dad weren't helping. They had some special embedded parent code, like invisible ink that shows up when two perfectly reasonable people have a child. Next thing you know, they're making their mostly normal kid attend a school for time travelers, even though she hated "real" time traveling—talking to strangers straight out of dried-up oil paintings about field dressings or the price of grain.

In my opinion, history and art could be learned while comfortably seated in a plastic chair in a classroom—no need to experience them in real time. But my teachers would say, "The best way to shape the present is to experience the past." How were we supposed to shape the present when we were practically never in it?

Truth was, all that separated me from the next person was the equivalent of a typo, and I wasn't special—or in need of a special school. The students at the overly high on itself, secret society of Windline Academy all had rare genes like mine. But 90 percent of them also had a supercharged extrovert one that made them the perfect go-getter time travelers. All those wow personalities in one place made for exhausting school parties.

Several insistent honks outside interrupted my thoughts, and I dragged myself out of the bathroom, running with heavy footsteps down the hardwood stairs.

"Good morning, Charlie!" Mom said brightly, a total morning person once she had two espressos on board.

"G'morning, Mom." Then, before I even hit the bottom stair, she pointed her camera and—SNAP.

"Come on, Mom. I gotta go," I said, blinking from the flash. "Quinn's outside."

SNAP, SNAP.

"Mom, how long have you had that camera? Does it use FILM?"

"Don't sass the camera, Charlotte Landers. How many times does a mother get to see her daughter off to junior year? You're so grown up and so . . . gosh, I don't know . . . stunning!" Mom stood staring as if she'd sculpted me out of clay.

"Stunning" was a classic parental exaggeration. I had spent extra time getting ready, surfacing dusty hair tools from deep in the bathroom junk drawer, the cords gummy from who knows what. A weird kind of magic had happened to my body over the summer, as if my seventeenth birthday was some kind of finish line for my growth hormones. I'd started June with spindly legs, gangly arms, overly large and wide-set hazel eyes, and zippo for curves. Then all my quirky parts miraculously came together with the icing on top of actual breasts. I almost resembled both a human and a female. Plus the summer sun had given my dark brown hair free highlights.

I wanted to make the most of the new me while I had the energy to care, which was probably a day, maybe three, tops. Plus, it was tradition for everyone to take tons of pictures on our first day of school. Soon everyone in my high school class would be scattered across time for their Junior Year Tests, and we might not see each other for weeks or even months. Some of us might never make it back.

"Where's the towhead?" I asked, referring to Sammy, who was starting sixth grade.

"Your father took him already."

"Excellent." One small annoyance down, another big one to go.

Mom lifted the camera one last time. "Love you, honey!" SNAP.

The horn sounded outside again. *Patience much, Quinn?* Quinn was sort of ever present, but not by choice. Mom had plotted with Connie, her college bestie, to throw

Quinn and me together from my first breath. It's like I was conceived to be his forever plus-one. Their plan wasn't working out too great at this point.

Grabbing my backpack, I blew Mom a kiss. She followed me outside, waving as if I were a first grader who'd never left home before. *Good thing I love that woman, because sometimes I really want to go back in time and discourage her from having children.*

I ran down the walkway, leaping over Sammy's skateboard—the only thing out of place on our manicured front lawn—and jumped into Quinn's white, open-top Jeep Wrangler idling at the curb. Thanks to the quarter inch of height I'd gained, I misjudged the entry and my head grazed the top of the doorframe.

"Easy there," Quinn said, never wasting a chance to give me crap. He was freakishly handsome as ever in an annoying European-soccer-player-turned-underwear-model kind of way, with beach-boy sandy brown hair that brushed his shoulders.

"I got it," I insisted, heat rising in my cheeks.

My own car couldn't show up soon enough. On my birthday over the summer, in between cake and Sammy's sad but adorable boy band concert in the backyard, Mom and Dad had promised to get me a car after I passed my Junior Year Test.

"You SURE you got it, Charlie Chicken?"

"You do realize you've literally called me 'Charlie Chicken' since I was six years old, right?" All because I wouldn't eat a goldfish when he'd dared me to. For the record, he wouldn't do it either, even though he'd said the fish was just sushi waiting to happen. Everyone knew you didn't name your sushi.

"Been that long, huh?" he said, shifting into drive. "Then it's sort of our thing. It's history."

I glared at him. "Yeah, history, as in past—not future," I said, defensive weapons coming online. "Might be time to move on from the goldfish incident."

"Nah," he said. "If the fish fits . . . and all that. Besides, somebody's gotta have a pet name for you. I mean, come on, it's a sign of love," he said sarcastically, stepping on the accelerator, "and someone's gotta love you besides your mom." He gestured with his head toward my waving mother as we pulled away.

"You love so many girls, Quinn. It's hard to keep track," I said, watching a house with a red tile roof slip by. "I'm just grateful you can fit me in."

"You're welcome." He laughed, cranking up UCLA's college radio station. Then he asked loudly over his tunes, "So you excited about your JY Test?"

Was Quinn actually making conversation? He'd grunted at me or talked on his phone to one girlfriend or another my whole sophomore year—at least when he wasn't away taking his own test.

"Not really excited, no," I replied.

Actually, I'd considered running away, which for a time traveler was as easy as sneaking into the family safe for a time pin. Money wouldn't be hard to come by either, considering a stock trading windfall could be whipped up with allowance money and a few short trips back in time. "Can you—uh—give me any hints about what to expect?" I asked, half trying to keep this bizarre thing called "conversation" going.

Another sideways glance. "You know I can't tell you anything about the test, Charlie. Just trust the process."

"Trust the process? Kids have died!"

"You won't die."

"So you're saying no one has ever died?"

"I'm saying that's rare. And you won't be one of them."

"Whatever," I said. "They probably sent you to 1970s Italy to drink wine and make out with gorgeous Italian girls. You know, so you'd have a little variety in your life."

"Doesn't sound too bad, actually, but you really think the one thing I needed to shape my future was girls? There are plenty of those here."

"Right."

"What about you?" Quinn's bright swim-in-me blue eyes stood out against the perfectly formed canvas of his tanned face. They scanned me up and down like he hadn't seen me all summer. In reality, he'd seen me when Connie had dragged him to my birthday party.

"What *about* me?" I asked. I did my own scan just in case, and everything seemed in order. I wore Windline's standard-issue white button-down shirt, navy "WA" crested blazer, and a plaid skirt. At least I didn't smell like a mixture of suntan lotion and over-applied cologne like he did.

"I don't know—you're different," he said.

"Maybe like I'm seventeen, not six, for example?"

Quinn went on, ignoring me. "You'd better be careful or you might get asked out or, God forbid, wind up with a BOYFRIEND." He laughed.

"Well . . . I hope my new boyfriend has a car and I can get out of riding with *you* every day," I replied.

"You'd miss me, though."

"Desperately," I said, rolling my eyes. "But I'd survive the pain."

"Maybe not. I'm like coffee. A little bitter but addictive."

"There are plenty of places to get a good cup of coffee," I said, "so no worries."

Not that I was keeping score, but I'd say that round went my way by a smidge. Best to quit while I was ahead. I smirk-smiled and grabbed my long hair, so carefully straightened earlier, hoping to stop its inevitable journey to becoming a rat's nest in the Santa Ana winds. With the top off, they'd blow through the Jeep like a hurricane once we hit the 101.

We wound our way out of the sun-dappled Malibu hills in silence after that, a random playlist blasting and glimpses of the blue-green ocean at every other curve. Sycamore trees clung to the steep slopes, a little parched, a little bent, as if bracing against a future fire or flood, common in this little slice of paradise. As for me, I was like those trees, clinging to today and bracing for whatever disaster lay ahead.

# two

Windline's long, tree-lined drive made the campus feel more like an old Ivy League college than a private school. The largest building housed the high school. It rose up like a modern castle, with three stories and three rectangular stained-glass windows. Each was a gift from a sister school, one from Ireland, another from Nepal, and the third from Ghana. They stood for the three pillars of the time-traveling community: stewardship of time, conservation of antiquity, and respect for nature.

Quinn weaved the Jeep through the school's crowded parking lot and whipped into a spot reserved for seniors. As always, I gripped the door handle, ready to jump out almost before he put the Jeep in park. I dreaded the embarrassing moment when half the crowd went to the driver's side to welcome Quinn like he was the long-lost homecoming king. This time, though, Quinn said, "Stay put."

When he opened my door, I squinted my eyes at him, hoping to discern if his newfound chivalry was genuine or the start of some junior year hazing ritual. Having no choice but to get out—and since Quinn was wedged between the door and the next parked car—I slid down, carefully avoiding any bodily contact. I walked ahead murmuring, "Thanks."

The crowd that usually gathered around Quinn's side had shifted to mine, and they all stood waiting like unusually attractive, school-uniform-wearing paparazzi. When an arm was casually draped over my shoulder, I almost jumped out of my skin. It was Quinn, smiling like we did this all the time. I looked up at him as we walked, an old-school *Twilight* movie flashback running through my head: Edward and Bella arriving at school for the first time as a couple—Edward all cool and smug, and Bella awkward and slightly embarrassed by the attention. Everyone stared at them, the same way *everyone* was staring at us. Only, Quinn and I weren't a couple, and my payoff wouldn't be immortality as a hot vampire with perfectly poofed hair and perma-make-up.

"Hey, y'all," Quinn said lazily. "Charlie's a junior now."

Half the people didn't know who I was, and the other half must not have recognized me, because the looks we got ranged from *Who the hell is Charlie?* to *Who's the new girl?* to *I want to rip her eyes out.* And just like that, I was somebody to the gaggle of Quinn-worshiping seniors.

By the time we reached the other side of the parking lot, the show was over, and Quinn and his arm disappeared without so much as a "see you later." Well, whatever that was, I was glad it was over.

~

The morning was a picture-posing, hugging, back-slapping blur in the Grand Hall. We took group pics in front of the completely unnecessary nine-foot-tall fireplace and low-angle selfies with the high-timbered ceiling in the background. Maybe the rest of the juniors enjoyed being the subject of a million photos to post on social, but I was over it. I worried that all the attention was the equivalent of a photographic Last Supper—that we were being captured now because we'd either never make it back from our trips, or never be the same after them.

Then the loudspeaker blared. *Attention, juniors,* the voice of god said, *please report to the auditorium for the Junior Year Test briefing.* Like sheep, we plodded as a group toward the meeting.

Ms. Featherwell took the podium. She was the school's headmistress—tall, thin, and, despite her unfortunate name, a semi-famous time traveler. Legend had it she'd been the one to whisper in Paul Revere's ear that the British were coming and was responsible for one of the record labels discovering several of the most famous 1960s bands. She'd broken the first rule of time travel—to avoid changing the future—and somehow had been commended for it.

Teachers stood at the back doors, blocking the entrance in case lower-level students tried to sneak in. A panel sat behind Ms. Featherwell, some of the members recognizable and some not. "Class," she began, "welcome back, and congratulations on embarking on your junior year, which, as you're aware, includes the Junior Year Test. We've called you here to unveil what has been a secret—and will remain a secret—for as long as Windline Academy exists. Before we get started, please raise your right hands."

We all obeyed.

"Repeat after me." She recited, with us as her echo:

*Upon penalty of expulsion from Windline Academy,*
*And from the larger community of travelers,*
*I hereby swear,*
*That from this moment forward,*
*I will keep secret the process,*
*As well as the experience and results of,*
*The Junior and Senior Year Tests,*
*From any and all who have not yet participated,*
*And I will do my level best to excel,*
*For the betterment of myself,*
*My school,*
*And my community.*

A slow murmur rose from the sea of blue blazers, gradually turning into a roar as if a hundred voices came together to say, "What Senior Year Test?" I'd never heard about any Senior Year Test! Did that mean we had to do the stupid test twice, once this year and again the next? I looked at my best friend, Tiana, sitting next to me. The warm undertones of her dark skin were turning ashen, and a silent glance back from her told me she was as stunned as I was. The fact that a Junior Year Test existed was an open secret, since kids were missing for big chunks of time, though all anyone knew was that it was some sort of test of time travel survival that was fashioned specifically for each student. But a Senior Year Test? The seniors were either on campus or doing self-study projects or internships. So we all thought.

Ms. Featherwell held up her hands to shush the crowd, her black teacher's robe billowing as she raised and lowered her hands in a "quiet down" gesture. I shrank low in my folding auditorium seat, putting my head on the back of it and staring up at the ceiling, a painted night sky with constellations drawn like creatures among the stars.

"Now, you may be wondering why I mentioned a Senior Year Test," she went on. "Allow me to explain, first about the details of your test and then about the test for seniors. They're related.

"For the next two weeks, each of you will be evaluated on skill level, aptitude, personality, fitness, and attitude. These results will be matched against the attributes needed to be a contributing member of the time travel community and of society at large. From there, the esteemed group of colleagues behind me," she said, gesturing to the group of pursed-lipped, black-robed adults seated in a row, "will confer with your parents and then determine where, when, and for how long you will be on assignment during this school year.

"Once we share your destination, you will then have a one-week preparation period before embarking on your journey. Your assignment will be to survive and thrive in the appointed time *and* accomplish a goal set forth by the committee. You will write and present a confidential report upon your return. As you should know from your years of training at Windline, you are forbidden to purposefully interfere in the time stream during your journey. Should you fail, you will face a repeat of the test.

"Now," she said, "allow me to bring up Mr. Peña. He'll provide you with information about the Senior Year Test. Virgilio?"

The podium traded one black-robed school official for another, this one the senior-class dean. "Juniors, welcome back, and welcome to an exciting and challenging year for you all," he said. "As you've just heard, senior year also has its excitements and challenges. You see, during the Junior Year Test, each junior will be paired with a senior as a Minder. The job of a Minder is not—I repeat *not*—to be your friend during your trip; in fact, the Minder should give you distance to achieve your goals, so much so that in some cases you may never see, or only briefly see, your Minder.

"Minders are there to make sure you follow the rules of

engagement and to ensure your safety to the best of their ability. Minders also have very strict rules that apply to their jobs. For example, should you become ill and unable to travel back here yourself, your Minder is required to return to school to report the illness so the committee can send appropriate assistance. Should you break a rule, the Minder is instructed to mitigate the damage as much as possible and to report the infraction in a final report to the committee about your test performance. In the end, if you fail, you will repeat the Junior Year Test, as Ms. Featherwell noted. However, should a senior fail, he, she, or they will not graduate, which of course means the student will receive neither a diploma nor a time pin.

"So, as you can see, the stakes will be high for each of you during these tests, and each should respect the role of the other. The tests are serious matters, and if you cannot take your role seriously, you will face the consequences."

The other black robes spoke in turn, but all I heard was that we'd be tested until we were nothing more than lab rats. Then we'd be sent away on a quest designed to whip us into top shape—our best selves—so we could go out into the world and represent the sanctioned time travel community with honor, dignity, and enthusiasm. Enthusiasm might be a tall order for me.

All I could think of was how my parents were handing the baton to Windline to turn me into what my genes dictated I should be. Time travel was like breathing to them—in and out, in and out, day in, day out. They'd rather be drooling over artifacts in some distant century than riding the ferris wheel on the Santa Monica Pier. Not me. No matter what I had to go through, I swore a silent promise to myself to be me, to choose what I wanted and not what my genes, my parents, or my school wanted me to be, even if I had to endure the polishing of my rough edges by the grinder of the Junior Year Test. And now I had the added bonus of a Senior Year Test, so that if I somehow made it through this year, next year I'd have to grind away at the free will of the class year below me.

They told us to look for an encrypted email with our schedule for the next two weeks. At the end of those two weeks, we'd be brought in with our parents and told one by one about our destinations and assignments. And we wouldn't find out who our Minder was—if we ever did—until we saw that person in the past. I made a note to study last year's junior-class yearbook section so I'd recognize all of this year's seniors. It suddenly occurred to me that Quinn may have pulled that stunt with the crowd in the parking lot so the seniors would know I was "okay." If so, I owed him one.

As we poured out of the auditorium, some of my classmates were laughing like this whole thing was a joke, and some were high-fiving like they'd made the Olympic team.

I could practically smell the adrenaline. The few who realized the test might be awful or dangerous had hunched shoulders and looked at the floor. Tiana and I huddled together at the rear, checking our phones for the emails. Nothing yet.

"I'm not gonna sleep until this is all over," Tiana complained, tucking her hair behind her ear out of habit. Her parents made mine look like pushovers, so they'd be all over her to pass with flying colors. "I hope they don't send me too far back," she said, "especially if I'm in this country or an English colony. Definitely not before the Civil Rights Movement."

"I know," I said, not really knowing but trying to put myself in her shoes. Just being a girl was dangerous enough, and Tiana had way more to worry about than just her X chromosomes. "They'd have to send you to some recent time for your safety. Or to another country."

"Maybe. God, who knows? I hope, wherever it is, it's at least not before the Industrial Revolution."

"Or before indoor plumbing," I added.

"Or bras!"

I laughed. "Totally."

"Which probably means they'll send both of us back to the Dark Ages—to get us out of our comfort zones?"

"Probably," I said, dejected. I felt like I had a metal band in my head, scream-singing with no autotune.

"Maybe if we figure out what we're missing, we can figure out what deficiency they're trying to address?"

"Somehow I doubt that'd work. I'm missing a lot, like a clue what I want to do. And maybe coping skills for dealing with my parents. Oh, and a boyfriend or girlfriend . . ." She gave a strained laugh. Her laughs always made me envy her perfectly shaped face, made even prettier when she smiled. *She really should be in toothpaste commercials.*

"The only thing you're missing is a modeling contract, my friend. You're already top of the class."

"Very funny," she said. "And what about you? The only thing *you're* missing is a regular high school and a normal future. How are they gonna fix that?"

"Oh, crap, maybe they'll send me back to a high school in the 1950s, like in that eighties movie *Back to the Future*. I'll have to fight off Biff and get my grandparents together so my mom will be born. Then if I'm not successful, I'll start disappearing out of the family photo I took back in time in my pocket."

"Girl, you gotta get out more. I've never even heard of that one."

I laughed. "Yeah, I'm digging deep. Saw it on family night. The parents love it for some reason."

"Remind me not to invite myself over when that one's up again," she joked. Actually, we were past inviting ourselves to each other's houses and had graduated to just showing up.

"Oh, you're coming next time. It's a rite of passage," I said.

"I think we've got enough of those going on at the moment."

# three

As I waited my turn for the fitness evaluation, I stood shivering by the side of the pool, the smell of chlorine burning my nose and goose bumps popping up on my arms. I couldn't tell if blood had stopped making it to my extremities as my test location announcement was getting closer or if I was embarrassed, standing in front of everyone in a bathing suit with new curves on full display. I caught a bunch of guys and a few girls looking at my chest. How a couple of boobs could generate so much attention was beyond me.

For that day's fun, we'd be racing against the other lanes in the fifty-meter indoor pool while also trying to best the others on distance. I had no idea why. It wasn't like we were trying to make all-state swimming. Each of us also wore a smartwatch to transmit our vitals. My heart was just fine, at least until Quinn and the actual guys' swim team walked out from the locker room, all Speedos and long, lean muscles. Worse, they jumped in the hot tub that had a picture-perfect view of our group.

"Team two, you're up," yelled the faculty monitor. He and several others stood with devices around the pool. I'd never been so happy for the chance to dive into a pool as I was at that moment. I stepped up onto the starting block.

“Crush ’em, Charlie!” Quinn yelled from the hot tub. His teammates then proceeded to laugh and whistle at me. I turned and glared.

At “Go,” I dove into the water, pushing hard off the block to land as far as I could into the pool. I glided until I was out of breath and started windmilling my arms. One. Two. Three. Breathe. One, two, three, breathe. Then, two breaths for every three strokes. I’d had plenty of swim lessons, but the ocean taught me everything I knew. I pictured myself paddling out for a wave . . . paddling, paddling. I knew how to pace myself, to save energy for the ride and the rest of the day. Swimming was like nirvana, my head down, listening to the rhythm of my heart and the cadence of my breaths. I lost myself, devoid of time or weight.

Finally, I heard a shout when I took a breath, then another shout. I paused to see the monitors with hands on their hips, the closest one motioning to me. I was alone in the water.

“Landers!” he yelled. “We get it. You’re a machine. Get outta the pool.”

The first thought that ran through my head was that I’d won—not that this was a legit competition, but still. I was definitely a fish in another life. No wonder I couldn’t eat Quinn’s goldfish. My second thought was that I was an idiot. Who wants to win the fitness test when it’s for a time travel evaluation? *They'd probably make me hike through Death Valley in the Mojave Desert before cars were invented.* Then, the third thought, as I popped myself out of the water, was . . . *Quinn!* He stood right above me on the pool deck, holding a towel.

"You trying to set a school record or what, Charlie Chicken?" He laughed, closing the space between us until I could feel the heat radiating from his chest. He slipped the towel behind me, then wrapped me up in it like a child and stepped back.

"Thanks," I managed, blood rising to my cheeks. "I could do that myself, you know."

"Yeah, I know," he said. "But what fun would that be?" He winked. Really? A wink? Either he was a fifty-year-old dude with gold chains, or I was six again. Dealer's choice.

"Plenty of fun," I said with attitude. "Fun for days."

"Well, have some fun and get dressed. I'm ready to go home."

~

Friday of that first week rolled around way too quickly, and Tiana and I stood with linked arms outside one of the classrooms. She was called in for her interview first, leaving me waiting in the hallway, smoothing down my post-Jeep hair for the fiftieth time that day. I leaned against the wall, lost in thought, until Gustavo—we called him Gorgeous Gustavo because, after all, he was friggin' beautiful—stopped inches away from me, his eyes locking with mine. "Hey, Charlie. ¿Cómo estás, linda?"

If he hadn't said my name, I'd have assumed there was another girl behind me he was talking to. "Bien, grácias, Gustavo. ¿Y tú?"

"Doing great," he said, thankfully switching to English. My brain was too shocked to speak Spanish, and, anyway, the only thing I'd be able to talk about was Don Quixote. Besides, Italian was my best language other than English. Actually, I was best at not talking to the likes of Gustavo at all.

"Cool," I said. *Oh God, I just said cool.*

Gustavo didn't seem to care. He went on, "Saw you the other day at the pool. Impressive." He inched closer. One of his hands held his schoolbooks, and the other floated over to touch my arm.

"Uh, thanks." Crap, he must've been with Quinn in the hot tub. I was catching on, now. The boobs had worked their magic on him.

"Hey, Quinn's having some people over tomorrow night. Want to come with me?"

I didn't expect Quinn to invite me to his parties, but, then again, I usually didn't know about them, so I never felt left out. Somehow, the fact that he hadn't told me about this one grated on me, so much so that I blurted out, "Sure, yeah."

Then, a new voice said, "Miss Landers?"

The call came from the classroom that Tiana was exiting, looking like she'd just finished a tough final exam. The silent friend message she telegraphed was *That sucked . . . and why are you with Gustavo?* I sent her a "call you when I'm done" look.

I grabbed a Sharpie from my backpack and wrote my number on Gustavo's palm. He flashed a smile, and I turned to face my interview. I needed to get my mind off the hot Argentinian and into the game.

At a long rectangular table at the end of the classroom, five grim reapers sat in black robes. In front of them was a single wooden chair. I guessed figuring out I should sit there was the first test. Probably told them I was self-confident in my choices, or some such crap. *Deep breath.*

"Welcome, Miss Landers. How are you today?" asked the one at the end of the table.

"Fine, thank you." I decided to play this like I was a murder suspect in a TV crime show, with a lawyer in my ear telling me not to give them anything more than what they asked for. I really wanted to say that I thought this whole process was insulting and that I was far from okay, but I decided to keep those thoughts to myself.

"Wonderful, then let's get started." Each member of the panel was introduced. Two of them were teachers. A human development expert, a curriculum designer, and a psychologist completed the group. I forgot their names as soon as I heard them.

A second black robe spoke up. "What do you want to do with your life, Miss Landers?"

*Wow, so much for the warm-up.* The metal arms of the fan above my head spun around, clicking at each turn. "Um, I'm not sure. Probably be a lifeguard or maybe a surfer."

Notes scribbled on a pad. "A surfer?"

"Yes, you know, someone who surfs." *Whoops. That sounded snarky.*

"Very good. What appeals to you about surfing?"

"I don't know. Being alone. The rush. The quiet. I love the ocean."

"What do you love about the ocean?" asked the third robe.

"I guess I like the way it's constantly in motion. Life came from the ocean. Our lives depend on it. It can destroy us, and at the same time, whole ecosystems thrive below the surface. And"—I realized I was saying too much but was unable to stop—"it brings me peace." I suspected they were doubling down on my Mojave adventure right about then.

"You like the ocean. What do you dislike?"

"You mean specifically?" I asked. I hate lima beans, but I suspected that wasn't what they were looking for.

"How about generally? Broadly—even philosophically?"

"Well," I said, shrugging my shoulders, "I like individual people, but I'm not a huge fan of the human race, I guess. There're too many of us. We're overrunning the planet. Polluting the oceans. Killing each other. We're so LOUD as a species." The imaginary lawyer in my ear told me to stop, but I ignored her. "And, if I'm honest, I'm not wild about being a time traveler. I don't really see the point in it."

"You'd rather not be a time traveler?" Robe Four.

Straight up. Why not be honest? I was in deep now. "Well, I like it so I can travel without getting on a plane. But otherwise, that's correct. I'd probably rather not be a time traveler."

"Why?"

"Well, we aren't supposed to change the past, so other than the travel benefits and making ourselves rich, I don't know what good it does. Sure, it's fun sometimes to go to different times with my class or with family, and it's better than reading history books, but no one at this school appreciates today—right now. Even being here in this room . . . it's not fun, but it matters because it affects the future. The past is dead, literally and figuratively. Today is what matters. And tomorrow."

"So if I could give you a pill that would target and deactivate the genes that allow you to time travel, you'd take that pill right now?" asked Robe Three.

I thought for a second. Surely this was a trick question

of some sort. "No," I answered, "because I don't know you. But I'd do my research, and then I'd probably take it."

"Very interesting," said the fifth robe. "Miss Landers, who are you?"

*Who are you?* That's way too deep for some school test. *If I run out of here right now and never look back, what would happen?* I glared at Robe Five and said, "Respectfully, sir, I'm my own person, no matter how many questions you ask me or how many trips you send me on. I'm not somebody else's to mold. You asked me why I like the ocean? Because there, I'm free."

~

I spent Friday night worried about my impending trek across Death Valley. I even went as far as researching survival in extreme heat. Gustavo texted to set up our date, which was freaking me out even more.

I'd been on dates of course, but usually with a group or with a guy who was either a friend or too scared to try anything. Gustavo was the REAL THING, a full-tilt, gonna-stick-his-tongue-down-your-throat-as-soon-as-possible kind of guy. Given my track record with guys with accents—including the shaggy-headed Australian surfer I'd made out with over the summer—and Gustavo's devastating bone structure, I was sure I'd be more than happy to oblige him.

Still, I already had a lot on my mind.

After four phone calls with Tiana, I finally decided what to wear to Quinn's party. His house had a pool, so I wore a bikini under white shorts and a semi-dressy black halter top. I started to wear sandals, but I felt stupid. I went with black Chuck Taylors instead.

When Gustavo arrived to pick me up, I almost ran back to my room to earn my "Charlie Chicken" nickname for real. Out of his school uniform, wearing dark wash jeans and a white T-shirt, he looked larger somehow and about twenty years old. When he leaned down to hug me, I smelled just the right amount of cologne, deep and musky. Suddenly, I felt like a little kid next to him. I needed to get out of my head, so I jumped into Gustavo's Porsche SUV like I owned it.

The orange sun was setting off a hazy coastline when we pulled up to the Daniels house, lit with exterior floods and uplighting that made the small palm trees out front look ghostly. I heard the beat of music from inside and wondered where Mr. and Mrs. Daniels were. Gustavo ushered me in, holding my hand. Did the guy even know my last name, I asked myself? *Who cares? He's cute, and I'm going to die in the Mojave.*

Before we'd made it through the entry hall, two girls ran up to Gustavo. I'd been studying the seniors in the week since school started, and I recognized them as Marla and Jackie, both volleyball players.

"Gustavo, you made it!" Jackie exclaimed. Did they think he was in some kind of danger in Malibu? Not exactly a big deal to make it across town, especially if you own a Porsche. "Who's your little friend?"

*Little?* I was five foot seven, so it wasn't like I was a pixie.

"Meet Charlie," Gustavo said as if he hadn't noticed the dig. Guys never do.

"Hey, Charlie," they said in unison and laughed, like they were twins.

"Hey," I said, unconsciously backing up to tuck myself behind Gustavo's arm. Maybe this wasn't such a good idea. Why the hell was I stressing myself out by going to a senior party?

In the background, I saw Quinn walk by, glancing our way as he did. At first he kept going, but then he stopped and did a double take. *Take that*, I thought, suddenly remembering why I was here. *I don't even need you to invite me to your parties!* We locked eyes, and I gave him a smirky half smile. He looked down, then kept walking. So much for a big welcome. I wasn't going to let him, or any of these people, ruin my fun. I was desperate to forget about everything.

Soon we found ourselves outside dancing, but when Gustavo excused himself to go talk to a clump of his friends, I was left alone by the pool. A guy with a Hawaiian shirt walked by with a tray of little JELL-O squares and offered me some. Self-conscious standing there by myself,

I wanted to look busy, so I grabbed a few and stuck them in my empty glass. I choked them down one by one. They reminded me of mouthwash, the kind that if you swallow, it burns all the way down to your stomach.

After a few minutes, the burning stopped, and I went in search of more. I didn't find the tray guy, but I did find a bar of sorts, where someone was pouring and chanting, "Shots, shots, shots," while the two girls we'd met at the door tossed them back.

"Charlie, right?" Marla said, laughing. "Here, have a shot." More laughter.

"No, uh, that's okay," I said.

"C'mon, Charlie. You're a junior, right? You definitely need to have a good time!"

That was all the prompting I needed, and two shots slid right down to join their gelatin friends. I was off to the races. I lost count of the shots, the music and faces a blur.

Marla and Jackie each grabbed one of my hands and pulled me to the end of the pool. The three of us kicked off our shoes—me clumsily trying to unlace my Chucks while standing on one foot at a time—and got on the diving board, where we starting dancing, jumping up and down with our hands over our heads.

Marla was the first to fall in the pool, a big splash following her high-pitched yelp. Jackie went in after her, on purpose, shouting about saving Marla, but they both were treading water, still laughing like falling in the water was the funniest thing ever.

"Charlie, get in!" Marla shouted my way, motioning me in.

"Yeah, yeah, I'm coming!" I remembered, barely, that I had my bathing suit on under my clothes, so while the music thumped, I unbuttoned my shorts and wiggled them down, tossing them onto the grass. My awkward stripping didn't go unnoticed, and soon I was ringed by a cheering mini-crowd. Off came my halter top, while I fumbled and laughed, too loopy to care about decorum at that point. I pushed the Mojave way back in my addled brain as I threw my halter in the same general direction as my shorts, leaving me in my blue-striped bikini. It was a little tight up top because I'd bought it at the beginning of last summer.

Gustavo pushed his way through everyone to join me on the diving board, taking up the dancing where Marla and Jackie left off. He grabbed my hands and spun me around, his arms around my stomach, my back to his front. I hadn't quite been in that position before, and I had to admit that the skin-to-skin contact felt really good. He spun me back around on beat, so that we faced each other, pulling me in with a hand on the small of my back as I laughed. For a moment, I was lost in his eyes, and he bent to kiss me. . . .

Gustavo was gone in a SPLASH, into the pool in a very much uncontrolled dive. I admit I was a little out of focus, but my brain couldn't figure out how he'd gone from about to kiss me to in the pool in a hot second. Then it all made sense. Out of nowhere, Quinn appeared on the diving board. He had pushed Gustavo into the pool fully clothed. And he was coming for me next.

I turned to dive into the pool to save myself the humiliation of being pushed when Quinn grabbed me from behind—and not in a slow, sexy way like Gustavo had. Next thing I knew, he had flipped me up as if I were a sack of potatoes, so I was over his shoulder with my head and hair hanging down his back and my butt next to his ear. *Oooh, he is going to get it when he puts me down!*

My fighting spirit didn't last long, though, because all the bouncing as Quinn headed for the house was making the mix of sugar and alcohol in my stomach swirl around, and not in a soft-serve ice cream yummy kind of way. "Quinn, I think I'm gonna be sick!"

Quinn took the stairs to the house two at a time, quite a feat with me flopped over him. We went through the open accordion glass doors and into the powder room off the living room. He lowered me down onto the cool marble and in position just in time for all the JELL-O and all the shots to reappear in the most unpleasant way.

How had I gone from having so much fun and almost kissing one of the cutest guys at school to worshiping the porcelain goddess with Quinn standing over me, watching?

I was never going to live this down.

When my stomach was empty and I sat back against the wall with my head in my hands, Quinn sat down on the floor with me. He scooted my way, but I put up my hands to stop him from getting close enough to see me. Gently, he moved my hands away and leaned in, a cool towel pressing against my cheek, my forehead, my mouth. I felt like a baby. Maybe I was. My first senior party, and I was in a heap.

"C'mon," he said quietly. "I'm taking you home."

"No!" I protested. "This is your party."

"So? Everyone will be fine. And Mom and Dad will be home soon to throw them all out. My parents don't need to see you like this."

"Roger that." Connie would tell my mom, and I'd be murdered before I could even set foot in the Mojave.

Quinn pulled me to my feet, and we wobbled toward the front door, his arm around my waist to steady me. "Wait," I said, "what about Gustavo?"

"He'll be fine," Quinn said, motioning to the party going strong out back. "He's made it most of the way through high school without you, so I'm sure he can find someone out there to talk to."

"Maybe Jackie and Marla will dance with him," I mumbled.

Quinn opened the Jeep's passenger door and helped me up. "Wait!" I said again, and Quinn rolled his eyes. "Have you been drinking?"

That got a laugh. "You're asking me if I've been drinking?"

"Exactly. You can't drink and drive."

"I don't drink when there are people at my house, Charlie. Somebody has to keep lushes like you under control." He snapped my seat belt, leaning over my lap. I was still wearing only my bikini. His closeness started my nerves tingling, or maybe that was the alcohol.

"Quinn—my clothes."

"I'll find them later," he said, straightening up. "Here." He pulled his polo shirt over his head in a quick gesture, then turned it right-side out. He unbuckled me and said, "Put your hands up." Then he slipped his shirt over my head, pulling my arms through the sleeves. It smelled like him, and since Quinn was at least six inches taller than I was, his shirt did a nice job of covering me. He buckled me again and jumped in the driver's side.

The wind swirling around me was California-evening cool. I fell asleep in the short distance to my house, and though I vaguely remember Quinn carrying me, in his arms this time, I have no idea how he got me inside and into bed without anyone noticing. I woke up the next morning still in his shirt and with a killer headache. I took off his shirt like it was on fire and threw it across the room. How could I ever face Quinn again? And how was I possibly going to face the Mojave Desert—or whatever the committee threw at me—if I couldn't even handle one senior party?

# four

That Monday, the trip to Windline was a family affair. Sitting in the back of Dad's hybrid, I flip-flopped between being glad I had an entourage to walk into school with after Saturday night . . . and being mortified to be seen with my parents. I was sure about one thing—I was relieved not to ride to school with Quinn that morning. As far I was concerned, I'd be okay if I never saw his face again, no matter how square his jaw was or how that widow's peak at the center of his part made his hair look casually perfect all the time. It should be illegal for guys to have such good hair.

I spent the first two hours of the morning waiting outside a classroom turned conference room. What could the committee and my parents possibly talk about for TWO HOURS? All I could hope was that a negotiation was going on, and my parents were fighting them over the Mojave plan.

As I sat in the busy hallway, Tiana was a welcome sight, our BFF-fly-by hug lifting my mood. Of course, I'd already downloaded the party fiasco story to her on Sunday, which had helped me put the whole thing in perspective. After all, I hadn't done anything wrong. It wasn't like I didn't have a bathing suit on, and I hadn't done anything with Gustavo except dance and almost kiss him. It was Quinn who'd embarrassed me, pushing my date in the pool and carrying me away like a piece of meat. And then there was the throwing up, but only Quinn saw that, which he could chalk up to more annoying pseudo-little-sister crap.

Quinn strolled by at one point, but he was talking to two girls, and I snapped my head down to concentrate on my phone so I wouldn't have to catch his eye. When Marla walked down the hallway a bit later wearing her volleyball team uniform, her hair in a ponytail, she looked at me like I'd lost my mind after I ventured a little wave. Then recognition dawned, and she beelined for me.

"Hey! Charlie—right? What happened to you Saturday night? You were there one minute and gone the next!"

How to explain myself? It hadn't dawned on me that anyone would care. "Uh, I had a little too much, and Quinn took me home."

One of Marla's perfect eyebrows went up. "Oh, well, that was nice of him, I guess. Just FYI . . . Gustavo hung out with us after you disappeared. I think he really likes you, but he doesn't want to mess with Quinn. You know how territorial guys can be. . . ."

Wait, what? I was Quinn's "territory"? What did that even mean? "I guess so," I managed. "But Quinn isn't—"

"Miss Landers?" One of the black robes had opened the classroom door to usher me in.

Marla smiled as I stood. "Good luck," she said in a pseudo-whisper.

I mouthed, "Thanks," and turned to walk in.

The robes were sitting in roughly the same configuration as when they'd interviewed me, only there were three chairs in front of them this time. Was it my imagination, or did my Windline-all-the-way parents look unusually pale?

I sat down next to Mom, who squeezed my hand. Dad leaned forward in front of her so he could flash me an encouraging smile. They'd been authorized time travelers for so long, time travel was routine for them, a constant when they weren't "working" in their antique shop. Their shop was really just an extra spot to store the historical treasures they were preserving before Windline could catalog them. They were like art dealers who'd never sold anything.

Robe One spoke. "Miss Landers, we've had a productive discussion with your parents about you and your needs, and it is clear that they have a great deal of faith in you and your abilities." Pause.

"Uh, great," I muttered.

"And we only have a couple of questions left before we begin our deliberations about the destination and goals of your Junior Year Test." Pause.

"Okay." Was this the conversational version of the inkblot test to see how my brain worked? Why did the robe keep pausing?

"Tell us what you'd like to do for your test—that is, what you'd like to learn."

If this were an inkblot test, that request would be a big, fat blob of amorphous ink. I took a deep breath. "If I have to do the test . . . which I'd rather not, but if I have the choice . . . I guess I'd like to learn about . . ." I trailed off to give myself time to formulate an answer. ". . . US peacetime in the post–Industrial Revolution era. Maybe small-town life. Ideally, life near the water, so I can compare it to my life here. I think I could learn a lot about why I'm so attached to this place and this time." I was quite pleased with my answer—no lack of amenities, not too many people to deal with, and a coastal town. Had to be bearable, right?

"Interesting," said Robe Two. "What about personal characteristics you would like to dial up or down?"

Another big blob thrown my way. I translated that question to *Which rough edges do you want us to grind down so you're smoothed and polished into a Windline time traveler who will travel responsibly and report those who don't?* I literally had no answer to that, so I said, "I like myself the way I am."

"I understand, Miss Landers, but this is your chance to provide input. Do you have any?"

*Well, if they really want input, I'll give it to them.* "I just want to be a normal human being," I said, a bit of anger oozing from a festering place deep inside me, "and I don't want some challenge to shape me into who the people in this room want me to be. I'm not a genetic formula. I'm not strong, I'm not brave, and I'm not interested in the folds of time.

"There are a zillion people in the world who try to center themselves and focus on the present. They do yoga, they meditate, they buy books. I'm already focused. I'm already centered. I'm right where I want to be." Of course, I didn't mention anything about my social life, which could use some work, but I didn't think asking for help figuring out guys would be an appropriate response. God knows where that might land me. "Oh," I added, "and I definitely don't want to trek across the Mojave Desert."

My mom patted me on the back. The robe said, "Noted. Thank you all for coming."

And just like that, we were excused.

~

The rest of the week crept by, like sands through an hourglass with a clog. I made Sammy sit in the front with Quinn every morning, making the excuse that I was deep into a new book on my phone. Sammy pestered Quinn with "Dude, can you show me some new surfing moves?" Then, "Hey, will you let me drive the Jeep down this block?" (The answer was no.) And "Quinn, could you come play video games with me after school?" Not that he could get a word in, but Quinn never mentioned the weekend, and neither did I. When in doubt, stick your head in the sand like an ostrich.

I bumped into Gustavo at one point, almost literally, because we were coming around the same corner from opposite directions. We both laughed, and I apologized for bailing on him. He hugged me, then said, "Let's do it again, without Quinn around to shove me in the pool." I nodded, thinking a future date with Mr. Hot Guy might just be the thing I needed to look forward to. Hopefully I wouldn't be gone so long that he wouldn't remember me.

Finally, the Friday of trip announcements arrived. Mom whipped up eggs, hash browns, and freshly squeezed grapefruit juice for me, as if a good breakfast would make all of this okay. She cooked bacon, too, and though the warm, wafting greasiness of it smelled heavenly, I had sworn off red meat—my first step toward eating lower on the food chain and saving the planet—so I resisted. Afterward, I was in the back of Quinn's Jeep, pretending to read my phone, which made me completely nauseated during the twisty part of the ride out of the canyons. The nervous butterflies weren't helping either.

Maybe I should've asked my parents to send me to a regular high school. So what if I didn't get the coveted Windline diploma, which came with my own time pin. You had one from either Windline or a sister school and you time traveled legitimately, or you didn't. You could live on the fringe with a black market one, but then you'd always have to look over your shoulder. If you were found out by sanctioned time travelers, you'd be stopped permanently by the SWAT-team-like enforcement group I'd heard Mom and Dad whisper about. But I was sure I could give up time traveling. I might not take that pill the robe described, but I could use a ton of self-restraint. No one would care if I snuck back to less crowded beaches to surf every now and again with my family's time pins.

Right before we walked into Windline, Quinn pulled me aside. "Come 'ere a sec," he said, taking my arm and guiding me out of the funnel of kids entering the building.

I glared at him. "I need to go in, Quinn." Not true, exactly, but my nerves were shot, and my defensive weapons were offline.

"Charlie, I want you to know that everything is going to be fine," he said, his baby blues drilling into me. "You're gonna be safe."

What to say to that? "You promise?" was all I could think of.

"I promise," he said, sotto voce. He stepped in, wrapping his arms around me, pulling me into him. Maybe because I needed the comfort, and since I didn't give myself time to think about the fact that Quinn—annoying and beautiful Quinn—was holding me, I wrapped my arms around him, too, glad for the surprising, solid comfort of his chest.

~

I slogged through the day, and at 1:55 p.m., a teacher came to fetch me from history class. *I'd rather stay and listen to the details of the Ming dynasty and native Chinese rule in the 1300s than face the robes.* But all I could do was stand up and walk to the door, with the rest of the class looking on. Some already knew their fates, but of course couldn't share them; others were still waiting.

The walk down the hallway to Ms. Featherwell's mahogany-paneled office felt like the high school version of a prisoner death march. My legs felt wobbly and my stomach was doing an Olympic gymnastics routine, which by the feel of it would've gotten a perfect execution score. When my escort opened the door and ushered me in at 2:00 p.m. sharp, I felt my shoulders slump. Mom and Dad both stood when I walked in, my dad coming to pull out a chair. He could probably see that I wouldn't make it on my own.

Ms. Featherwell looked over her reading glasses with such a sympathetic look on her face—eyebrows raised, head tilted—that I nearly broke into tears. At least someone I admired was giving me the news. Half the class would get theirs from the crabby junior-class dean. I took deep calming breaths. She began.

"Charlie, Mr. and Mrs. Landers," she said, "before I share the destination and parameters of the Junior Year Test, allow me to go over a few administrative details. We find that students don't hear much after the announcement."

She picked up a piece of paper and read it. Since she'd do this about fifty times that day, she probably wanted to be sure she remembered all the points.

"Your destination and goals have been carefully crafted based on input from the committee. Once determined, your course cannot be altered, unless you choose to withdraw from Windline. Your passing or failing grade will be determined based on a number of factors, including your accomplishment of the goal or goals set for you, and your adherence to the school's rules of time travel. We will not reveal to you specifically why your destination was chosen, nor what general lessons we expect you to learn. Your final written and oral reports, in addition to a factual account of your trip, will focus on the perspectives and skills you've gained through the experience. More information, along with certain items you'll need for your travels—such as clothing—will be provided to you next week during Preparation Week. The junior and senior bon voyage celebration a week from today will be the last official school function prior to your traveling the following Monday. At no time are you allowed to discuss your destination with anyone other than your parents. This weekend, we suggest you begin your own research about the time and place to which you are being sent.

"For your safety, the Windline Testing Committee has assigned a senior student to be your Minder during the test. This person is in place to monitor you and to ensure your safety, not to participate in the experience with you. You are not to interfere with the Minder. The Minder is also being tested. Those Minders with failing grades will not graduate from the academy, nor receive the associated time pin for authorized time travel. Lastly, juniors are forbidden from seeking the identity of their Minders before the test has begun, and you may not reveal details of your test or post-test examinations to other junior or senior students until the entire process is complete." She removed her glasses and held them suspended above her large wooden desk.

"Do you understand, Charlie?"

I nodded, looking past Ms. Featherwell to a framed sepia-toned photograph of her posing in front of an airplane like the one Amelia Earhart would've flown in. I held my breath. *Here it comes.*

"Very well." Ms. Featherwell picked up another paper and put her glasses back on. "Charlie, for your Junior Year Test, you will join the inaugural voyage of the RMS *Titanic* on April 10, 1912, from Southampton, England.

Your goal is to retrieve a famous bejeweled book of Persian poems from the ship before that book finds a home at the bottom of the Atlantic. Barring illness or injury, you will return on or around midnight on April 14, 1912, before—I repeat—before the *Titanic* begins to sink. More details will be forthcoming during Preparation Week." She put down the paper slowly, removed her glasses, and clasped her hands.

My father stood, all six foot three of him, ready to argue, but my mother grabbed his jacket and motioned for him to sit down. I guess my destination was as much a surprise to him as it was to me.

"Charlie, dear, do you understand these instructions?" asked Ms. Featherwell. I looked at her familiar face, noticing the intricate map of wrinkles across the grooves of it for the first time, as if my eyes suddenly had zoom lenses.

"Miss Landers?"

"Yes—yes, ma'am," I said, finally, my mother squeezing my hand. I barely recognized my voice as my own. "I—I, uh—I'm going to be a passenger on the *Titanic*—to witness a ship full of people sail into one of the worst disasters in maritime history, while I locate a book of poems."

"Exactly."

# five

My parents pep-talked me all the way home. As soon as I could escape, I locked myself in my room for about sixteen hours, spent mostly with my duvet pulled over my head. I tried to block out all my thoughts and emotions, which was successful . . . as long as I was asleep. Otherwise, I went from despair to fear to denial and back again. Then I'd spend a while beating myself up for the input I gave the committee. . . . I might as well have straight-up asked for the *Titanic*—water, coastline, "small town." It all fit.

On the bright side, my journey would last a matter of days, and I'd be back in Malibu in under a week from departure while some juniors would be gone for months. Also, my goal didn't seem too tough. How hard could it be to find a book of poems?

Once I forced myself out from under the covers, I watched the *Titanic* movie over and over until I just couldn't listen to Rose say, "Jack!" one more time. And why they didn't both get on that floating piece of debris, no one will ever know. Still, I cried to the bitter end each go-round, until my eyes were puffy and red and I looked like an alien. They itched, too, and all my rubbing gave me blurry vision.

Finally, I took a thirty-minute shower that turned my skin the color of a lobster. After, I went straight to the kitchen to make a pile of nachos with extra cheese and jalapeños—my go-to comfort food—then asked Mom for her time pin. We were allowed to use our family's devices with permission, and Mom never hesitated. She always seemed pleased I was making an effort. In this case, I set Mom's to send me back a few days to the New York Public Library on Fifth and Forty-Second, known for its historical collections. The epic Beaux Arts building always made me feel close to history as I sat in the main reading room with its dark, ornately carved wooden ceiling, getting lost in the pages of a dusty old book.

I pored over the stack of volumes in front of me and jotted notes. I took pictures of the ship's layout on my phone—first-class cabins on top, of course, the dining rooms, storage, boiler rooms—and read some more. I quickly figured out that for such a famous ship, the details were a little fuzzy, with one book quoting a statistic that was contradicted by the next one. I supposed most of the documentation had gone down with the ship.

I memorized the sequence of events on April 14 and into the early hours of April 15, which were corroborated by other ships as well as passengers who'd survived the disaster. By the time I finished my research, I could've taught a college course on the *Titanic*, or more properly, the RMS *Titanic*, for "royal mail ship." More importantly, my despair and dread had turned to acceptance, and I decided to take control of my attitude and get some perspective. All I had to do was find that poetry book and hunker down in my room or stroll the deck, then I'd leave well before the ship met its fate. Nothing required me to interact with people. I could wing it with the committee about lessons learned.

When I wasn't depressed or bent on learning more details that weekend, I was at the mercy of my parents. Dad started shopping for a post-test new car for me, occasionally showing me this model with advanced aerodynamics or that model with some awesome new interior tech. Sadly, I wasn't giving him much positive reinforcement, and his expectant face would fall each time I frowned at his excited efforts. I knew I should've been grateful. After all, a car was a pretty big deal, but as much as I wanted one, my mind was squarely on a seventeen-story-tall ship that would soon set sail with me on it.

Mom pitched in by baking cookies and pies, in between bouts of checking on me with chipper words like "What an opportunity," and "It's really quite an honor to receive this location for your test," and "You are so brave" (not true, by the way), and, digging deep, "Think about the fashion." At least the house smelled like apples, cinnamon, and sugar. I had to call Tiana to come over and save me from their good intentions.

"Oh my God, I have never been so happy to see you!" I said, practically attacking the poor girl when I opened the front door to find her standing there, her face ashen and her hair far from its usual polished perfection. The two of us could've gone trick-or-treating with no costumes.

"You too," she said, squeezing me back just as hard. "I'm desperate to talk."

"We can't say much, though, right?"

"No, but who cares? We don't need to say things to SAY things," she said, one eyebrow raised.

I grabbed her hand and pulled her up the stairs to my room.

"Okay," I said, sitting in a wicker hanging chair by the window, swaying slightly. "I'll ask questions, and you answer . . . but not about your test."

"Gotcha," she said, sitting opposite me in the mirror image of my chair. When we both swayed the same direction at the same time, we almost bumped knees.

"Here goes," I started. "If you take a vacation next summer, would you stay long?" My heart beat faster. For Tiana's sake, I wanted her trip to be short. Plus, I knew we'd need to put each other back together again when we got home.

"You know my parents like vacations that last a few weeks," she responded, without a trace of a smile.

*Not good but could be worse.* "But they always pick great destinations, don't they?" I asked.

"They do a really good job, usually, like bucket list stuff. It could be way worse, and the facilities will at least be modern." *Thank God.*

"What about YOUR summer vacation plans?" she asked me, turning the tables.

"It'll be a quick trip this year, but a really intense one. I've always considered myself lucky that I don't live with depression, but our next vacation has situational depression written all over it." What other state could the *Titanic* possibly put a person in?

"Damn," she said, "this is actually making things worse." We both nodded. Pseudo-information was nearly as bad as no information. Though we excelled at nonverbal best-friend communication, these details were a little above our skill level. "Are we both gonna be okay?" she went on, her voice quiet, as if we could be overheard. Like mine, Tiana's family expected success on the JY Test—but even more so. They believed the right inputs should equal the right outputs, within a slim margin of error, which didn't give Tiana much room to screw up. Her parents were both scientists, a common time traveler profession, along with professor, art historian, and the like.

Tiana and I also shared the same fears—of failure and the unknown. "I've heard that a couple of kids didn't make it back," she said. "You remember hearing about Elsa Chao?"

"Yeah, I remember. I think the rumor was that she was poisoned at Spain's royal court. There was also Phil what's-his-name. Remember?"

"Oh, crap. I forgot about him. Everyone said he was killed by a samurai or something, right? Oh God, please tell me you'll come back, Charlie—"

We finally bumped knees. "I will, definitely. What about you? Promise me?"

She pulled her legs up and sat crisscross applesauce. "Definitely. I'm sure I'll be fine. No poison or swords in my future . . ." She sounded only semi-convinced.

"There's always our Minders. I wonder if Elsa or Phil had them."

"I don't know, but I wouldn't trust my safety to many of the seniors at our school. All they do is party."

"I've seen THAT up close," I said, heat rising to my cheeks as I remembered being the one who partied a little too hard at Quinn's house. "I'm actually hoping for Marla as mine. When I first met her, I thought she was a snob, but she's actually pretty nice."

"Who knows if we'll even see our Minders."

"Unless it's Marla, I'd rather not," I said. I couldn't think of any senior I'd want to hang out with on the *Titanic*. Of course, I only knew a few seniors, really, and of the ones I knew, half were guys. I imagined they paired girls with girls and vice versa for obvious reasons.

We sat in silence for a while, swaying and looking at each other, so many questions unasked and unanswered. Finally, Tiana asked, "What's up with this junior and senior bon voyage celebration? Who wants to celebrate their JY Test before they finish it?"

"Not me. Wish we could skip it."

~

Preparation Week flew by in a whirlwind of activity. Normally clothes just showed up in our classrooms for us to use during class trips. This time, we were finally allowed into Windline's mahogany-paneled artifacts room, basically a museum students didn't get to see up close until . . . surprise . . . you're going on your own massive quest and needed stuff. If I could have, I would've wandered for hours, looking at the treasures from various centuries.

There was even a ticket for the *Titanic*. Turns out that in 2000, Christie's auction house sold an unused first-class ticket from the maiden voyage of the *Titanic* to a generous Windline Academy donor. The cost of that ticket at auction was close to $8,000. Tickets in 1912, especially for the best-of-the-best, first-class parlor suites, were only affordable for the super rich. In current dollars, those tickets were the "mega shopping outing on Rodeo Drive" variety of expensive.

Windline's precious ticket resided in a glass case in the artifacts room. Printed on vellum and marked with the White Star Line sailing flag, the ticket read:

WHITE STAR LINE
YOUR ATTENTION IS SPECIALLY
DIRECTED TO THE CONDITIONS OF TRANSPORTATION IN
THE ENCLOSED CONTRACT.
THE COMPANY'S LIABILITY FOR BAGGAGE IS
STRICTLY LIMITED, BUT
PASSENGERS CAN PROTECT THEMSELVES
BY INSURANCE.
FIRST-CLASS PASSENGER

If I had to travel on the *Titanic*, traveling in first class was definitely the way to go. According to my research at the library, the first-class cabins were located in the center section of the ship, where the waves would create less movement, and they had "modern" amenities like telephones, electric heaters, and lamps that stayed level in high seas. They also had hot and cold running water, private baths, hardwood floors, and, of course, staff to see to the passengers' every need.

Unfortunately, after showing me the ticket, the curator put it right back in the glass case. Then he reached for a nearby metal box and handed me a second-class boarding pass, a fresh-looking replica that even the White Star Line wouldn't be able to tell from the real thing. Until I started researching at the library, I didn't even realize there was a second class on the *Titanic*.

It was up to me to invent my own story about who I was and why I was sailing. Knowing I would hold a second-class ticket narrowed down my possibilities. The quest for the poetry book would be more challenging from second class, too—since first-class passengers had certain privileges on the *Titanic*—but I'd figure out something. I made a mental note to ask that my wardrobe be suitable for first class. I'd need all the flexibility I could get to move around the ship.

The Windline gym had been turned into a clothing shop extravaganza, with everyone getting measured for the first time since summer. Our clothes were fitted, and, if needed, we were schooled on how to wear our particular period-appropriate outfits. Unfortunately, I already knew how to wear a corset from studying the history of fashion and taking class trips in one, but I'd never paid much attention to the particulars of the *Titanic* era.

This was the best glimpse we'd get into where everyone was being sent, though of course we had no clue about their assignments. Tiana and I went for our fittings at the same time, so while I was being pinned in late-Edwardian-era long dresses and hats, I kept peering around the privacy curtain to get a glimpse of what Tiana was trying on.

I spotted flowy skirts, flowery shirts, and vests handed to her behind a curtain across the room. There was no doubt about it—she was going back to the 1960s. Not perfect, but close to what she wanted. I breathed a huge sigh of relief.

Time was such a funny thing. Sometimes it went by so slowly that I felt suspended in it, like when I was sitting on my surfboard, bobbing up and down, alone with my legs in the water and my head in the clouds. Other times, the noise level rose, the sounds of life buzzing by, and time moved so quickly that it was like a film in fast forward. Preparation Week was a head-spinning mix of both. But each evening, when I marked off another day on my National Parks wall calendar with a red Sharpie, I could've sworn time had sped up, like a runner kicking into the finish line of a race. Our finish line—or start line, depending on how you looked at it—was Monday.

~

Friday's bon voyage celebration was a hush-hush event. All we got was a note stating that we shouldn't wear school uniforms—news worthy of a celebration any day—but instead should dress as if we were attending an "elegant" evening event. There was an asterisk defining the word to mean no short skirts or tank tops, and they added at the bottom, "Think of something that your 'greats' would approve of."

Windline students understood the reference, since most families spent time with their greats. We'd use our parents' time pins to travel back as a family to see them at holidays, at a different point in time each visit so we didn't run into ourselves. Sammy and I had met our greats, our great-greats, and our great-great-greats and so on. Christmas in Malibu was vastly different from Christmas in New York City in the 1890s, all darkness, snow, and horse-drawn carriages.

Mom helped me create an updo with skinny braids that were swept up with the rest of my hair into a side knot, a few naturally wavy tendrils pulled out for effect. I wore a black, fitted, below-the-knee skirt with black skinny-heeled pumps, and a flowy white cropped top with sleeves that landed right above my elbows. I added large silver hoop earrings, even though the greats might disapprove.

Tiana grabbed my arm and pointed as we walked into the dining hall, the tables and chairs moved to the walls to make room for both the junior and senior classes. "We're leaving school," Tiana said over the din of chatter. Placed around the room were stands with time pins—the mysterious tech that allowed us to move in time. Each would be programmed for the time and location of the event.

"I wonder where we're going. Hope it's someplace fun. I can't take any more challenges right now."

"No kidding," Tiana said as Ms. Featherwell stood on a step stool in the middle of the room. Someone whistled, one of those two-fingers-in-the-mouth kind of whistles that can bring a whole room to a standstill.

"Thank you, Mr. Jarvis," she said to the tall, lanky junior with the whistling talent, then she turned to address us all. "Obviously, class, you are surrounded by time pins. Please, in orderly fashion, with seniors first, then juniors, make your way to one, and we will see you soon for the celebration. Please conduct yourselves with the utmost decorum at the bon voyage party, reflective of your class and the Windline Academy of today.

"For those of you who have not attended this event before, you will find yourself in the good company of junior- and senior-year students who have participated or will be participating, each in their own timelines, in the tests you are facing. We come together on this day, at a different location and time period each year, to celebrate a legacy of challenge and excellence. I have great faith that you"—she swept her arms around the room to include us all—"will be your best selves today and in the tests that lie ahead of you."

Tiana and I stood back while the seniors crushed toward the small time pins around the dining hall. I spotted Quinn across the room as I shuffled forward. He was about to reach for a time pin when he looked up, sweeping the room as if he were looking for someone. When his eyes caught mine, I smiled weakly and gave a little wave. Without a hint of a smile back, he touched the device and disappeared.

Finally, Tiana and I couldn't stall any longer. The time pin on our side of the room was an ornate gold one with swirls on the face of it. The little device would have been programmed to direct us to the specific time and place of the party. To return, we would simply focus on the location where we'd started, and like homing pigeons in heels, we'd be back at school later that day. With only a few people left in the hall, we both reached out and touched the time pin.

In a blink, we were standing inside an expansive room, tapestries alive with teal, crimson, and orange hanging from the stone walls, and candles burning in holders around the entire place. I had assumed we'd go back to Windline in the late 1800s, when it was founded. But Windline's roots, and the roots of its sister schools, all ran deep in time because once time travel was discovered, the early pioneers reached back out to ancestors and alchemists, improving the runway for family wealth in the present. Clearly, wealth building was an exception to the "don't alter the time stream" rule.

Looking around, I realized we weren't at Windline after all. We were in Europe in the late sixteenth century, or early in the seventeenth, though the musicians at one end of the expansive room were playing the music of Chevalier de Saint-Georges, who we'd learned about in music history. He was born a slave in the Caribbean and had risen to fame in Paris in the eighteenth century.

The flickering candlelight cast a pale glow over the scene, and the air was warm with so many people standing nearly shoulder to shoulder, especially before our group started to push for the fresh air beyond the exits. Nothing like a field trip to a medieval castle for a party during first period.

"We should find people who're from the time periods we're being sent to," Tiana suggested, yelling in my ear.

"Good idea," I yelled back. "I'll meet you at this spot in an hour, if I don't see you before?"

"Roger that!" Tiana said, turning on her heel and ducking into the crowd.

I decided to find higher ground and beelined for the stairs on the other side of the room to find a good vantage point. Once I did, I spotted a group—probably a class like ours, clumped together off to my right. I couldn't tell exactly, but I figured they were from the early 1900s. Close enough.

I moved toward them and wedged myself in between two girls in the group, tripping slightly on the delicately embroidered train of one of their flowy, draped dresses. "Hi," I said awkwardly, catching myself using one of their shoulders to steady myself.

"I beg your pardon," said the girl who owned the shoulder my hand was sitting on. I removed it like it was on fire. The satin gown that flowed over her shoulders into folds of material below her waist felt cool and smooth to the touch. Cost a fortune, no doubt.

"I'm so sorry," I said, fumbling. "I was wondering what year you're from?"

The girls looked at one another. One spoke. "We came from 1911."

The other asked, "Are you a student, or are you an attendant?"

I was actually just confused. "An attendant?"

"Yes. Your clothing resembles that of a servant."

I looked down at myself. "I guess it does." I laughed. "I'm wearing black and white, which is fashionable in my time. But no, I'm a student, too, and I was wondering about your time. I'm very interested in the period between 1900 and 1915." I couldn't say why, or where I was going, though I wanted desperately to spill everything. Instead, I drilled them with questions about their time period until I bordered on annoying.

The taller one, Epiphany, said eventually, "If you do visit our time, you should try to use fewer contractions, so you do not sound overly casual, especially in mixed company. Young women of . . . breeding . . . express themselves with a bit more formality than must be the case in your era."

She wore a beautiful rose-colored velvet choker that kept drawing my eye as she spoke.

"I agree wholeheartedly," said the other, nodding. "And I suggest you never use phrases like 'you guys' should you visit."

I was so in trouble. How was I ever going to make it on the *Titanic*?

"You must also know how to dance properly in our time," said a guy who'd just entered our conversation. He wore a crisp black tuxedo with a long jacket, a white vest and bow tie, and his hair was slicked down. Wow. *That* whole getup never goes out of style. "Do you?" he prompted.

"Uh, do I what?"

"Know how to dance?"

Dance? I mean, I could jump up and down, shake a few things, or slow dance—the kind where you stand there and sway, maybe with a twirl or two. But real ballroom dancing? I'd seen *Cinderella*, but that hardly counted. Luckily, the only dancing on the *Titanic* was in third class.

"No, not really," I said, "but that's okay. I can just avoid dancing. Really."

"Please, I insist." He held out his hand.

"Well, now you have no choice," said Epiphany. "He asked so nicely, after all." Her friend giggled behind a gloved hand.

"But this music, it's—I mean, it is—from the eighteenth century," I said.

His hand remain extended, an expectant look on his face. Tentatively, I put my hand in his. It was warm.

"Admittedly, ragtime is a much more upbeat sound, but we will make do. For teaching purposes." He smiled. Okay, the teeth needed some modern help, and he was a smidge short for me, but overall quite a specimen.

Specimen or not, I looked around for someone, anyone, to save me, but I was on my own, under peer pressure from Mr. Mostly Fabulous 1911. His group cleared some floor space for us.

"Now," he said, taking my hands as I faced him, "This is called the one-step." He put one of my hands on his shoulder and held the other out, like we were going to waltz. "The man starts on the right foot, the woman on the left, and we step together. Step, step, step, step. That's it!" All I was doing was lifting one foot, then the other.

I smiled and tried not to laugh at the thoughts in my head: *This is more like the one stomp,* or *This is the two-step, minus one cowboy*. But then he started to move us around, which required concentration—and the ever elusive foot-brain coordination. I was practically tripping at the turns. My cheeks burned.

"May I cut in?" It was Marla, tapping on my shoulder. She was wearing a black tuxedo, like a man's, except fitted at the waist and with a silk shirt unbuttoned across the top of her chest.

She gave me an I-got-this look, and I said, "Of course, be my guest." I mouthed *thank you* as she moved to take my place.

Mr. 1911 quickly realized that Marla didn't need teaching and was a veritable ragtime queen. Her one-step was less stomping and more gliding, and soon they were one-stepping all around the circle, opening and closing their stance, the crowd clapping a beat until the musicians gave up and took a break.

The Windline crowd from my time caught on to the dancing idea. Someone whipped out a phone and a speaker and started playing our kind of music. When a slow song finally came on, I felt a tap on my shoulder and turned to see Quinn behind me. "Dance?" he said. The noise level was pretty high between the music and the voices bouncing off the high walls of the room, so I wasn't sure whether he was making a statement, asking a question, or inviting me to dance with him.

"I guess," I said, figuring that was a safe response no matter what he'd said. I got my answer when he stepped toward me, his hands moving to my hips just under my cropped top.

I'd known Quinn my whole life, and he was as familiar as the ragged teddy bears I'd had since I was a kid or the light hanging from the ceiling in my room. He was a fixture, a constant, nothing more and nothing less. Since we were little, he'd never really touched me, except when he tried to practice by kissing me on his eighth birthday, or when he needed to push me aside or throw me over his shoulder. So his touch on my body was the equivalent of one of those old teddy bears suddenly coming to life and prancing around the room with jazz hands. It wasn't *natural.* Only, as my hands went to his shoulders and the shock began to wear off, it felt like we'd done this a hundred times before and might a hundred times after.

I had to rein in my thoughts and remind myself that I was just the closest familiar female in his line of sight. While my brain was noodling all over the place about his intentions and how I actually felt about them, he was probably having guy thoughts like *I want to dance, and there's a girl,* or *She'll do until I spot a better girl,* or, most likely, *Booyah.*

I kept my mind blank, as blank as someone with out-of-control hormones could while in the arms of a guy with piercing eyes framed with slightly sloped eyebrows. I moved toward him when he shifted his hands to the small of my back and applied a subtle amount of pressure there. I stood looking up at him, forcing myself to meet his gaze and suppressing hysterical laughter, an unwanted byproduct of awkward intimacy.

He cleared his throat and leaned down so I could hear. "You know, Charlie, I'm not your brother."

Not that I was expecting him to say anything in particular, or really anything at all, but I wasn't expecting that. "I'm aware" was all I could think of in response.

A few beats went by. "You're really a pain in the ass, though." Ah, there he was, the Quinn that resembled the light fixture in my room.

I couldn't let the insult go unanswered—fair was fair, even in dim, flickering candlelight with close bodily contact going on. "Well, I may be a pain in the ass, but you're just a straight-up ass." *Though you do have nice cheekbones.*

"You really hate me, don't you?" He moved closer, so I couldn't look up at him anymore, unless I wanted a sore neck and a good look at the underside of his chin. I put my head on his chest, cheek to heart. I didn't answer. It would be too complex. I randomly started thinking of words that mixed love and hate—*late* didn't work, and *hove* sounded ridiculous. Again . . . I had to stifle laughter at the absurdity of all this.

When the song ended, Quinn released me, still close. "Thanks for the dance," he said. He ran his fingers through his enviable hair. "I guess I won't see you for a while."

"No, I guess not," I said. "Good luck on your Senior Test."

"Yeah—and you be careful during yours. Listen to your Minder. Seriously. Promise me?"

My Minder was going to be bored and possibly seasick.

Plus, I didn't expect to need much minding while lounging in my room on a luxury ship nicknamed the "Millionaire's Special." I answered, "I will," anyway, trying to rush through this awkwardness so I could dissect it all in the privacy of my own room.

He stared at me, like he was trying to figure out if I was lying. "Good," he said slowly, pulling the word out into two long syllables.

While I contemplated how to get as far away from him as possible, Quinn lowered his head at the same time as his hand reached behind my neck, pulling my head in his direction. With no time to duck and run, I braced for impact, not sure if I wanted him to kiss me at all—or more than anything in the world. Then he broke right and kissed my cheek—a slow, slightly lingering, sensual kiss with soft, warm lips. My hormones started screaming at me to pounce on him, but I stood frozen, not daring to move. If I did, I would definitely embarrass myself. And I had enough to stress about with the *Titanic* looming.

# Six

Sometimes the expectation of something is more frightening than the thing itself. I hoped that would be the case for my Junior Year Test, but I seriously doubted it as I stood with the other juniors in the beehive-buzzing gym, lined up in rows. I saw classmates wearing armor, scuba gear, ball gowns, kilts, kimonos, extreme weather hiking gear, colorful saris, and military uniforms. Tiana stood next to me wearing a short orange skirt and a macramé vest that hung down below her skirt's hem.

Since almost everyone had luggage of various sorts, each of us was ushered to an X made of blue painter's tape, spaced about five feet from each other. Time pins were placed on the floor in front of each of us, checked and double-checked against a master list.

I could barely breathe, not just from nerves, but because I was wearing a corset—since I could hardly wear a modern bra in the early twentieth century. I also wore a heavy cotton day suit with a tie and high collar that covered me from neck to feet, with stockings underneath, secured to garters that hung from the bottom of the corset. A black, fur-trimmed wool overcoat, leather gloves with more buttons, and an ornate large-brimmed hat that sat atop a loose updo added to the weight of it all. *Maybe if I pass out, they won't make me go.*

Ms. Featherwell stood in the front on a riser so we could all see her, her eyes sparkling with the adventure of it all. "Class," she called out when the clock high on the wall behind her ticked over to 10:00 a.m., "the time has arrived for your departures. Remember the rules of the test, including those that prohibit intentionally impacting the time stream, and of course, place your safety above all else. Please do not take your time pins with you, since you risk losing them and do not need one to return. Open your minds to this adventure. I wish you all a safe journey, and now, you may go. Godspeed, everyone!" With that, people began to disappear around me. Somebody started wailing. Tiana had her arms crisscrossed in front of her chest like she was shielding herself. She and I stole one last BFF we-got-this look, and she was gone, too. Grabbing up my luggage, I sucked in a breath and touched my time pin. In an instant, as easy as walking into the next room, I was in 1912, in the port town of Southampton on England's south coast.

~

A chilly fifty-something degree morning breeze stung my cheeks as I turned the corner from the side street where I had arrived near Queens Park. No roller bags here. I held a heavy embroidered bag and a trunk-like leather suitcase with straps I'd taken from the school's supplies.

Using a map I found on the Internet, I started to make my way the short distance to the White Star Dock, specifically Berth 44. My long skirt was so narrow at the bottom that I shuffled instead of taking my usual long strides. My boarding pass, along with some money, was tucked in the top of my corset, in case I was robbed. In the movies, women in strange places always get mugged first thing and have to make their way with only their wits to rely on. I hadn't spent too much time in the distant past by myself, so I wasn't about to rely only on my wits, no matter how itchy my boobs were at that moment.

Every photograph I'd seen of this real place and time was in black and white, so the Technicolor spectacle in front of me was a minor shock, like thinking you're taking a sip of an iced latte and getting hot chocolate instead. There was also a cacophony of unexpected sound, a mixture of horns and shouts and laughter. Men on bikes wearing bowlers, women with ribbon-adorned hats, and children in flat caps or curls bustled along, navigating around cars straight off a Hollywood lot. A horse-drawn carriage even moved slowly down the street. All appeared to be headed to the end of the rail line and the docks that created the hub of activity at the intersection of the River Test and the River Itchen.

I smelled the sea, the kind of salt-water-mixed-with-civilization, slightly pungent odor found at docks everywhere, with gulls circling overhead.

"Pardon me," I said countless times as I weaved my way toward the so-called ship of dreams. The path became increasingly congested as passengers and well-wishers funneled down the docks toward the *Titanic*, sharing space with the long, low White Star Line building that ran for hundreds of feet. An idle crane was visible high above, having already done the work of lowering the ship's cargo.

When the *Titanic* came into full view, in its ten-deck, seventeen-story-high majesty, I stopped moving, unable to take one more step toward it. It wasn't as big as modern cruise ships, but it was a deep-charcoal-gray-and-white technological marvel against this backdrop of time, a ship for the ages. I felt like I had fallen into a movie, with the *Titanic* as a main character and all the actors in period costumes. All I'd have to do was play my part. *If only Windline's "Titanic test" were all cameras and lights and make-believe.*

As I stood there gawking at the vibrant and bustling scene in front of me, the harsh reality set in that this was all *real.* Pressure gripped my chest, and with zero help from my brain, tears welled up, stinging my eyes and spilling down my cheeks. I'd promised myself I'd compartmentalize the end of this ship's story, storing it in a sealed box in my brain, like one of those watertight compartments that were supposed to make the *Titanic* unsinkable. But my seal failed, just like the *Titanic*'s would, and the horror of the ship's journey spilled over and out into my consciousness. The 882-foot-long ship, with its three million rivets and propellers the size of windmills, was a testament to human ingenuity—the best and biggest of its time—but was also a colossal human failure, a floating soon-to-be tomb that would live only in history books and movies while it decayed at the bottom of the Atlantic.

I barely noticed as people broke ranks and flowed around me like I was a boulder in the middle of a stream. I also didn't notice that a car had pulled up behind me, its doors opening and closing. "You look like you could use a little help," said a woman beside me with a clear American accent. I recognized her instantly as one of the most famous passengers on the *Titanic*, the "Unsinkable Molly Brown." Her brown hair and full eyebrows sat atop blue eyes and rounded cheeks. Her hat was slightly askew, which was adorable, or, for all I knew, fashionable. The light behind her eyes made her incredibly attractive, in the full sense of that word, and I felt awkwardly large next to her. After all, I was much taller than the average woman in 1912.

I'd read all about Margaret Brown's life at the library in New York. She was born to Irish immigrants in Missouri. She'd worked in a tobacco factory, and also as a housekeeper and a seamstress, before marrying a miner who'd struck gold. With that money, they'd made even more, buying mining properties across Colorado, Utah, and Arizona. She was a suffragette, too, even running for office.

"Hello," I said, trying to wipe the tears off my cheeks. "I beg your pardon." I planned to use the word *pardon* in every other sentence, so I would sound semi-period-appropriate.

"For what?" she asked. Valets flitted around her, gathering her trunks. "Are you cryin' about leavin' here or gettin' on the ship?" She laughed amiably, her head motioning to the *Titanic*.

I'd fabricated a whole backstory while trying to go to sleep on Saturday night. I'd say I was a schoolteacher working abroad for a French family, but my uncle in New York had gotten sick. But now that I was here, remembering Ms. Brown was rushing to the side of a sick grandchild back home, I made a game-time decision to change my story.

"Both, I suppose," I said, forcing my face muscles to move my mouth into some semblance of a sad smile. "My older brother died in an accident in Africa, and now I have to return to the States without him." That sounded plausible and much more interesting. I thought about saying it was my fiancé who'd died, but I figured since I'd never even had a serious boyfriend, my authenticity might be low on the believability meter.

"I am so sorry to hear that. Well, here," she said, "let's help you get on board." She motioned to one of the men working on her bags. He hurried over. She pointed, and he went for my luggage.

"What's your cabin number, miss?" asked the man, with a heavy English accent.

I remembered right where my boarding pass was, tucked close to my heart, so to speak. But how to retrieve it from my corset without looking like a mannerless wench in front of Ms. Brown? "Ah, yes, let me see," I said, twisting to rummage through the small bag I carried like a crossbody purse. I undid one button of my suit and reached in my corset quickly to grab the paper, shielded, I thought, by my coat. "It's E-76," I said, straightening the paper.

"Very good, miss. I'll see to it." He tipped his hat and disappeared with the other men into the fray.

Ms. Brown didn't try to hide a big grin. "I can tell we're going to get along fine," she said, taking my arm. "Now let's get goin'. Time to check out this fancy hunk of metal."

"Thank you so much," I said sincerely. If I had to board the *Titanic*, I was glad to do it with someone who would live through the ordeal. "My name is Charl—Charlotte Landers," I said.

"Pleased to meet you, Charlotte," she said. "I'm Margaret Brown, but my friends call me Maggie." I wasn't sure exactly how Margaret, aka Maggie, got to be Molly, but I was glad our paths had crossed.

Boarding was on the port side, or the left side when facing the front of the ship. Maggie saying, "She's with me," got me on the first-class gangway, which felt like a parade of 1912 style and glamour. We went through the gangway door on D-Deck and into first-class Reception, where everyone received a deck plan in the form of a booklet entitled "White Star Line, Southampton-Cherbourg-New York Service, First Class Accommodation."

Just like that, I was aboard the *Titanic*, my junior-year fate in its hands. I scanned for my Minder, hoping to see Marla. I didn't recognize anyone from back home, so I focused on the passengers, particularly the handsome gentlemen and overly well-fed mogul types, very few of whom would make it out of this alive. Looking at them, I couldn't help feeling lucky. No matter how my test went, I would survive to see my parents and little Sammy, Tiana, and even confusing and annoying Quinn.

Another stroke of luck was the location of my cabin. Turns out some of the second-class cabins on the E-Deck were overflow in case first-class demand outstripped first-class availability. When I walked into E-76, I saw two beds, one of which had already been claimed by a small trunk sitting open on top of it. *Uh-oh* . . . I had a roommate, which meant that hiding in my cabin alone the whole trip would be less appealing than planned.

The room definitely looked like it could be a first-class cabin. It was large and airy, with natural light, mahogany beds, and rich wood paneling. It also had a dressing table, a wardrobe, a couch made of horsehair, and a marble-topped washstand with a basin that could be folded back into its cabinet to save space. Shared bathrooms were down the hall, segregated by gender. I'd give it four-and-a-half stars, even by modern standards. I could see my review now: *Highly recommend the first- and second-class accommodations on the White Star Line's new ship, Titanic. Everything is so fresh and perfect, with comfortable and high-end accommodations that include all the amenities of the time. I'd give the Titanic five stars, except for the whole iceberg, likely-death bit.*

I plopped down in a heap on my bed, wondering how in the world I was going to find a book of poetry on this gigantic ship. One step at a time, I reminded myself. Thanks to Maggie, my luggage had been placed just inside the door. I unpacked what little I had, hiding the few modern items I'd brought with me, like a large plastic zip bag for my toiletries and precautionary medicine, including seasickness patches. I'd stuck a few notes about the *Titanic* in the bag, too, in case all the facts I'd memorized got jumbled. I was glad I had—I was already desperately missing my smartphone. When I checked the clock, I was shocked to realize it was nearly noon. I hustled above deck to watch the ship depart.

With another "pardon me," I squeezed between a family with two young children and an older couple, finding a sliver of rail space for a good viewing spot. The little boy wiggled in front of me to be able to see, and I felt his shoulder solid against me, sending a jolt of dread up to my brain. I couldn't think about what would happen to kids like him, or I'd never make it through the week.

At noon, we cast off, and everyone on and off the ship cheered, waving hands, hats, or handkerchiefs at each other in the cool spring sunshine. So many people. So many goodbyes. It was a scene that would be captured in pictures for posterity, more important than anyone here realized. Now I'd be in that picture, just another passenger in a black coat and hat. I waved and cheered, too, swept up in the excitement as six tugs guided the *Titanic* slowly out and away through the narrow channel. No one and everyone waved back at me.

From my research, I already knew that a disaster almost happened at the very start of the voyage, when the backwash churned up by the *Titanic*'s propellers caused several ropes from the American liner *New York* to snap, making loud popping sounds like gunshots. The *New York*'s stern swung around and almost collided with the *Titanic*. When it happened, passengers on the deck were startled, and we had a one-hour delay. Unfortunately, one of the tugboats saved the day. If only it hadn't.

Off we went toward our next stop eighty miles away in Cherbourg, France, where 274 more passengers would board. Smoke from three of the four elliptical-shaped funnels—each large enough to fit two trains—billowed into the breeze. The fourth was a dummy, added for looks to provide a more balanced profile for the ship. I felt like the fake smokestack . . . not really doing anything here. I didn't even provide balance.

The rugged coastline slid by, with only a few well-wishers noticeable on the shore. Those who were there would always be able to say they'd seen the *Titanic* in its short-lived glory. If the trip had been in July instead of April, the banks would've been more crowded. And the icebergs in the Atlantic might not have been in the *Titanic*'s path. It would only take one change in the timeline, one small twist of fate, for the *Titanic* to sail on safely to New York. Just one.

# seven

## 1912
## on board the Titanic

As I dressed for dinner, struggling with the stays of my corset, I had a hell of an inner monologue about the history of the subjugation of women through their undergarments. Body styles went in and out of fashion, and if women's natural bodies didn't cut it, fashion would. In the 1910s, a slender, straight figure was in, so the relatively unstructured corsets of the day were mass-produced of single-layer cotton with reinforcement around the steel boning to smooth the body's shape and support good posture. My undergarments were twenty-first century made, more for show than anything else. Still, an engineering degree would've come in handy, since I could barely figure out how to dress myself. Plus, there were so many layers. Over my corset was a "princess petticoat," like a long precursor to a slip. I was getting claustrophobic, so much so that I considered stripping, sticking to my original plan, and staying in my room. But Maggie had invited me to dine with her in first class, and as much as I hated the idea of parading around with the likes of the Astors, I was both curious and hungry.

I also had to figure out how to get to my assigned goal of rescuing Omar Khayyám's *Rubáiyát*. I'd never read it, but I knew it was translated and published in 1860 by Edward FitzGerald. The edition I was after was encrusted with rubies and other jewels by British bookbinders, and I had to venture out sometime to find it. Besides, for once being with people sounded marginally appealing. Homesickness was starting to circle around the edges of my mind, since nobody was there to remind my subconscious what a short trip this would be. From my perspective at that moment, there was an eternity of the journey still ahead. After all, whole books were written about the night the *Titanic* sank, though I wouldn't see all of it. I'd been instructed to sneak home before the ship sank, with my heart still beating.

My roommate bustled in while I was slipping into a deep-burgundy gown made of a synthetic material that wouldn't wrinkle and looked like silk. Much of my wardrobe was thin, so it could be squeezed into my luggage. Unlike the first-class passengers, I didn't have large trunks to hold my things.

"Good evening," my roommate said as she closed the door behind her. "I am Rosalee Dunner."

I turned to see a young woman in her mid-twenties, with freckles sprinkled across her nose and cheeks and corkscrew curly red hair coming completely undone from its pins. Her eyes were emerald green, striking in a makeup-free face.

A wool shawl was wrapped around her shoulders, pinned in the front.

"Good evening," I responded. "My name is Charlotte Landers. You are American?" I tied a velvet ribbon around my neck as a choker, a tip I'd picked up from Epiphany's outfit three days ago.

"That I am," Rosalee said, removing her shawl and tossing it on her bed. "Though I have been in London for so many months that I would like to think I could pass for an Englishwoman. And my folks are Irish, if you could not tell." She held up a few errant twists of her hair. "You?"

"Yes, American. From California," I replied. "What brings you to make the crossing? Did you get tired of London?" I laughed. *Who gets tired of London?*

She sat down heavily on the couch, stretching her legs in front of her. "I was training there. Now I am returning home to Boston to put my learnings to good use."

"Oh? What sort of work do you do?"

"I am a physician, though I was studying midwifery techniques in London."

"How wonderful!" *And impressive for 1912!*

"Thank you, yes. Surgeons back home have tried to push aside the art of midwifery, which has been practiced with great success for ages. And they do not take non-traditional medicine seriously in the slightest. Someday I would like to study Eastern medicine, too."

"Wow, impressive," I said. "You must be extremely smart."

"Wow, you say? I have not heard that word used quite in that way before. In any case, we are each smart in our own ways. Mine just happens to be in science and anatomy." She looked me up and down. "You know there is no requirement to dress for dinner in second class, do you not?"

I looked down at myself. If only she could see my preferred clothes—shorts, a tank top, and flip-flops. "Oh, yes, but I have been invited for dinner in first."

"What a treat, Charlotte," she said.

"Please, call me Charlie."

"Well, how marvelous. Who says a woman cannot use a man's name?" She crossed her legs. "Charlie," she said with gusto, "your dress is lovely. By the looks of it, you should be staying in first-class accommodations, as well as eating there."

"Oh, yes, this . . . I had a wealthy aunt who decided she needed to clean her closet, and voilà, here I am, a girl with modest means in a rich girl's clothing." I shrugged.

"How very lucky! I am not sure your aunt would approve of your hair paired with her dress, though. . . ."

I looked in the mirror, not realizing quite what the wind on deck had done to my hair, with strands ratted from flying around the hat I'd worn. I grabbed my hairbrush, an old one with a sterling silver handle, which my mom had brought out from my parents' antique store for this trip. "So you'll know I'm with you," she'd said.

"Oh, it *is* awful," I replied. "I had better do something with it, or they may not let me into the first-class Dining Room!"

"My younger sister is forever asking me to help with her hair. Do you need a hand?"

She had no idea. I was okay at ponytails and flat irons. But I could only do a bare-bones updo, and if I hadn't watched twelve YouTube how-to videos before I'd left home, I wouldn't have been able to do that much.

Rosalee sat me down at the dressing table, and as if we'd known each other for years, she went after my hair until it was swooped up and piled high on my head. Some women in this period even saved hair from their hairbrushes to stick into their real updos for added volume.

"One more thing," she said, rummaging through her bags. "The pièce de résistance!" She held up a beautiful comb, sparkling with rhinestones in the light of the cabin. She placed it in the back of the nest at the back of my head and stood back to admire her work.

"I am stunned," I said. I looked, well, like I belonged in 1912. Amazing what a hairstyle could do. "You must be a wonderful doctor because you saved both my life and my hair. Thank you!" Careful not to show my contraband plastic zip-top bag, I patted on a light dusting of powder and nothing else, since makeup wasn't fashionable in 1912. I added my long, cream-colored gloves, then headed for the door.

"Enjoy your evening," she called. "And good luck!"

~

The *Titanic* had been described as a floating palace. I fully understood after seeing the grand staircase with its carved oak railings and bronze cherubs, and a span of sixty feet from the landing to the domed glass skylight above. Even the Hollywood versions didn't do the ship justice, and no amount of 3D video could substitute for what it felt like to actually walk on those steps.

With ten named decks, most corresponding to a letter, A through G, it was easy to get lost. After a couple of detours, I found my way to the Bridge Deck's À la Carte Restaurant, run by a famous Italian chef of the day. I was shown to Maggie's table, and as I walked toward the far end of the room, I drank in the Louis XVI–style decor that I'd read about. The paneling was French walnut, and large bay windows made the room airy and spacious. The floor was covered in a rich carpet, and the ceiling was plaster with flower patterns. I felt like Dorothy, waking up in Oz. Even though there was no place like home, this ship was pretty awesome—at least for the moment.

I caught a few stares as I walked, which I chalked up to my height, especially given that the two-inch heels on my satin slippers put me at five feet, nine inches. Plus I still had a bit of a summer tan, which probably made me look a little exotic for the time. I had the urge to slouch, to make myself less visible, but I felt certain that slouching wasn't done in first class. So I held my head up and shoulders back and tried not to trip.

When I arrived at the table for eight, I took the seat next to Maggie, who welcomed me warmly as the gentlemen stood and then retook their seats.

"Everyone," she announced, "this is my new friend, Miss Charlotte Landers. We boarded together this morning."

Then she began to go around the table, introducing me to each of her dinner companions. I didn't hear much after the introduction of Mr. Guggenheim—Benjamin Guggenheim—who was semi-attractive for a late-forty-something man. He had a baby face, a high forehead, and hair that waved slightly. His "companion," which I took to mean "mistress," was French singer Léontine Aubart, whose big smile lit up her face. Even I could figure out that these two must be scandalous. Still, they looked so refined as they nodded my way, clearly not impressed by this stray Maggie had picked up, although I did notice quite the "checkout" from Mr. Guggenheim. Except for Maggie, I didn't imagine many of the diners in the restaurant broadened their circles very often, but I got the creepy vibe that Mr. Guggenheim would gladly broaden his if he thought it might lead to some fun. *Ick.*

Another guest arrived not long after I did to complete our table of eight. I was glued to the menu, sipping water when he appeared at the opposite side of the table from me. As Maggie greeted him, I looked up.

And my heart jumped right out of my chest. . . .

"Quinn?" I said way too loudly to be mannerly, nearly choking on the water I'd just swallowed. He looked every bit like Quinn but also not at all like him. His shoulder-length hair was gone, now trimmed neatly, shorter on the sides, and slightly longer on top, and parted on one side and slicked down so that it looked semi-shiny. His tuxedo was right out of 1912 Windline central casting, with a vest and tails, and as flattering as almost everything was on Quinn. He looked every bit the upper-crusty first-class passenger.

"Well, Mr. Daniels, it appears you have given Miss Landers quite the fright," said one of the women. "Do you two know each other?"

Without taking his eyes off me, almost as if he didn't recognize the 1912 me either, Quinn took his seat next to the French singer. He placed his napkin in his lap before answering lazily, "Indeed I do, yes. We are well acquainted, but it has been some time since I have had the pleasure of seeing Miss Landers." Then his gaze turned to me, and he said, "I hope you are well?"

I was sure I'd floated out of my body and was levitating above the table. Quinn was my Minder? Why in the world would Windline allow that? Why didn't he give me some kind of hint? He'd had every chance to come clean. Was this his way of torturing me, of paying me back for some perceived slight in our childhood?

Worse, he'd specifically told me to listen to my Minder. He'd pulled me in, just to surprise me in the worst way. Like suddenly realizing two plus two equals five, it occurred to me that his dancing and kissing and helping me since school started had most likely been all about him. Did he go to that much trouble to make sure he passed his stupid Senior Year Test? It made sense—the stakes were high for him, too.

The seed of doubt about Quinn's motives quickly became a full-blown tree in my mind. Like a fast German car, my suspicions—fueled by embarrassment—raced from zero to sixty in a nanosecond. I couldn't stop them or argue with them. Why should I? Everything made sense.

There had been no big change in our usual relationship over the summer. He cared about me, if at all, only because our mothers were best friends, and he wouldn't get close to me or become my Minder out of some kind of family obligation. And who better to use than me as a compliant junior who'd hang on his every word, making his job as Minder that much easier—a slam dunk passing grade for graduating, complete with a time pin.

So much for thinking he'd introduced me to other seniors to help ME. All of it—the attention, the dancing—was an insurance policy for HIM. Heat ran along every nerve in my body. I curled my hands into fists in my lap and clenched my teeth. If he thought I'd be easy to "handle," then he didn't know me very well after all!

Everyone was looking to me for a response. Swallowing hard to choke down my double-jalapeño-hot level of anger, I fell back to my 1912 utility word. "Pardon me, everyone," I said slowly, afraid curse words might come out if I didn't concentrate. "I did not expect to see Mr. Daniels here on the *Titanic*, but what a nice surprise. He turns up in the most unlikely places." I took another sip of water to cool the flames inside me. "I am well, Mr. Daniels, though you may have heard of my older brother's passing in Africa." I raised one eyebrow for emphasis.

No one else would've noticed, but Quinn looked down at the table and his lip curled up slightly for the tiniest moment before he shot a serious look of concern in my direction.

"I had not," he said, "but I am truly devastated to hear of it. My sincere condolences to you and your family. Your brother was a great chap." Another infinitesimal semi-smile.

Chap? Damn, he didn't miss a beat. I was dying to murder him, yell at him, or at least pepper him with questions, but the meal dragged on and on, ten courses of dishes like chilled spring pea soup, chicken in cream sauce, and oysters à la Russe. My "no red meat" plan went out the window somewhere along the way, though I nibbled just enough to go along with the group. In between courses, we drank Punch à la Romaine, a shaved-ice cocktail made with rum and champagne. It was a citrusy and refreshing "palate cleanser."

I wasn't used to eating so much food at once, or drinking, so my head got lighter at the same time my corset got tighter. By the tenth course, I was barely holding myself together, though other than telling a few made-up tales about my long-lost brother, I didn't have to say much. I was a seat filler at best for this group, meaning silence was golden as long as I laughed in the right places or asked a polite question now and then. Quinn, as a seemingly well-to-do and self-assured young man, had to work a bit harder.

"Where are you from, Mr. Daniels?" asked one of the men.

"California," Quinn answered.

"And your family?"

"They are also from California," he said innocently, though I knew he was baiting the man. "We are in the travel business."

"Railroads, then?"

"Indeed, though travel is so much more than railroads these days. Just look at the *Titanic*, for example. No one could have dreamed up a ship like this ten years ago. Imagine what the future holds."

"And what do you see in our future, Mr. Daniels?" I asked, doing my own baiting that would fly over everyone's heads except Quinn's.

Quinn took a sip of his drink. "Aviation, Miss Landers. One day, we'll be flying from London to New York." He gestured with an arcing motion of his hand.

"I can't imagine," I said, glaring as a contraction accidentally slipped out.

"Sounds like wishful thinking to me," said another guest. And so on. Quinn never flinched. Of course, it's easy to forecast when you're from the future, and he was blessed with an easy self-assurance that had to come from his good looks. All eyes were usually on him.

Quinn's job on the *Titanic* was easy. *He* didn't have to find the *Rubáiyát*, and he had clearly been given a first-class ticket. I imagined Quinn spending his trip luxuriating in the gym, or the indoor pool and Turkish baths, while I was trouncing around the ship with a crowbar trying to pry open crates of books in the hold.

When dinner finally concluded, we all stood, and I found myself a bit wobbly on my feet. Quinn appeared behind me. "Miss Landers?" he said, offering his arm. Reluctantly, I slipped my hand through the crook of his elbow.

"Mr. Daniels," I said, conscious that the group could hear us. "What an odd coincidence to see you here. You might have mentioned something."

"I am afraid I could not."

"But you were able to make sure all would go smoothly for *you*."

Quinn stopped walking and turned slightly to look at me. "What is that supposed to mean, Miss Landers?"

I glared up at him, about to unleash my inner beast smack dab in the middle of this fancy room full of the who's who of 1912. "You—"

"Mr. Daniels, care to join us in the Smoke Room?" called Mr. Guggenheim, interrupting my plan to take Quinn down a few pegs right then and there.

"Indeed I would," Quinn called back.

"Indeed you would," I mocked under my breath. If my one word was "pardon," he had two—"chap" and "indeed." Of course he had to one-up me.

Quinn knitted his eyebrows, probably trying to decide if I was so tipsy I'd fall overboard. If I did, he'd fail his test, which was clearly all that mattered to him. I guess he figured I could make it to my cabin on my own, because he dipped his head in a pseudo-bow and said, "Good evening, Miss Landers."

I didn't respond, and he turned to join the men. Well, fine. I didn't envy anyone going into a room full of cigar and cigarette smoke anyway, even if it was with the rich and famous. Besides, almost every single man in that room would be dead in a few days. He'd be hanging out with ghosts.

Quinn thought he was on easy street, that he'd fly through the Senior Year Test with me drooling at his feet. But I vowed to get back at him, if not on the *Titanic*, then somewhere, someday. He might play a nice guy, but he had used me—had used our families' relationship to make sure he graduated, to get his own time pin. He thought he could pay attention to me for a few weeks and that I'd fall all over him when he somehow wormed his way into becoming my Minder? He had another thing coming. But revenge would have to wait. If I didn't get some fresh air, I was in danger of hurling up that fizzy drink all over the place—not a good look for my first night aboard. Luckily, Maggie was ready to turn in, so I thanked her profusely and said my goodbyes for the evening. I headed for the deck.

~

The *Titanic* was almost as long as three football fields, and the grand staircase was closer to the bow than the stern, in front of the second of the ship's four giant smokestacks.

Since the *Rubáiyát* was in storage somewhere below the stern, next to the third-class cabins, I decided to walk in that direction, breathing in the night air to clear my head and cool my anger. The moon cast a muted glow over the ship and the water beyond. A ghost ship full of ghosts. I shuddered.

I passed through the second-class Promenade, through the third-class one, and then arrived at the deck that led to the far rear of the ship. When I arrived, I had to blink to clear my vision. Was I hallucinating? I was alone except for one woman. She appeared to be on the *outside* of the railing, leaning over the water, nothing but her hands and feet keeping her on the ship. Was I having flashbacks to the movie, having watched it so many times that I was confusing Hollywood with reality? Or was she real—and in actual danger of falling to her death? I kept walking toward her, hoping she would disappear into thin air, a figment of my imagination from too much fizz in my bloodstream.

This girl was no illusion, though. She also wasn't a first-class passenger trapped in a smothering engagement to a tall, dark, handsome millionaire. Judging by her dress, she was a third-class passenger, contemplating a jump to her death.

I briefly considered turning quietly and running for my room. After all, I had no plans to engage with the people on the *Titanic*, and somebody—anybody—would be more qualified to do something than I was. . . . I looked around. All quiet. On a ship filled with people, I was it. A string of choice profanities ran through my head. Then, reluctantly, I approached the girl as ninja-like as I could, trying not to spook her. She heard me as I got within a few feet.

"No!" she yelled into the wind. "Please leave me alone!" I could tell she wasn't from Western Europe or the States from her accent, but I couldn't place it.

"Where are you from?" I asked in as soothing a voice as I could muster, hoping she spoke some English.

She looked at me with a mixture of anger and fear. Her face was pale, and despite the cool night, beads of sweat stood out on her forehead. Her raven-black hair blew loose in the wind, a scarf flying behind her as if she had wings. Coal-black lashes framed dark eyes.

In a heavy accent, she said, "Syria."

"Syria, oh that is wonderful." She probably spoke Levantine Arabic, which I had no clue how to speak, not even the "where's the bathroom" kind of stuff. Thank goodness she spoke English.

"It was," she said, adjusting her handholds.

My mind raced. Here was a third-class passenger. Only about half the people in her class would survive. She was female, which would increase her chances of getting into a lifeboat, but the odds were still against her. Should I leave her alone so she could take her own life in peace? At least she'd have some sense of control over her last moments. . . . Or should I try to help, to talk her back from the brink, knowing she might die a horrible death from injury or cold or drowning in a few short days?

A few years ago, my family witnessed a wreck on the freeway. We stopped to help, and my parents ran to pull the driver out of the window of his smoldering car. Now I was the one watching a car on fire a few feet in front of me. Shouldn't I try to help?

I had no right to intervene, and in fact was forbidden to interfere in the timeline, but I quickly realized that the human instinct to survive can extend to others, almost involuntarily. My better angels won the debate.

"Syria was wonderful?" I asked. "Are you sad to go to America?"

"It does not matter," she said, bristling at being drawn into conversation. "Now leave me alone."

"I am afraid I cannot leave. I know four things about you now. You are from Syria. You are smart because your English is very good, and it is a hard language to learn. I can clearly see that you are very sad. And you are very pretty. That's four things. Once an American knows four things about you, she cannot leave you when you are in danger. It is a rule, really."

"I do not think so."

"No really, it is true. In fact, you will have to swear to it when you enter the country. What is your name, by the way?

I will need to know, so I can tell your family if you accidentally fall into the freezing cold water."

She frowned at me, then looked down, far down, to the churning ocean below her. "My name is Rima. Please go now."

"Rima, my name is Charlotte, but my friends call me Charlie."

"Okay, Charlotte. I want to be alone."

"I promise to go away if you will just tell me why you want to jump."

With good reason, she cast me a doubting sideways glance. "It is not for you to know, but it is because I am in love and will never see my Farid again." Tears gathered in her eyes as she spoke.

"He is still in Syria?"

"Yes."

"That is very sad. Could he come to America, too, someday?"

"It does not matter."

"Why not?"

"Because my family has made a match for me in the United States." More tears.

I couldn't think of how to make her situation sound hopeful, but I kept going. "Now I can understand why you are hurting. Will the match your parents have made be so bad?"

She nodded.

I couldn't imagine an arranged marriage. Mine would be to Quinn, no doubt, knowing my mother and his. *Talk about a disaster. . . .*

"That must be really hard," I said, speaking slower than normal to make sure she could understand my accent, "but there is hope. In the long run, it is your female friends who stay with you, and you will love all the friends you will make in America. Women have lots of options there, too, like education. I am sharing a cabin on the ship with an American doctor, for example. She delivers babies. And women can divorce, too, so you do not have to get married or even stay in the marriage if you do not want to."

"You cannot understand. My family—" Her voice trailed off as if carried away by the wind.

"I imagine they will pressure you. But take one day at a time, then you can make your own life when you are ready. You do not want to end it tonight. Not in that freezing cold water, if you even live long enough to feel it." *Oh God*, I thought, *why am I doing this? She might not survive anyway!*

She looked down again at the *Titanic*'s wake, then back at me. I watched her breathe heavily. I watched the uncertainty in the downturn of her mouth and the furrowing of her brows. I imagined I could hear her heart pounding . . . or maybe that was mine.

I held out my hand. She looked back and forth from me to the water below, weighing her options. I kept my hand out until my arm started shaking. Finally, she reached out for it and began to pivot so she was facing the deck.

Her palm was sweaty in mine. I wasn't taking any chances that she'd fall, so I took her hand and grabbed her arm above the stack of bracelets she wore. She hooked a leg over, a difficult maneuver in her long cotton dress, and when she got halfway, I got in front of her to help pull the rest of her body over, holding her in a half bear hug. But her shoe slipped, and her weight shifted dangerously toward the water. I leaned back hard to make sure we went the right direction. We both screamed as we fell onto the deck in one flailing lump, me underneath her.

My head hit with a loud *crack* sound on the hard wood-over-metal surface, and the wind was knocked out of me as the weight of Rima's body forced out all my air. I gasped to fill my empty lungs as she rolled off me and onto the deck, now more concerned about my survival than her pain. When I curled into a ball on my side, Rima started screaming. I wasn't sure why. Oxygen was my first priority.

As my breathing normalized, I was able to do a quick system check. Left elbow—*fair*. Ribs—*sore*. Head—*stinging like it was on fire*. None of it mattered. Rima was safe, for the moment anyway. But the system check of my conscience revealed an inner conflict with guilt bubbling up. I'd helped her save herself, only so she'd live to face a death she had no control over. *Did I do something wonderful or absolutely horrible?* I couldn't be sure.

I heard men's voices—heavy English accents—and footsteps. But I was deep inside myself, thinking through what I'd just done. The *Titanic* was determined to get its pound of flesh, from me, from Rima, from the men with Quinn tonight. This whole ship was a burning car, and I was a passerby watching it burn. I thought the people on this ship wouldn't matter, that they wouldn't seem real to me. But tonight, I realized I was wrong. Rima was real. I'd felt the depth of her sorrow and the weight of her very bones. Her pain and her family's dreams of a better life in America were real, too.

Rules were rules, though. I almost always followed them. I'd been told more than once that I'd have to redo my Junior Year Test if I interfered with the time stream—if I tried to change the past.

Failing would have consequences for me, perhaps for my family, and definitely for Quinn, who would most likely fail his test. But how did any of that amount to anything in the grand scheme of time? It was nothing. Nothing in the face of Rima dying of hypothermia. Nothing to children in third class dying in their beds because US immigration required segregation of passengers to stop disease from spreading. Nothing to women and children in lifeboats watching their loved ones go down and living with that image their entire lives. Sure, the sinking of the *Titanic*, and all the hearings that took place after it, meant more strict safety rules were put in place for ships. But history could sort that out.

In that moment on the cold, hard deck, something began to shift in me. I realized the reaction I'd had when I saw the *Titanic*, when I'd cried, wasn't about history. It was about the moment I was living in—in 1912. It was about each human like Rima on the ship. This wasn't a movie to cry over with popcorn. This wasn't a theme park version of some event that made the papers in 1912. This was a ship filled with flesh-and-blood people, and most of them would be dying soon, terrified, cold, shocked. I cried over puppies in cages at the pound back home, and here I was planning to spend this trip in my room, ignoring the very lives of people like Rima?

# eight

⚓

A crew member, who had come running when Rima screamed, arrived and gave me instructions, his voice shaky. "Miss, I'll be fetching the ship's surgeon. Do not move, miss. Please, stay right there." He covered me with his dark wool peacoat, which I gladly accepted because I had started to shiver uncontrollably.

Another crew member grabbed Rima by the arm and pulled her aside.

"What is going on here?" the sailor demanded. "You have injured this passenger."

"I—I, it was an accident, I swear it!"

"How did this happen?"

"I was just on the railing, and I fell—we fell," she said, wringing her hands as she spoke and casting frightened glances my way.

"She is right," I said, my teeth beginning to chatter. "She was looking over to see if we could see the propeller, and her skirt got caught. Then we crashed on top of one another. It was merely a silly accident, really. . . ." Good thing I'd dressed for that dinner, so at least I looked like a first-class passenger. If I'd been on my feet, I would've had a few choice words for the guy manhandling Rima.

The crew member stared at me as if physically weighing my words against his own prejudice, but he let go of Rima, who ran to my side. I reached for her.

"Can I get up now?" I asked. "Really, I am fine. I only have a bit of a headache, and my elbow hurts—nothing to worry about."

"But, miss, you must stay there and wait for the surgeon. He will just be a moment."

Rima added in her accented English, "Charlie, your head, it is bleeding. It would be better if you did not move."

Okay, I could take direction as well as the next person, but being told to lie still on a ship's deck with a head wound was a hard pass. Someone needed to put pressure on the wound and get me to my cabin. After all, my roommate was a doctor and my cabin was so much warmer than the deck.

"Rima, if I am still bleeding, do you think you could rip off a piece of your dress—I will pay for the damage—and press it against the wound to stop the bleeding?" My shakes hadn't stopped, but the adrenaline of doing something helped a bit. Rima reached for her dress hem.

"Will this do, miss?" asked the seaman, quickly offering his handkerchief instead.

"Is it clean?" I asked.

"Yes, miss."

"Then it will be perfect."

Rima grabbed it and lifted my head gently. I sucked in my breath when she pressed against the cut. I should've realized a wound had been causing the stinging.

"Great, Rima, thank you. Now let us see if I can sit up. We will go slowly, okay?"

Rima nodded and took an arm, and the crew member came to take my other one. Slowly, I rose to a sitting position and did another system check. I was a little woozy, but then again, I'd been a little woozy since drinking at dinner. My head hurt, but it was nothing my secret stash of name-brand pain relievers couldn't handle.

Then we heard, "Over here, Doctor!"

Dr. William Francis Norman O'Loughlin, a stout older man with white hair and a ginormous handlebar mustache, trotted across the deck toward me, followed by two crew members and—God, no—Quinn, plus another one of the men from dinner. Looks like the doctor had been in the smoking room with the gentlemen when he'd gotten the news of my accident. I hoped he was sober.

I couldn't focus on what the doctor was saying at first because Quinn stood over him, practically doing hand signals. I knew what he was trying to do—his job as Minder was to make sure that if I were hurt, modern medicine would come to the rescue. He obviously wasn't able to travel back to our own time with human cargo, but he could get help to come back here if needed.

I held up my hand in the universal signal of "stop." Thankfully, Quinn backed up a bit.

Dr. O'Loughlin took over from Rima, looking at the back of my head. "Head wounds tend to bleed in a disproportionate amount relative to the size of the wound, miss. You will need three or four stitches, but you will be right as rain in no time." His brand of English accent was quite comforting. "Now," he said, moving in front of me, "let me have a look at your eyes."

He propped open one eye, then the other, with his fingers. He asked me to follow his finger up, down, and sideways.

"Your eyes look normal. Judging from the wound on the back of your head, you must have hit the deck decently hard, perhaps landing on a pebble brought on board by an errant boot. I would hazard a guess you have a minor head injury. I can give you aspirin powder to help."

*I think I'll stick to my secret stash of acetaminophen*, I thought.

"Does anything else hurt?"

"Only my elbow." I offered my arm.

He bent my arm back and forth. I winced. "Good range of motion," he pronounced, "but a nasty bruise. The powder should help with the pain. Now, gentlemen," he said, looking up at Quinn and his new friend and ignoring Rima entirely, "get her to the Hospital for the stitches. I will dash on ahead to get things ready, and you can take it slowly. The

Hospital is on D-Deck at the starboard side close to the second-class Dining Room. You can also enter above on C-Deck. After that," he said, turning to me, "we will get you back to your cabin for a good night's sleep." He looked over at Quinn, who nodded.

"Wait," I said. "Rima can come with us and help me back to my room—really." The last thing I wanted was for Quinn to pinpoint my cabin.

Dr. O'Loughlin spoke up. "I am sure she will be missed by her traveling companions belowdecks. Best to say goodbye here."

Of course. Third-class passengers couldn't just wander through the ship like I had. The doctor and Quinn helped me stand, and after steadying myself and handing the crewman his coat, I went to hug my new friend. As I pulled away, I said, "Remind me, Rima, of your cabin number." I wanted to be able to check on her. "Thank you," I said, after she told me. "Everything is going to be okay, Rima. I promise." I smiled and squeezed her hand.

~

The doctor shaved a small spot underneath the thick hair on the back of my head. When he stitched the wound, I felt like a football with the laces being sewn in. Maybe I should've let Quinn call for a Windline-affiliated doctor to come to my rescue with some numbing medication and a pediatric needle. But I'd gut it out.

Quinn stayed through the ordeal, which included Dr. O'Loughlin's heavy breathing behind me as he concentrated. He'd definitely been drinking bourbon, and the smell of it mixed with the fresh paint scent of the room.

I told Quinn to go several times, but he ignored me:

"Quinn, thank you, but there is no need for you to stay."

"Quinn, I will be fine. I am in good hands. You should get back to your friends."

"Quinn, really, I would feel much better if you would go."

"Quinn, when we get home, I am going to have a word with our mutual acquaintances."

Nothing.

I was his assignment, and he was taking it very seriously. Why couldn't Marla have been my Minder? Or, if guys were allowed, Gustavo? Or really . . . anyone else?

When the doctor said, "All done," I slid down off the table, intending to make a getaway from Quinn. But he stood in front of the door like a well-dressed Oscar presenter.

"Now, Mr.—" the doctor began.

"Daniels."

"Yes, Mr. Daniels, make sure she mixes no more than one tablespoon with a glass of water, three to four times a day." Quinn took the famous "powder" in a small glass vial from the doctor. "She will need to rest and stay quiet tomorrow."

"Of course," Quinn said, ignoring my eye roll.

"And if she starts having any other symptoms, ask the steward to ring me right away."

"Will do."

I wanted to shout at both of them that I was sitting right there with perfectly functioning ears, but this was 1912. Women weren't exactly considered rocket scientists, especially after a knock on the head, so I refrained from making myself any angrier. Besides, when my satin shoes touched the floor, I realized how exhausted I was, as much by the accident as the whole night and, well, the whole *Titanic* thing. I needed rest. And time to think.

"Quinn," I said when we hit the brightly lit passageway outside the door to the Hospital, "we can stop pretending now. I'm going to my cabin, and you're going to leave. You aren't supposed to interfere with my JY Test, and I'm clearly in no physical danger now. Plus, my cabinmate is a doctor. I'll be fine."

Without saying anything, Quinn accelerated ahead of me. "Good and good riddance," I muttered under my breath. Then he stopped and came back at me, pointing.

"Charlie, get a grip! I'm trying to help you! But you're too damn stubborn to accept anything from me." He shook his head. "God—you're the MOST annoying girl I've ever met!"

"I'm annoying? At least I don't play with people's feelings to get what I want. You're the most SELFISH, self-centered, egotistical, narcissistic guy on the planet—at any TIME on the planet!"

"What are you talking about? You MUST have a concussion because you've totally lost your friggin' mind!"

We were getting louder and louder. "Oh, so you're going to blame head trauma for words that nail EXACTLY who you are? Next you'll blame your lack of character on my period or my hormones. Take a good look at yourself instead of at ME!"

If this dialogue had happened in a movie, the two main characters would suddenly stop arguing and passionately kiss each other as the soundtrack swelled and the camera panned. In our case, I would've murdered Quinn if he'd kissed me. I was actually considering kicking him in the groin when the surgeon bustled out of the Hospital to break us up.

"Mr. Daniels, Miss Landers. Please." He wedged himself between us. "Perhaps I should escort Miss Landers to her cabin?" Again, directed at Quinn.

Quinn started to run his hand through his hair, but quickly realized most of it had been cut off and what was left was pasted to his head. I rolled my eyes and snickered.

"A good idea, indeed," Quinn said to me. There was that word again. Hadn't he read books? Watched an old movie or two? Then, to Dr. O'Loughlin, he added, "My apologies."

Quinn made a slight bow with his head, then turned on his heel as if he were a soldier and strode away.

~

The next morning, my roommate woke up early. She tiptoed around inside the cabin, but when she left for the bathroom, the sound of the door opening and closing woke me up. I groaned and turned over to put a pillow over my head. Unfortunately, I forgot about the stitches and sat bolt upright when I felt a stinging pain. But I had to use my abs to sit up, which reminded me that my ribs were sore. And my elbow felt creaky. I wondered briefly if this was what old age felt like. If so, I'd aged decades overnight.

In addition to my body scan, I also did a gut scan. Was I embarrassed at how I'd behaved with Quinn? For a split second, I felt a wave of guilt, but it was quickly replaced with anger as I thought about how he'd been plotting his own success and manipulating my feelings.

In the cold light of day, the most logical explanation for his behavior was definitely self-interest. Otherwise, he wouldn't have changed his tune just when school started.

He wanted me to be an easy traveling companion, careful to follow the rules so he'd pass his test and get his time pin. I'd been an easy target for his "make nice" plan, given our history. What better way to get me under his spell than to try to make me feel special? Our history and his good looks would do the rest. He might even enjoy his test, watching with smug satisfaction from his perch in first class as I fell deeper into his trap.

I stood up in slow motion. My body was a mess, but my mind was worse. I desperately needed some fresh air. I gingerly shimmied into a dress, skipping all the extras, and threw my coat on top. I left a "be right back" note for Rosalee and headed for the deck.

Leaning against the railing, looking out at the expanse of ocean, I took some deep breaths and revisited the thoughts I'd had about the *Titanic* the night before. Now that the alcohol and excitement had worn off, I needed to decide what to do. I wasn't used to making such weighty decisions. And even if I were brave enough to interfere with the time stream and try to stop the *Titanic* from sinking, could I do it? And could I face my parents when I got back, telling them I'd broken the biggest rule of all?

I turned to look down the deck. People were moving about now, and I spotted two small children in stockings and leather lace-up shoes playing catch, running my direction, and laughing. One missed a catch, and the ball bounced and rolled toward me. I scooped up the ball and tossed it back, and as thanks I got a sheepish grin. I couldn't help smiling back.

Like the boy at the railing when we set sail, this child was real. Innocent. And all of these children were facing terror at best, and potential death at worst, in just a matter of days. At the same time I felt the pain of that reality in my gut, a strong resolve flowed from the ship's deck, up my body, and into my heart until my internal monologue stopped questioning and silently screamed, *NO!*

I would not let it happen! I would not let this ship sink. I couldn't. If fate—or my genes—or whatever—got me here, then I was going to use what I knew to change this timeline. I was going to stop this tragedy, with its insufferable loss of human life.

How could I live with myself, safely back in my own bed at home while I thought of children dying in these waters, thrown from the very ship under my feet? Rima and Rosalee bobbing in life jackets, frozen and lifeless? I was going to stop the *Titanic* from hitting that iceberg, instead of crawling away back to my time for a good grade and a pat on the back.

I'd saved Rima last night, unsure if it was the right thing then. Now I knew it was. And I would have to do it again. There was really no choice to make.

I was going to change history. Consequences be damned.

And if, because of me, Quinn failed out of high school, then . . . bonus.

# nine

The *Titanic*'s dining rooms were also called saloons. I'd always thought of saloons as those dusty places with swinging doors found on every corner of every town in the Wild West—or at least in every old Hollywood movie version. The *Titanic*'s second-class dining saloon had deep brown wood paneling, pillars, and heavy swivel chairs that were bolted to the floor. Long tables were dressed neatly in white cloth. The place smelled like a mix of syrup and meat when Rosalee and I walked in, making me realize I was hungrier than I'd thought. The sea air and my newfound purpose must have kicked my appetite into overdrive. There were a lot of regular breakfast choices—fruit, oats, scones, buckwheat cakes with maple syrup—but also super weird foods like Yarmouth bloaters, a type of whole cold-smoked herring, and grilled ox kidneys. I was in a daring mood, so I tried a bite of the herring. I drew the line at kidneys.

We sat next to a friendly man who said he was a "confectioner," which I figured meant he was a baker. He was sailing to join his brother in Connecticut and had left his wife and children, who would follow him once he got settled in the States. He dabbed his mouth and excused himself, saying he wanted to make the post with a letter to them.

When he left, I asked Rosalee nonchalantly as I nibbled some fruit, "How do you think I could meet the captain?"

"Why in the world do you care to meet the captain?" she asked, a heaping bite of creamy potatoes going into her mouth.

*Because I'm planning to tell him about the iceberg that's gonna sink us.* "I am just so curious about the ship, and who better to give me the details than the captain?" I responded.

"Maybe you could ask the surgeon?"

"Great idea," I said, taking a last sip of my coffee. "I will try to catch him."

~

At sixty thousand tons, the *Titanic* was the largest man-made object ever built in its time. Around 11:30 that morning, April 11, the technological marvel arrived in Queenstown, Ireland, where we dropped anchor for our last stop before setting sail for New York. More than one hundred and twenty-three passengers would join us, bringing the total souls on board to over two thousand. I stood on the Boat Deck—the deck with promenades for first- and second-class passengers where the majority of the lifeboats were housed—in the brisk wind with my coat wrapped around me. I watched our arrival against the backdrop of the Irish town, a cathedral standing tall above rows of buildings with uniform windows. The *Titanic* was welcomed like a celebrity, people lining the shore for a glimpse. Small boats buzzed around us, selling local goods such as lace and linen.

"How's your head?" It was Quinn, appearing next to me out of nowhere and somehow replacing the woman who had stood there a moment before.

"Stalking me much?" I asked, continuing to look out at the scenery.

"Maybe." We were quiet for a moment. Then he added, "I'm your Minder, remember?"

The wind seemed to pierce through me, giving me a chill. "How could I forget?"

"Look," he said, "I don't know why you're so mad at me, but any possibility we could call a truce? I could be helpful here, you know."

I turned to look at him, and in the muted light of the late morning, he looked like the best version of himself. His hair moved slightly with the wind, his high-collared black coat accentuating his square jaw and perfect cheekbones. I had the urge to lean into him and beg him to throw his arms around me, to erase the dread of the *Titanic*'s fate from my bones, but Hell would freeze over before I did that. Just because someone's outsides were beautiful didn't mean what was on the inside was worth the trouble.

"What could you possibly help me with?" I asked.

"Well," he said, "for starters, I could help you find the *Rubáiyát.*"

"I thought you weren't supposed to interfere? You're here to make sure I follow the rules and don't die, and that's it, right?" It crossed my mind that he could be springing a trap of some sort.

"Do I want us to both pass our tests? Yes, of course I do. But what Windline doesn't know won't hurt them. If I can help you, then I want to."

"And Windline would've known if you'd told me you were my Minder?"

"That's different."

"Yeah. Like an apple and an orange are different. But they're both still fruit."

Quinn paused. "I literally have no idea what that means, Charlie."

"Whatever."

"So are you gonna let me help or not?"

I wasn't about to let him in on my plan. After all, the rule I intended to break was *the* rule, and breaking it would mean we'd both fail. But maybe I could take him up on his offer, and by the time he found out about my plan, it'd be too late to do anything about it.

"Can you help me get to the captain? I want to meet the man who kills most of the people on this ship. And,"

I added, to be sure I wasn't being too obvious, "I'd like to ask him for a tour, so I can figure out exactly where the *Rubáiyát* is stored." Quinn was a bona fide first-class passenger, and even though I could move pretty freely dressed as one, I couldn't go everywhere. Having him with me would help with access. Sadly, in this era, having a member of the male species by my side might also give me more credibility.

Quinn looked at me like he was trying to peek inside my brain and figure out what was going on in there. Then he said, "Sure. What did you have in mind?"

"I thought I might ask Dr. O'Loughlin for help first. Then maybe Maggie?"

"Okay, if those don't work, I could ask Guggenheim."

"Great. I'll let you know. In the meantime, maybe you could check around with the crew—find out who's in charge of the cargo manifest—then we meet back here at around three this afternoon?" Adjustment to life without texting was annoying. It was amazing any human progress had ever happened without cell phones.

Quinn shook his head. "No way, I'll come with you."

"We can get more done if we divide and conquer."

"We can get more done if we work as a team."

"Fine, but only if you promise that you'll leave if I ask you to."

"Sure."

I didn't believe him for a second. "Cross your heart?"

"Whatever—yes."

Best I was gonna get. We left the deck and headed straight for the Hospital.

~

Dr. O'Loughlin was working in the Hospital when we arrived. We waited in silence on hard, straight-back chairs for what seemed like ages. A child had slipped while spinning a top on the "poop deck" in the rear of the ship, which, ironically, was where the dogs of the first-class passengers were walked.

Health requirements on ships were established by the British Board of Trade, so the *Titanic*'s medical facilities were comparable to most state-of-the-art small hospitals of the era in the United States and Britain. Still, I was glad my injury hadn't been worse. No matter how state of the art, nor how many instruments the ship's surgery had, this place couldn't compare to a modern-day hospital.

"Ah, my dear, come in," the doctor finally said when the little patient limped out with his father. "Let me have a look at you."

I obediently presented myself, at which point Dr. O'Loughlin repeated the eye check from the night before. Then he sat me down and dug into my mass of brown hair, which hung halfway down my back with a simple ribbon tying the front sections in the back. Not at all fashionable at my age, but with the stitches, I couldn't manage much more.

"Looks just fine," he said. "Any headache?"

"No, sir," I said, which was only a little white lie. The smell of antiseptic in the Hospital wasn't helping. "I feel surprisingly good. In fact"—I looked over at Quinn—"we were wondering if you might know how we could meet the captain—maybe even see the Bridge? That would be such a special adventure!"

"You two?" He looked back and forth between us. "I got the distinct impression you were not on, shall we say, the best of terms last evening."

Quinn jumped in. "Yes, and we sincerely apologize. Our families have been friends forever, and sometimes we fight like brother and sister."

I nodded and smiled. *More like gladiators, but close enough.*

"I can understand that," the doctor said. "So you want to meet the captain, aye? I can tell you for certain that you will not be able to go on the Bridge. It is accessible to crew only." He looked at our expectant faces. "But let me call up and see where he is this afternoon."

I clasped my hands together over my heart in a sign of thanks. Dr. O'Loughlin stepped away to the other room, then after a few minutes, he came back. "Good news. He is dining in the Café Parisien with some of our most illustrious passengers. Perhaps you could catch him there." He added, "It is on B-Deck starboard just off the aft grand staircase."

After I gave the doctor a spontaneous, no-real-body-contact hug, which he tolerated stiffly, I started away from the surgery at a run. Quinn followed suit, then nearly ran into me when I stopped abruptly. "Sorry," I said as he grabbed my shoulders to stop his forward momentum, "running is hurting my head and ribs. Let's walk fast."

The Café Parisien was a popular spot, so I hung back while Quinn angled for a table, using his first-class credentials. With my hair down and a simple dress on, I looked decidedly second class.

The long, narrow room with sea-facing windows bustled with voices, movement, and clinking plates. Apparently, many of the younger first-class passengers enjoyed the feeling of an outdoor French bistro. The walls and ceiling were clad with latticework, with arches, crisscrossed slats, and circular centerpieces. The chairs were wicker, and greenery grew up the center wall.

Our table was near the entrance. We lingered before sitting, trying to spot Captain Edward Smith, commander of the nearly nine-hundred crew aboard. He was an unmistakable figure, a tubby man with a neatly trimmed Santa Claus–like white beard and mustache. He carried himself with an air of authority as the highest ranking and most experienced officer on the *Titanic*, having been a captain on seventeen ships. Ironically, the *Titanic* was supposed to be his last posting before he retired. If I had my way, he'd live a long life with his wife and their dogs in the Southampton suburb they called home.

He was dining with a small group of men at the far end of the room by the window. Quinn and I settled down to order, both of us on the same side of the table so we could keep an eye on our target. If he moved, we'd know it, and I'd intercept him. All I needed was three minutes. Three minutes to tell him what was coming. He'd think I was out of my mind, but maybe he'd change one thing, like the ship's speed. I just needed one change.

"Merci beaucoup," I said to our waiter when he departed with our order.

Quinn sat back in his chair. "This sounded like a good idea when you suggested it, but now I'm confused. How is ambushing the captain gonna make him want to help us find the *Rubáiyát*?"

I willed my face to stay neutral, but color rose to my cheeks despite my efforts. "Well, it's a long shot, but at least I can ask him who's in charge of the items in storage, then drop the captain's name when I find that person. Otherwise, it's me and a crowbar."

"Us."

"Us?"

"Us and a crowbar. Though I don't know where we're gonna find a crowbar."

"We'll think of something," I said, my eyes trained on the captain.

"In the meantime, are you gonna tell me why you're so mad at me?" Quinn reached over to put his hand on top of mine, but I slid it out and tucked it under the table. "Case in point," he said, frowning, which gave him a puppy dog vibe. More like a *dog*, come to think of it.

I took a deep breath. "Are you sure we should have this conversation here? We need to watch the captain."

"I don't know about you, but I can use my eyes and ears at the same time. I won't let him get away."

"Fine." Another deep breath. This was gonna sting a little. "Look, Quinn," I started, "you've never been nice to me—like barely ever in our whole lives. And that's cool. It's you doing you, and I got used to it. But lately—before this" —I gestured around the room—"you started being nice. . . . More than nice, even."

I took a sip of water and continued in an angry tumble of words. "It took me a minute, but when I saw you here, it all became so clear. You knew you'd be my Minder. You turned on the charm so I'd be easier to 'handle' and probably more fun during your Senior Year Test. All the kindness, the hugs, the dance . . . it was all about you passing your test." I paused. "And I want to murder you now."

"Are you finished?" Quinn asked, with a flat, deep tone, pursing his lips together like a dad who knows you're saying something ridiculous and is waiting to tell you why.

"No, I'm NOT," I said, now in a full-on spiral. "All that's bad enough, but you did it to ME. We may not be friends anymore, but our parents are, and you shouldn't treat me like that. You shouldn't use me. It's mean, and it's selfish, and your mother will be ashamed to face my mother after I get back and rat you out." I wanted to storm off, but I couldn't let the captain get away. So I said, "NOW I'm finished." I stared at Quinn like one animal stares down another. I wasn't going to concede the high ground.

His hands were on the edge of the table, and he balled them into fists. I braced for an outburst, but instead, he said quietly, "You're wrong."

"Oh, really? I'm wrong? Tell me you didn't know you were going to be my Minder!"

"I didn't know." He raked a hand through his hair, and this time it didn't get stuck in product. "I lobbied your panel to let me, but I didn't know my assignment until the morning of the bon voyage party."

"So? You were already lobbying for some unknown reason, and the day you found out for sure was when you asked me to dance and . . . you know . . . kissed me."

"I kissed you on the cheek."

"Operative word there is *kissed*."

"If I'd been trying to cast some kind of obedience spell on you, would I have kissed you on the friggin' cheek? I was trying not to be an ass!"

"Well, you failed. And why were you lobbying to be my Minder anyway? You barely tolerate me—you don't even invite me to your stupid parties!"

Just then, the captain stood, and my stomach did a somersault. I wasn't sure how to feel about the conversation with Quinn, but it didn't matter. Just thinking about ambushing the captain of the ship was A LOT. I'd much rather huddle in the corner by myself and leave the hard part to others, but extraordinary times called for extraordinary measures. Even I could play a hardcore extrovert when absolutely necessary. I'd decided on the right thing in this situation, and I would do it, no matter the cost. It was go time.

I got to my feet. "Quinn, stay here, please," I said as I scooted around him and out.

"Oh hell no," Quinn said, but I barely heard his words because I was out the door in a flash.

The captain was strolling out of the restaurant with his group and appeared to be saying his goodbyes, with handshakes all around. I took a deep breath. *You can do this. You can do this. You can do this.* As he broke from the group, I approached him on wobbly legs, standing right in his path.

"Captain Smith!" I said with a croaking sound. I cleared my throat. "Captain Smith," I said again more clearly. I'd read that he had a daughter at home, so I hoped he might see her in me. I looked particularly young today, with my simple dress and my long hair waving and loose.

"Yes?" he said, his hat under his arm. "How may I help you?" He seemed friendly enough, warmhearted even. I had assumed he'd be cold and indifferent.

Quinn arrived behind me. "Sir," he said, extending his hand, "I am Quinn Daniels. It is a pleasure to meet you."

The captain looked from Quinn, clearly a first-class passenger, to me, clearly a second-class one.

"And this is a family friend of mine, Charli—Charlotte Landers. She wanted to ask you about a bit of important cargo."

"Intriguing," said the captain, though he looked antsy to leave, shifting the weight of his feet and taking his hat from under his arm.

It was now or never. For a split second, I nearly chickened out, the scenario playing out in my head like a movie reel. I'd just ask about the *Rubáiyát* and the cargo, like a star-struck poetry lover who simply had to be near it.

He'd think I was cute for being in awe of a silly book while standing on the most marvelous feat of human engineering in the world, then he'd give me some tidbit, maybe even a name of someone to talk to. Quinn and I would carry on, find the *Rubáiyát,* and return to Malibu to live out our lives while these people froze in the Atlantic.

I steeled myself.

"Captain, actually, the important cargo he is talking about is your passengers."

Quinn gave me a puzzled look, his brows knitted, but I ignored him, staying laser focused on the captain and my objective. Forgetting any finesse, everything tumbled out of my mouth, word-vomit style.

"You are likely to think I am crazy, but please hear me out, sir. Even though the *Titanic* is truly a marvel, your passengers are not safe. On the night of April 14, the lookouts are going to spot an iceberg just before 11:40. But the ship will be going too fast to avoid it, and the iceberg will hit. It'll slice through the hull and flood too many of the ship's watertight compartments." I stopped to suck in a quick breath, like a singer who couldn't quite hold a long note. "The *Titanic* will sink, sir. Over half the people on board will die, since you do not have enough lifeboats for everyone. You yourself will not live through this trip, sir, unless you change—"

Captain Smith's face turned beet red and got more and more red as I spoke until, with his eyes wide, he roared, "What in God's name is the meaning of this?"

The people standing nearby turned our way.

"Young lady, you must be unwell," he snapped. "I will not have such nonsense spoken in my presence or the presence of my passengers, and if we were still in port, I would have you put off this ship!"

Then he turned to Quinn, who stood mute and stiff, like a pale version of a wooden statue. "Sir," the captain went on, "I suggest you confine your friend to her quarters, because if I see her again, I WILL!" With that, he brushed past me, muttering to himself about "damned girl" and "my ship" and "good mind to" as he strode away, shaking his head.

I yelled after him, "Please do not ignore the iceberg warnings!" He didn't even turn around.

Quinn stared after the captain. Then he came back to life with a vengeance, snapping his head toward me, his eyes wide. "Charlie," he spit through gritted teeth at me, "what the hell have you DONE?"

# ten

I flushed hot from my total failure to sway the captain. Quinn's anger and a gathering of people staring at me like I'd lost my mind didn't help either. I had just done the worst semi-introvert, good-student nightmare combo, EVER. I forced myself on a stranger, broke the rules, and yelled across a crowded room.

Still, I managed to stay in control. If the captain was a fool, there were other ways to change the *Titanic*'s fate.

Quinn repeated, "Well? Are you going to answer me?"

"The answer is that I haven't *done* enough. Not yet."

Quinn grabbed my hand and pulled me along behind him. "Where are we going?" I asked, struggling to keep up without trotting, which would hurt my head. "Slow down!"

"We're going to my cabin so we can talk."

As we weaved through the passageways of the ship on the Bridge Deck, I had a flashback. My tenth-grade classics teacher took us sometime and somewhere each week to illustrate our textbook chapters. During a trip to Marrakech, I got lost in the labyrinth of souks. At least on the *Titanic*, if Quinn deserted me, the stewards would help me find my way out.

In fact, a steward stood just outside Quinn's cabin. "Good afternoon, Mr. Daniels. Welcome back." He opened the door for us.

"Good afternoon, Felix," Quinn said, moving me ahead of him into the room and closing the door behind us with a "Thanks very much."

As for me, "Holy crap" was all I could say. We'd entered a sitting room that reminded me of the French palace at Versailles, from the walls to the ceilings to the burgundy-and-gold brocade fabric covering the settee. The exotic hardwood paneling on the walls enveloped me like a warm hug. No wonder the first-class passengers wouldn't be in a hurry to abandon ship after the *Titanic* hit the iceberg; surely a company that could construct this room would have built an unsinkable vessel. Hard to imagine this gorgeous work of craftsmanship at the bottom of the ocean.

Stalling, I asked Quinn, "Okay if I look around?"

He held his palms up and lifted his mouth into a half grimace, as if to say *Can I stop you?*

I walked through a bedroom with ornate headboards and a marble dressing table and a fresh-air veranda with ocean views. If only I'd been given Quinn's first-class ticket. Maybe I could've stuck to my plan of staying in my room the whole trip. But then, I'd probably never have met Rima or Rosalee or the baker at breakfast. Funny how one small pebble can have so many ripple effects.

I'd meant to be that pebble with the captain earlier, but I was more like a wrecking ball. I doubted anything I'd said made the least bit of difference. Time would tell.

Quinn slumped in an armchair in the sitting room, his coat and jacket gone, his shirt collar open. He looked so comfortable here, like he was a regular passenger, maybe one I'd met on the deck—one I'd remember with butterflies as "the boy from the *Titanic*." Unfortunately, he was the boy from home instead, the boy who was enraged, a time traveler whose future as a guardian of time was starting today. And, to him, I'd gone from patsy to villain in our particular story.

Having burned up as much time as I could, I finally sat on the edge of the settee, steeling myself for my tongue lashing. I could hardly blame him. He was on the side of the rules of time travel. I was on the side of mercy. We were both right.

"So, Miss Landers," he said, still in 1912 mode, "would you care to explain your actions?" He was too calm. It was scary.

I bit my lip before answering. "No, I really don't care to."

He shifted in his chair. "Let me rephrase. Explain yourself, now."

"Or?"

"Or I'm going to assume you have a severe concussion and return home for medical help."

Maybe I did have a concussion, because I hardly recognized myself. Now that I'd made the decision, I couldn't visualize anything except my new mission to save the ship. But I'd gambled on the captain and most likely lost. How could I neutralize Quinn while I carried on with my plan B?

"Well, Quinn, I suppose it's simple. Windline could've sent me to serve the poor with Mother Teresa or to the Nazi occupation of France. But they didn't. They sent me to the friggin' *Titanic*."

"So it's Windline's fault that you've lost your mind?"

That question was a no win, so I didn't answer, exactly. "If I'd been sent to France, I couldn't have defeated the Nazis on my own, but this is the *Titanic*. If just one variable changes—if the *New York* had hit the *Titanic* in the harbor at Southampton—if the captain paid attention to the iceberg warnings—if the weather had been different—if the ship wasn't going so fast—if a proper lifeboat drill had been done—if, if, IF!

"Maybe I can be the catalyst to change that variable, because, like it or not, I've grown a conscience. I can't stand by and do nothing, knowing that fifteen hundred people on this ship will wind up fatally injured, drowned, or frozen. I won't be a party to it. And if you think you can stop me by snitching on me to Windline, then do it. But no one can force me to travel home, and I won't go. Do you hear me? I won't go until this ship sails in one piece past 11:40 p.m. on the fourteenth."

I softened a little. "I know this trip is a test for you, too, Quinn, and I'm incredibly sorry," I said, suddenly feeling the weight that must be on his shoulders. "If you fail, it'll be on my head, but I can live with that if I have to. What I can't live with? Children drowning. Third-class passengers not standing a chance because they couldn't afford all of this." I swept my hand around the sitting room. "And if you were a real passenger, you know you'd die, too, because you wouldn't be able to get in a lifeboat. Imagine what that would feel like!"

"So that's it," he said flatly.

"That's it."

We sat staring at one another until the silence became awkward. I stood to go. "Well, this is goodbye, then."

"Sit down, Charlie."

I remained standing.

"Charlie, please sit down."

I sat down.

"I don't know what to do," he said, leaning forward, his forearms on his thighs. "Our families, our teachers—they've all taught us that messing with the time stream is wrong—it's bad. Like what if the *Titanic* sails on to New York, and it turns out she's carrying a serial killer or some new disease? What if a widow whose husband dies in the disaster never marries the new husband and has the child who invents something that saves lives? What if the hearings about the *Titanic* disaster never happen and a different ship goes down with too few lifeboats and even more people on board?

"You've always lived in the moment, like neither the future or the past really matters. That's your gift—but also your weakness. Sometimes you have to think about the bigger picture, Charlie. It's what responsible time travelers are supposed to do, as awful and heart wrenching as it is sometimes."

"And you—you don't want to fail your Senior Year Test." I got back up and started pacing behind the settee.

"Of course I don't wanna fail. I'll never graduate high school if I do."

"Or get your time pin."

"That too."

"I know, and I'm really sorry."

"If you fail, you'll just have to do another test, but I'm done, Charlie. Ostracized from the legitimate time traveling community. And you accused ME of being selfish and treating YOU like crap!"

"First of all," I said, pointing at him as I reached a conclusion in my own mind, "I will *never* do another test like this. Never." I'd make a life for myself. I'd take the GED and work my way through community college. Whatever it took to make my own choices. "And I do—I admit that I'm being selfish, okay? I'm paying you back for how you've treated me and dishing out a whole lot more. You can hate me for the rest of your days, and that'll be totally fair."

"I couldn't hate you, Charlie." He put his head in his hands so I couldn't see his face. I walked over to him and slowly, tentatively put my hand on his back. I could feel the heat of him through his shirt, and it traveled up my arm and through my whole body. As much as I was mad at him, I was truly sorry that the consequences of my actions would hurt him—that they'd alter his future. He'd been a jerk, true, but now that I was calm, I was sorry I was taking a match to his future, even if I couldn't make a different choice.

Quinn shrugged off my touch and stood. "I need a little time to think. Can we meet up for dinner?"

"You're not going back to Windline to tell them?" Not that I could be sure he'd give me the truth, but I really wanted to know if I needed to watch my back. One of the teachers could travel here, and together with Quinn, they could lock me in a room to neutralize me. Come to think of it, Quinn could handle locking me up on his own. If he did, I'd go down fighting. Suddenly I realized that I might already be trapped. I backed toward the door.

I guess I wasn't too subtle because Quinn said, "I don't know if I'm gonna go back home, but you don't have to be afraid of me, Charlie. I'm not going to keep you prisoner. You'd make a lousy one, by the way." He smiled, but only his lips moved, not his cheeks or his eyes. At least he was trying.

"Thanks—I think."

"You know, it's not like I don't care about what's going to happen to the people on this ship," he said.

"I know." Really, anyone who wasn't a sociopath would feel something.

"It's horrible."

"Yes, but it doesn't have to be."

"I should've seen this whole thing with you coming, by the way," he said, moving closer.

"Really? Why?" I put one hand on the doorknob, just in case.

"Because, Charlie Chicken, you care too much. You wouldn't even swallow that stupid fish."

"Ah, but you wouldn't either. We're not so different, you and I." I pointed at his chest.

"Maybe not, though I've always liked our differences. I'm not so sure now." He reached for the doorknob, and I held my breath, still wondering if he might try to silence me. But he took it in his hand and twisted it to open the door for me. "How about I meet you in the second-class Library this evening before dinner? We'll go to the main dining saloon?"

"Sure."

"Okay, it's a date," he said with little enthusiasm. The normally bright light in his eyes wasn't there. I'd dimmed it.

~

Since leaving Queenstown, the *Titanic* had slid past the coast and made it into open water. The temperatures grew cooler. Rosalee and I spent the afternoon on the Shelter Deck, which housed the enclosed promenade for second-class passengers. We whipped up a rousing game of cards as we lounged.

At some point, we were joined by a Mrs. Irene Corbett from Utah. Turns out she was also studying midwifery at London's General Lying-In Hospital, the pioneering maternity infirmary where Rosalee had been studying. Irene had gone against her husband's wishes and those of her church to follow her passion, even leaving her three children with her parents to make the trip. I admired her from the moment I met her.

"So many men think women will not be women anymore if they get the vote," Rosalee said.

"And that we would have to fight wars," I added, hoping my argument was relevant to the period. After all, World War I was on its way.

"Exactly, as if women are not already fighting on every front—for civility, for education—" Irene said.

"As well as the ability to work at professions that fulfill us," Rosalee added.

"So true. And the biggest fight of all . . . for better futures for our children," Irene said, pulling out her knitting.

I was in awe of the two women as I listened. Yeesh. And I thought women still had a ways to go in my time. . . . History sure hadn't been easy on my gender.

After a while, I excused myself to go exploring, though my exact mission was to find the Marconi Room, which was located on the Boat Deck near the first-class entrance hall and the forward grand staircase.

I tried to force Quinn out of my mind as I made my way across the ship. Stressing about his feelings and his future would only make both of us miserable. I'd have my whole life to be eaten by guilt. At that moment, I only had three days to execute the new mission—my real test.

After a bit of maneuvering to cross into first-class territory, I almost made it to the radio room. But I was stopped short.

"Miss," said a tall, fair-haired crewman with pretty blue eyes as I approached the first-class entrance, "this area is reserved for first-class passengers and crew, and the second-class Promenade is aft."

"Oh, thank you, sir," I said, adopting a sweet tone, "but I was merely taking a stroll."

"Then your best bet is the second-class Promenade." Wow, the clothes—and the hairstyle—really did count on this ship. It's like I'd landed in some Orwellian world where class determined what you wore, where you lived, what you ate, and even how you died. Come to think of it, society back home wasn't too far off. The lines were blurred a little more, but the same prejudice still existed.

I needed some way to get this guy out of my way. Suddenly, it came to me. When intellect, subterfuge, and everything else you could think of failed . . . flirt. I was terrible at it, but I'd certainly studied flirting enough from afar. I moved a little bit closer to the twenty-something British guy.

"Thank you for your help and kindness. You do have a truly kind face, did you know that?" Maybe "kind" wasn't very flirty, but I couldn't go twenty-first century on the guy or he'd think I was some kind of sea-faring prostitute.

He stammered, "I—why, thank you, miss."

I went for it. "You remind me of a sweetheart I used to have back home, except you have a nicer accent." I had to stifle a giggle—flirting was close enough to awkward intimacy that it activated my laugh reflex. I did cover my mouth with my hand, dipping my head as if I were embarrassed to be so forward.

"Well, that is awfully nice to hear, miss." He blushed.

I shuffled closer, touching his arm. "You know, my brother made me swear I would look for the wireless room on the ship. He is one of those mechanical kind of men, you know? He would probably love to have an interesting job like yours."

He straightened. "Well, it is an enviable post, and a pleasure to serve on the *Titanic* for its first crossing."

If only he knew. "Say," I said, "since the radio room is near here, would there be any chance you could escort me there for a quick peek? I would be so grateful, and you would be my hero forever!" Major stifling of giggles. If Tiana were watching this, she wouldn't believe it, especially that I'd managed to keep a straight face.

"Well, it is close," he said, scanning the area for anyone who might see him breaking the rules. I held out my hand while smiling up at him to push him toward the right decision. It worked.

He took my hand, and his palm was warm and thick. Once we went through a door past the elevator banks, he dropped my hand and instead put his arm around my waist, a little low for my taste, but I kept a smile pasted on my face. He beamed down at me, like we were going out for a night on the town rather than into the wireless room.

"Wait here," he said.

I stood in the hall like a groupie backstage at a concert waiting to meet the headliner.

He opened the door, extending his hand from inside the room. I took it, and he pulled me in.

"Boys," he said, "this is Miss—"

"Miss Landers, Charlotte Landers," I said in a singsong voice.

"Yes, Miss Landers," he said. "This is the on-duty wireless operator, Harold Bride. He works for Marconi's

Wireless Telegraph Company. That is the company that manufactured the wireless we have on board."

My knees suddenly felt like they couldn't support my weight. Harold Bride was a hero—or he would be if April 14 happened as history books described. To me, having read all about him, he was a headliner, and I felt a little like a real groupie. I extended my hand. "It is truly an honor to meet you, Mr. Bride. Thank you for your good work here."

"Not much to thank me for, Miss Landers," he said with a laugh. "I am mostly sending telegrams for our first-class passengers. It is quite the fashionable thing."

"Ah, but you do so much more, I know. My brother is a huge fan of the Marconi." I looked around the room, bathed in light from a skylight. I'd always pictured this room differently. The white-paneled room had clocks, knobs, and brass equipment on the walls and the desk. Clipboards and stacks of paper sat neatly at Mr. Bride's fingertips.

"You know of the Marconi?" Harold seemed pleased that a girl might know something about the equipment.

"Indeed I do!" I said, adopting Quinn's word.

My crewman was not enjoying the attention I was getting from or giving to the wireless operator, and, like a man waking up from a nap, he went back into crewman mode. "Well," he said, "we had better get you back before you are missed." Translation . . . *before you are caught out of your designated class.*

"Of course," I said, moving with the seaman toward the door. Then, turning to Harold Bride, I said, "I hope to see you again, and thank you for taking the time to say hello. Be sure that if you get any iceberg warnings, the captain takes them seriously!"

Everyone laughed like I was funny, including me. It wasn't like the wireless operator was going to convince the captain of much. But, I did have a plan to return to the Marconi Room on the fourteenth. *Pebbles in the water.*

When we were back in our original spot, the crewman made a pitch. "Perhaps I could see you after my shift this evening?"

"I am afraid I am at a disadvantage, sir," I said. "I do not even know your name."

"It is Ruston Bean, Miss Charlotte. But you may call me Russ."

"Well, then, Russ, as much as I would like to see you this evening, unfortunately I am otherwise engaged. But," I said, throwing good sense to the wind, and on the heels of wanting to touch Quinn earlier, I stood on my tiptoes and reached up, locking my hands behind Russ's neck. Then I pressed my body to his, pulling him into a real hug, feeling his hands resting tentatively on my back. He smelled like the sea. This contact was nothing in my time, but here, it was probably obscene. I stepped back. "Thank you, Russ. I will not forget your kindness."

With that, I turned back toward second class. Maybe I was getting better at flirting, or maybe I was just desperate for physical contact.

~

I stood in the second-class Library, with its sycamore wood paneling and mahogany furniture upholstered in tapestry. It was elegant but didn't have nearly the detail and regal refinements of the first-class common areas. With help from Rosalee, who moved seamlessly from doctor to hairdresser—and at times both as she tried to avoid my stitches—I had transformed into a first-class passenger, complete with long gloves and a steel-blue beaded gown that was meant to display cleavage, thinly veiled with layers of a translucent fabric that flowed over my shoulders and tucked into the gown's bodice in the center.

Rosalee had joined me in the library. I wanted to introduce a "real" person to Quinn, so he could understand who I was determined to protect, and Rosalee was anxious to meet my "date." I had tried to explain that he was only a friend, but she didn't believe me. I think she could sense there was more to us than I was saying, and, yikes, was that an understatement. How about, *We're from the future, and we've known each other our whole lives, and he's trying to stop me from saving this ship from an iceberg?* That might be more than she had in mind.

Quinn arrived in his full tuxedoed splendor, with his hair glued down again, making him look like a bona fide privileged gentleman. I whispered, "That's him," under my breath to Rosalee as Quinn strode toward us.

"Oh my heavens" was her response.

"Good evening, ladies," Quinn said, giving us a formal bow. "Charlie, you look . . . amazing . . . and you must be the famous physician who is sharing a cabin with our accident-prone Charlotte?"

Rosalee stared, then remembered to answer. "Yes, that I am."

"Dr. Rosalee Dunner, please meet Mr. Quinn Daniels, a long-time acquaintance from California. Mr. Daniels, please meet my cabinmate, Dr. Rosalee Dunner." I was getting the hang of this 1912 thing. I hoped I could still talk like a normal seventeen-year-old when I got home.

We chatted for a few minutes, pleasantries mostly, though Quinn did ask, "Dr. Dunner, in your professional opinion, does Miss Landers have a concussion? If so, is it possible that it has affected her decision-making ability?"

I folded my arms in front of me, a caustic remark hovering on my tongue. But I stayed quiet. I knew Rosalee wouldn't rat me out.

"In my judgment, any concussion she might have is so mild as to have no significant effect, though I will admit that medical science is just beginning to understand head injuries. That said, I examined her last night and this morning. If one were to see behavioral change, it would likely be in the form of disorientation, and given that Miss Landers is the one who led me to this library as if she had lived on this ship for months, I find her to be perfectly in command of her faculties."

I wanted to yell *Take that!* but instead I only said, "Thank you, Rosalee. It is a privilege to have a learned physician right at my fingertips during this voyage. Now, will I see you after dinner, as planned?"

Quinn cut in. "Oh, do we have plans after dinner this evening?"

*Crap. I shouldn't have said anything.*

I started to answer, but Rosalee jumped in. "In fact we do," she said. "We are going on an adventure to the third-class cabins to find Charlie's friend Rima. Will you join us?"

*No, no, no*, I thought, helpless to derail the train of Quinn barreling right down the tracks at my plans.

"Indeed, with such a kind invitation from a new friend, how could I not join? Besides, I can see to it that you two avoid getting into any trouble."

"Trouble . . . me? You must be joking," I laughed. Rosalee laughed, too. She knew me—or at least the new *Titanic* me—quite well already.

We said our goodbyes and left Rosalee behind as we

made our way toward the Saloon Deck and the first-class Dining Room, which stretched the full width of the ship and could seat more than five hundred guests. The ceiling had an intricate pattern on it, and the walls were a soft white. Columns divided the room, which was decorated in an English style, with oak furniture that looked super comfortable—great for long, long, long meals. No fast food here. I'd have killed for a grilled chicken sandwich and sweet potato fries. Or a kale smoothie. I couldn't imagine eating fancy like this all the time.

We were seated at 7:00 p.m. in a recessed area that gave us some measure of privacy. Quinn held out my chair, then took the seat across from me at the table for two. With my back to the wall, I could watch the diners stream in, wearing the latest fashions straight from Paris. It was like being at a very retro fashion show.

I counted more than ten utensils at my seat, and I braced for course after course of rich food, with wine pairings and the famous palate-cleansing cocktail in between. I vowed to stay sober this time. As the saucy and sublime food started to arrive, I breathed in the rich smells, and Quinn and I chatted about each dish, making a game out of trying to guess how much butter was in each one. After a few courses, the game was getting depressing, so we abandoned it. Besides, eventually we had to stop with the pretending and get to the business at hand.

"So, Charlie, I've spent the afternoon thinking about our situation," Quinn said at last.

"And?" I realized I was wringing my hands in my lap. Quinn could make things very hard for me.

"And it finally dawned on me. . . . The reason a Minder is sent back with each junior is because if the junior alters the time stream, Windline would never know about it, right? The Minder is there to either stop the junior from changing the time stream, or to report back what happened, in which case Windline could undo the changes by sending someone else back."

I hadn't thought of it that way. Of course. Only the time travelers who were in the past when events were altered would know what had happened originally, before the change in the time stream. For everyone else, the future would unfold in a whole new way. The altered past we were creating would be the only one they'd ever know about. In the case of the *Titanic*, there'd be no headline newspaper accounts, no books from survivors, no Hollywood movies. The *Titanic* would be remembered not for its tragedy but its achievement—as a footnote in the history of engineering and artistry, an improvement for all classes of travelers in the early 1900s.

Sometimes the intricacies of time travel made my head hurt, like trying to play chess with a very tricky opponent while balancing on one leg. Another wrinkle occurred to me. "Wait. . . . Then how do sanctioned time travelers police the unsanctioned ones?"

"I asked myself the same question," Quinn said, "and the only explanation I could come up with is that either I'm wrong about everything I just said or they're policing the actual time travel and not the resulting changes to the time stream."

"Hmm. Fair point. It has to be the time travel. Somehow they must be able to detect when an unsanctioned traveler goes back." We sat quietly for a moment, even though the room buzzed with noise around us. Finally, I asked, "Have you ever changed the time stream?"

"Sure, small stuff when I was a kid, like dyeing the dog's hair purple. My parents had no clue."

"I'm not sure what it says about you that you dyed your dog, but I suppose you've got a point," I answered. "What does that mean for us?"

"Well," he said, taking a sip of wine, "I want you to know that I completely admire you for wanting to save the *Titanic*. . . ."

*Uh-oh. Here it comes.*

"However, I have to assume the rules of time travel have been tested and proven to be right over generations." I felt my heart beating faster. He went on. "I also know that I can't stop you, unless I take extreme measures, which I don't plan to do. Maybe I would if you weren't . . . well . . . you, but that's irrelevant. The best I can hope to do here is make sure you don't get yourself hurt in the process. . . . Well—I mean, hurt again." He shifted in his seat, reaching for my hand. "When we get back, I won't say anything about changes to the time stream, unless for some reason the changes make things worse. So," he finished, "we can do it your way, but we still have to find the *Rubáiyát* so you'll pass your test."

My heart nearly jumped out of my chest. I wouldn't have to fight him after all, and he'd even help me with my treasure hunt. I took the offer of his hand as I bounced with excitement and relief in my seat.

I compared the feeling of holding his hand to the crewman's earlier. There was no contest. With Quinn, I felt more than warmth. Like it or not, I felt electricity, as if he were a power generator and I were a lightbulb. Even though Quinn had used me, I'd also used him. He was going to help me, so he couldn't be all bad. Touching him wasn't bad either.

"Thank you, Quinn," I said, squeezing his hand for emphasis. Then it occurred to me that there was still the matter of his Senior Year Test. "Do you think you can still pass your Senior Year Test? If no one knows I changed the time stream and I get the book and come back in one piece, you should pass your test, right?"

"That's the hope," he said. He did look lighter than he had earlier. Hope suited him. And I could be lighter, too, knowing my decision wouldn't ruin Quinn's future.

I reached for one of my glasses. "A toast," I said, "to you, to the *Titanic,* and to passing our tests, together!"

"Hear, hear," Quinn said, clinking his glass to mine. "And to the most stubborn girl on the planet." His smile lit up his eyes once again. I wanted to drink in this picture for the *Titanic* Junior Year Test yearbook—though it would exist only in my memory.

# eleven

Rosalee, Quinn, and I wandered the narrow, white-washed passageways of the *Titanic*'s third-class section in search of Rima's cabin. In this part of the ship, I could feel the *Titanic*'s movement more acutely, and after I bumped into the wall, Quinn looped my hand through his arm. Our trio got a few surprised looks from other passengers: Quinn in his starched black and white, me in a beaded gown, and Rosalee in a simple deep-cream dress with her red hair upswept. Given the stringent segregation of the different ticket holders on the *Titanic*, I figured it was almost as strange for us to be roaming the lower levels as it would be for third-class passengers to be hanging out in the first-class hallways.

Accommodations and dining facilities for third-class passengers were actually considered to be quite advanced compared to other ships of the day, where passengers were required to bring their own food for the voyage. The passageways were clean, neat, and of course, new. Still, I shuddered to think about how far we'd come to find Rima, and therefore how far away she was from the Boat Deck. The bulk of the lifeboats would be launched from there in a few short days—or not, if I had my way.

"Here it is." Rosalee pointed when we arrived at Rima's cabin door.

I knocked on the freshly painted door and received a quick answer in the form of Rima's mother. Her face gave away her relationship to Rima—mostly because they both had these amazing, soulful eyes. Looking into the cabin, I could see two of the room's bunks and a basin. A young child slept in the lower bunk, his thick, dark lashes feathered over round cheeks. My stomach clenched at seeing the child. I desperately hoped he would live to see his next birthday.

"Good evening," I managed. "May we speak to Rima?"

"Rima?" I guessed she might not speak English as well as Rima did, so I nodded instead.

Her mother pointed and said with a thick accent, "The hall."

After wandering around for another ten minutes in search of the hall and asking for directions from a crew member who was walking down a passageway, we learned that the third-class General Room, the gathering place for passengers in steerage, was on the ship's starboard side.

If we'd appeared out of place in the passageways of third class, we were even more so in the General Room. It was comfortable, with linoleum flooring, long wooden benches, and plain white-paneled walls. Passengers of all ages were crowded in, laughing, arguing, and singing, the sounds of lively music coming from the instruments that had been brought on board and the piano at one end of the room. The place smelled of smoke and alcohol and real people. I'd take this place over the stuffy first-class Lounge any day! As we would say in Spanish class, "La vida está con la gente"—life is with the people. Pushing out of my head what was likely to become of these people, I zeroed in on the moment, and I began to relax for the first time since boarding the *Titanic*. I got the same sense from Quinn, who immediately started stripping off his fancy jacket and bowtie.

I spotted Rima across the room with a group and beelined for her.

"Charlie!" she shouted above the din.

"Rima! We found you!" I took her hands.

"I am so very glad, but whatever are you doing here?"

"I wanted to check on you. Are you all right?" She sure seemed okay, with a rosy natural blush in her cheeks and a big smile that could light up a room.

"I am feeling much better—still sad, but I have some hope," she said. "Thank you for helping me."

"No thanks are necessary. Your friendship is repayment enough."

"And what about you? How is your head?"

"My head is on the mend," I said. "And everything else is, too." I rubbed my elbow. Then I asked, "Would it be okay if we joined you?" I motioned for Rosalee and Quinn to come over. "I want you to meet my friends."

After official hellos and introductions, I explained that Rosalee was a doctor and Quinn was in "transportation," which was hard to spit out, since the only transportation business he was in was driving me to school every day. We learned that Rima was a teacher back home. No wonder she spoke English so well.

Our conversation stopped when guys with fiddles, Irish flutes, and tin whistles started playing an Irish jig. Quinn dropped his jacket and tie on a chair and extended his hand, and I had another *Titanic* movie flashback. "I'd ask you for the honor of this dance," he said formally, "but thank God we don't have to talk like that here. You wanna dance?"

I was over acting like a prim and proper society debutante. I wanted to forget the *Titanic*'s story and just be, for this one night. "Oh yeah!" I said, taking his hand. "Let's do this!"

Neither of us had a clue how to dance an Irish jig, so we held hands and did side shuffles and spins until I thought I'd throw up. The world swirled around us like we were the only two people in it. I'd never seen Quinn laugh so hard. I figured he was as tired of playing a transportation mogul as I was of being a proper young lady, 1912 style.

Rosalee and Rima joined us. We all locked arms in a small circle and continued with our dancing, four people from wildly different places and times, all connected. Just when I thought my dinner might make another appearance, we broke apart to watch a group of Irishmen as their legs and feet moved in unison. The whole room started clapping. We tried to imitate their steps, which resulted in us crashing into each other and laughing even harder. Quinn jumped in the line with them and did a decent imitation, kicking up his heels to the beat. "It's like playing soccer!" he yelled my way. I pressed my thumb and forefinger together, stuck them in my mouth, and in a decidedly unladylike manner, whistled at him.

We met people from Rima's neighboring cabins, along with her older brother, Arash, who asked Rosalee to dance. Rima stood watching and smiled, even though I suspected she was still hurting deep down. No one could bounce back so completely in such a short time. Not that my feelings mattered, but I wanted her to get to New York and live the American dream. She—and most of the people in that room—were the backbone of the country I called home. We needed them.

After more dancing, laughing, and clapping, we finally left our new friends, vowing to meet up again. We wound our way up and outside, where the temperature had dropped to the thirties. Quinn slipped his jacket over my shoulders. Maybe some of that first-class gentility was wearing off on him.

"I hope we did not shake up your poor brain too much tonight," Rosalee said as we leaned over the rail. Always the physician, she declared, "Dancing was probably not the best medicine for you." She tucked stray wisps of red hair behind her ears.

"Oh, it was absolutely the best medicine," I answered. "My brain might be scrambled eggs, but my heart is happy!"

Quinn laughed. "I hate it when your brain turns into scrambled eggs."

"Well, let us hope they unscramble soon. I imagine you will need them when you have to do more than dance," Rosalee added. She wrapped her arms around herself. "I think I will say goodnight, you two. It is entirely too cold out here for me. Quinn, it was such a pleasure to meet you. Charlie, see you in the cabin?" With more of her hair escaping in the wind, she was fighting a losing battle to keep it out of her face.

"Of course," I said. "I am so glad you came with us."

"May I walk you to your cabin, Rosalee?" Quinn asked, continuing to outdo himself on the chivalry front.

"No, no," she said, "I will be perfectly fine. But you can see to it that Charlie makes it. We do not want her to wind up with the surgeon again."

"Amen to that," I said as Rosalee waved and walked back inside.

We turned back to the railing. "Are you cold?" Quinn asked.

"Yep," I said, holding his jacket together with one hand, "but I'm not ready to go in. I don't want this night to end."

"Because reality will be back in the morning, or because you're alone with me?" Quinn put his arm around me, hugging me to him. I fit so well, nestled just under his shoulder.

"Hmm . . . Are you saying we aren't going to be alone tomorrow? We have a book of poetry to find," I said.

"Fair point. We should look for it late tomorrow, when the ship is quiet."

"Agreed. And tomorrow, I want to meet Thomas Andrews."

"The guy who designed the *Titanic*." It wasn't a question. He'd done his homework, too.

"Yep. He can help me."

"Maybe."

"You still aren't sold on changing things, are you?"

"I can understand why you want to, for Rosalee and Rima and all those people tonight. I get it."

I looked out at the water, the lights of the *Titanic* reflecting off the waves as the ship sped through the Atlantic at about twenty knots. If I blinked, the sea would change, always moving, always dancing. "I love the water," I said as much to myself as to Quinn.

He was looking up. "I love the sky."

I tipped up my head to see.

"All those white stars . . ." I said, trying to spot the constellations.

". . . against such a black sky," he added. He turned then, and we stood facing each other, the wind swirling around us. I looked at him, this friend, this enemy, this co-conspirator.

"You really do look beautiful tonight," he said.

"You must've had too much wine, Quinn. You've never said anything about how I look before—except that bit on the first day of school about my finding a boyfriend."

"Maybe I haven't said it, but I've thought it."

"Thought what?"

He moved infinitesimally closer. "That you're perfect." And then, with a swift movement, Quinn leaned down to kiss me.

It wasn't a soft, tentative first kiss. It wasn't a sloppy, eat-your-face kiss. Not at all. It was like a "two long-lost lovers reuniting as they run to each other from the opposite sides of a field" kind of kiss. Almost desperate. Hungry. Rough but not in a mean or unwelcome way. I wanted that kind of kiss, too. I didn't know how much until it happened.

One of his hands held the side of my head to maneuver it, deepening the kiss. His other arm wrapped around me, pulling my body forward. I gladly leaned in, the feel of his warmth and his solidness both comforting and jangling, the musky scent of him all around me. Every nerve ending in my body seemed to reach for every one of his. Sensory intake flooded my brain, and I was lost.

For the first time ever, intimacy didn't make me want to laugh. Instead, I had other urges to contend with. I never, ever wanted to unwind myself from this closeness, this two-pieces-of-a-puzzle fit that had my hormones dancing their own Irish jig.

But it was Quinn who pulled back. "Charlie," he said, breathless, "I—"

"No." I pulled him back down to me, this time for a slow-burn kiss, the kind designed to set your hair on fire and take all the oxygen out of your lungs. I didn't want to talk. Didn't want to think. Didn't want to hear any high school crap. We were on the deck of one of the most famous ships in the world. He was a guy in a tuxedo. I was a girl in a glamorous gown. We'd danced the night away.

It was our movie moment.

When we finally stopped, we stood forehead to forehead, breathing in rhythm together. I wanted more, but I was starting to shiver and the movie credits were rolling. My head started to ache, thanks to the whole dancing-with-a-head-injury thing.

"You're cold," he stated.

"Only on the outside," I answered.

Quinn breathed a laugh. "I hear that." Then, "Should we talk about this?"

I sighed. *What's with him constantly wanting to talk about things?* This was a situation-induced affection—a "summer camp" fling, only the summer camp happened to be headed for an iceberg.

"No, let's not," I said. I looked at him. Damn those eyes of his, that face. "You used me for your test, then I hurt you back. Not exactly solid footing. So let's just 'be.' And by 'be,' I mean this. . . ." I brushed a kiss across his lips, one more time, softly.

# twelve

After the excitement of the night, I slept like the dead. No dreams of kisses under the stars. No nightmares of water flooding into the *Titanic*. Just nothing. When I opened my eyes, I gave thanks. Sweet dreams wouldn't seem right on this ship, and the nightmare of what was to come would be real soon enough . . . if I didn't stop it from happening.

Quinn wasn't with me on my plan, but he wasn't against me either. That was something. I could find comfort—and brief escape—in his arms. If only our mothers could see us now. They would be so thrilled we'd found each other, only to be disappointed to find us even farther apart once our tests were over. After all, if the frigid ocean managed to swallow fifteen hundred people, it would surely kill the spark of romance between me and Quinn. We needed each other—for now.

Today was April 12, two days until the *Titanic* would rendezvous with the iceberg. I'd tried to warn the captain and had failed. I needed to do better. I was pinning a lot of hopes on Thomas Andrews, who designed the ship. He'd been given the honor of traveling on its first voyage to see to any last-minute issues.

I considered my approach. The one thing I couldn't do was tell him I was from the future. If I did, he'd think I was way worse than some fanciful girl. . . . He'd think I needed immediate medical attention and wouldn't listen to a thing I had to say. Even if I could manage to go home and bring back a book or newspaper article on the *Titanic*—which I clearly couldn't—he'd still believe I was crazy. I hoped I could appeal both to his brain and his heart. After all, he knew the *Titanic* inside and out, and he had to love his master creation. He'd seen men die to create it. Besides, he wouldn't survive the *Titanic*, any more than the captain would. Self-preservation was a powerful force, if only I could tap into it.

I watched Rosalee sleep, her thick red hair spread out like a wild halo on her pillow. If the *Titanic* did hit, she should make it out alive, since the majority of second-class female passengers did. I wondered what the future might hold for her after the ordeal. Getting to know her and others here was like being a reader who was starting multiple books, books that I could never read beyond their first few chapters. The rest of their stories would simply disappear into the folds of time.

I pulled the heavy coverlet up to my nose and stared at the ceiling. I was in no hurry to see Quinn, though we'd planned to meet up after lunch and spend the afternoon searching for Mr. Andrews. How would we greet each other? Since it was likely to be awkward, I hoped I wouldn't start laughing, given my usual response to touchy-feely situations.

If I did, he'd think I was laughing at him. Although Quinn might be a lot of things, he definitely wasn't laughable.

I desperately wished Tiana were here. She'd reason through what I should do—or would at least help me turn over every possibility. She might say, "You should kiss Quinn again first thing so the rest of the day won't be awkward." Or "The smartest thing would be to ignore last night like it never happened." Actually, that last one seemed like a reasonable approach, considering the alternatives. We could be like romantic vampires, only kissing after dark.

As for Tiana, as much as I'd tried, I couldn't figure out what Windline would want her to learn, to become, any more than I could figure out what their point was for me. Tiana could use some help finding herself on the relationship front, maybe. She was interested in both guys and girls, though she'd always dated guys and even then, usually with a group. Surely not Windline's top priority . . . She wasn't the best at standing up for herself with her parents. But, really? Maybe Windline was trying to help her find her passion, since she was good at almost everything. She could be holding a sign at a Vietnam War protest, celebrating President Kennedy's election, or helping Martin Luther King Jr. write a speech.

I turned on my side, blocking out Quinn and my own JY Test, and imagining Tiana, bent over a desk, writing.

"Dr. King," she might say, looking up, "how about 'I have a dream' as a theme?"

~

Quinn and I met in the second-class Library again, hardly a romantic spot for a post-kissfest reunion. He wore a gray day suit, still looking like Mr. Transportation Mogul, and I wore my finest first-class-worthy day dress, form fitting with a nipped-in waist and layers of material that floated down to my ankles in a swirl of embroidered flowers. I longed for sweatpants, but I had to admit my mom had been spot-on about the fashion.

My eyes locked on Quinn as soon as he strode in, and it took me a second to realize I was smiling from ear to ear, like his arrival had lit up my world. In fact, it kinda had. "Hi," I said as he walked up.

"Hi," he said back. "How're you? How's the head?"

"Good. A little sore, but it survived the dancing."

"Great." He shifted on his feet. "So, I've been thinking this morning. . . ."

"'Bout what?"

"What to say to you after last night."

Well, we had one thing in common. "What'd you come up with?"

"It was very," he said, narrowing his eyes, ". . . nice."

I raised my eyebrows expectantly. "'Nice' was the best adjective you could come up with?"

"It was the only G-rated one, yes."

I laughed. "And what was your favorite one that hit the cutting-room floor?"

I swear, he blushed. "'Hot.' It was definitely—'hot.'" He looked down at his shoes, then back up at me. Our eyes met.

My turn to blush. "Well, I'd say that about nails it."

"Maybe we should try it again at some point—you know, just to make sure. . . ."

I moved a step closer. Something about this ship made me brave. I said, summoning my best 1912, "Well, sir, I am sure that could be arranged."

~

The first-class Lounge on the Promenade Deck was the most luxurious room I'd seen on the *Titanic*. The steward told us it was decorated in the French Louis XV style, which basically meant it was fit for a king. The wood paneling was not only deep and rich, but ornate, with decorative swirls. The light fixtures attached to the wall panels resembled candelabras, and even the chairs had fancy claw feet.

The room was relatively empty given the sixty-degree day, with many passengers choosing to stroll or lounge on deck.

Quinn and I still turned a few heads as we entered, and I had one of those moments where it felt especially odd to be a time traveler, a future girl among people in their proper time. To the passengers in their finery, Quinn and I looked like any other well-bred young twosome, full of promise and ready to carry on the legacy of wealth. They would never guess that we knew their fates from books and movies and had sucked down JELL-O shots by a pool in California. But that was in the future, in a time when Quinn and I weren't lying to literally everyone around us.

"Hey, you two!" beckoned Ms. Brown, waving us over. She sat alone at a table for four, sipping a cup of tea.

We hurried over, genuinely glad for her always-upbeat company. "Maggie," I said, "may we join you?"

"Of course, sit yourselves down. I haven't seen a bit of you since dinner the other night. How are you enjoying yourselves?"

Quinn held my chair and then dropped into his. "We are taking full advantage of the *Titanic* experience," he said, "but dinner with you has been the highlight so far."

Such a suck-up, but an effective one, I had to admit.

"Aw, you are too kind, or perhaps you're tellin' a lady just what she wants to hear," she said.

I loved the way she talked. If I'd started out speaking that way on the trip, I could've avoided the stilted no-contractions approach.

"It is so true, though! And I am in love with this ship. It is truly a marvel," I said, counting the number of contractions I could've used. I looked around the room for emphasis. "I am dying to meet the designer—is it Mr. Andrews? I have heard he is on board."

Maggie slapped her knee, handkerchief in hand. "Well, have some tea, and we'll take a stroll and see if we can't rustle him up." If only I could tell Maggie about her legacy as a celebrated survivor of the *Titanic*. She was remembered for arguing with the crewman on her lifeboat about going back to save passengers from the water. There would be a Broadway musical about the "Unsinkable Molly Brown" that would run for two years in the early 1960s. Not that I dared tell her, but I figured she might be the only person on the ship who'd remotely believe I was from the future. Even if she didn't, she'd at least appreciate the tall tale.

We all left the lounge to stroll along the deck where the temperature was perfect and the salty wind felt like a caress. Maggie took my arm, and Quinn walked behind us, since it was difficult to walk three abreast on the busy promenade. It was about five hundred feet long and open to the sea. The Boat Deck directly above provided some shelter.

As we strolled and talked, I saw the captain walking with a couple of his officers and coming directly toward us. My heart sank to my feet, which immediately stopped working. If he recognized me and said something, Maggie would never help us find Mr. Andrews.

"Oh, dear," I managed. "I believe a ribbon has fallen out of my hair. Quinn, please keep Maggie company while I go back and retrieve it. I will only be a moment."

Quinn stepped up, taking Maggie's arm and walking on as if nothing had happened, but I caught his eye when I turned to flee. I took the nearest door and looked around, desperate for a place to hide in case the captain came through. Then, I spotted Mr. Andrews himself, standing right outside of the first-class Smoke Room talking with two other men.

I'd seen his picture in books, and they didn't do him justice. He had dark hair and a clean-shaven face with a perfect cleft in his chin. In a dark suit with a pocket square and a collar that folded above his neatly tied tie, he looked every bit the handsome professional with a business-first kind of vibe. To design something as monumental as the *Titanic*, he had to be devoted to his work. I immediately liked him, even from ten feet away.

As his group broke up, I pulled a ribbon out of the back of my hair and took my shot.

"Mr. Andrews?"

He turned in my direction and walked a few paces toward me. "Yes, miss?"

"Sir, pardon me, I know this is quite forward, but I was

just strolling the promenade with Mrs. Margaret Brown, and we were actually looking for you." I smiled brightly. "Then I came back to collect a ribbon I dropped, and here you are!" I held out the ribbon I'd pulled from my hair.

"Then what a stroke of good luck for us both," he said with a lilting upper-crusty Irish accent, putting me at ease. "And you are?"

"Charlotte, Charlotte Landers," I said. "And if you do not have to rush off somewhere, would you have a few moments to tell me more about the ship?"

"Of course I can spare a few minutes for you, Miss Landers. By all means. Shall we go enjoy a bit of the good weather, perhaps take a turn at the railing?" This guy was pure class, and not of the first, second, or third variety. If he'd been ten years younger, I would've been crushing on him.

"That sounds lovely."

He bowed and held out his hand for me to go in front of him. Then he stepped around me to open the door. I prayed the captain had passed by already.

We waited for a group of ladies in ginormous, completely unnecessary hats to pass by, then took our place at the railing. Mr. Andrews leaned over to see the view, propped on his forearms. I held on to the railing with my gloved hands.

"So what can I tell you about the *Titanic*? She is a beauty, is she not?"

"Oh, she is, Mr. Andrews. She most certainly is. You did a wonderful job in designing her."

"Thank you. She is a dream come true, in all honesty."

"I do have a few—I guess—'technical' questions, if you would indulge me?"

Unfortunately, even a seemingly sweet man like Thomas Andrews was raised in a chauvinistic society where women didn't ask technical questions. So his furrowed brow wasn't a big surprise.

I went on. "My father is an engineer turned businessman, you see, and he would be so pleased to get a few answers from the ship's foremost expert." Mr. Andrews's face lightened. Damn, I was getting good at this making-up stuff.

"Ah, then of course," Mr. Andrews said, more comfortable now that a man was behind the questions.

I took a deep breath of salty sea air and started in. "The ship has a double bottom but not a double hull, right?" I tried to sound innocent and sweet. How annoying to be a female in this era.

"I can see that your father is an engineer. . . . That is correct, Miss Landers. The double bottom is there in case the *Titanic* were to run aground."

"And the ship has sixteen watertight compartments, so it would stay afloat if it runs into something and, say, the first four compartments were breached?"

I was getting close to losing him, since no random engineer would know this stuff. "Did you say your father is a shipbuilding engineer, Miss Landers?" Mr. Andrews asked. "I am honestly quite surprised at your level of knowledge about this ship."

"I know," I said, patting his arm playfully and laughing off his comment. "I am forever getting teased about my memory for details, which I come by honestly from my father. Studying ships is his hobby."

"Oh. I see." I don't think he did.

"But, Mr. Andrews, since we *are* entering an area with icebergs, what would happen if, say, the ship were heading straight for one? It would be better to run straight into it than to sideswipe it, right? Because if too many of those watertight compartments were breached, then the *Titanic* would surely founder. . . ." I could only hope Mr. Andrews was too nice to bail on me at this point, but he was starting to turn a little red around the ears—not a good sign.

"It is highly unlikely that she'd be put to such a test, so you need not worry about a thing. The *Titanic* is a strong ship with an excellent crew." He smiled weakly, standing with his back up straight as if contemplating his escape.

"Oh my goodness, yes, of course. But I have done a little bit of math, and the ratio of lifeboats to passengers is quite low. I know I would feel safer if the captain would slow the ship or at least instruct his crew in the best way to handle the ship if an iceberg were spotted.

"I mean, we are going so fast that at night, we might not see an iceberg until it is too late to turn away from it safely, do you not agree? As I understand it, most of the danger of an iceberg is found below the water, where those watertight compartments would be at risk in a sideswipe."

No response. I could almost see the inner struggle between manners, anger, and interest, given the fact that my logic was sound.

I went on. "I can tell you are truly a good person and you would do anything to avoid a disaster on your ship. If we could go slower, say below twenty knots at night, and if the Bridge knew how best to take advantage of the *Titanic*'s safety features, we could all be sure of a perfectly safe journey. I get the feeling the captain must think us unsinkable, and —as you know better than anyone—no ship is unsinkable. Besides, I, for one, do not want any of our children on board to be at risk when help could be too far away to save us. . . . Do you?"

Again, no response, but I didn't fill the void this time. He just stared out at the water, so I did, too. After a few beats, he said, "Miss Landers, you are quite a young woman, and I am delighted to have had the pleasure of speaking with you. But I must attend to some ship's business, so I will bid you good afternoon." He moved to go, then turned back to me. "You can sleep soundly on the *Titanic*, Miss Landers."

"Thank you, Mr. Andrews. Oh—and one last thing . . . If you were going to speak to the Bridge crew, the evening of the fourteenth would be best. Word has it there will be a particular danger of encountering icebergs that evening, and the weather will be quite cold."

He frowned, then nodded and walked back indoors.

I turned back to the water and rubbed my temples. I had no idea if I'd done any good—if I'd gone too far or not far enough.

"There you are!" It was Maggie, with Quinn towering at her side.

"Yes!" I said. I held up my ribbon. "I was lucky enough to find my ribbon *and* Mr. Andrews. What an interesting and talented man. He obliged me for a couple of minutes to discuss the ship." I wondered briefly if "obliged me" was grammatically correct. I was starting to talk like the characters in old Western reruns my grandmother watched in the middle of the night on free channels for insomniacs.

"He built us a hell of a ship, that's for sure," said Maggie.

"Did you know the ship could run right into an iceberg and still stay afloat?" I asked.

"Really?" said Maggie. "Sounds like we missed quite the conversation! What else did you two discuss?"

"I am quite sure Mr. Andrews thinks the sea air has taken my good sense. I told him I cannot help that my father is an overly well-read connoisseur of shipbuilding and has been in my ear about the *Titanic*. I passed along a suggestion that we slow the ship at night since we will soon enter iceberg territory. Oh . . . and that Mr. Andrews speak to the Bridge crew about how to steer the ship safely if we come upon ice." Even I would think I'd lost my mind if I heard myself.

"And how should they steer, my dear? Do tell," Maggie said.

"As preposterous as it sounds, if they cannot avoid the iceberg altogether, they should ram the iceberg head-on and not expose the side of the ship."

"How intriguing. Why is that?" She appeared to be genuinely interested.

"Because if an iceberg does too much damage to the side, the *Titanic* could sink."

"Oh my Lord," Maggie said. "That's a hell of a thing."

"Indeed," Quinn said, not surprisingly.

"Let me guess. . . . Mr. Andrews didn't take too kindly to a young woman telling him what to do with his ship?" Maggie could've sounded condescending, but she actually sounded sorta proud of me.

"He was too polite to show it, but I think you are right. I simply want him and the Bridge crew to be careful on the fourteenth. Did you know we are heading into 'Iceberg Alley' as we get closer to Newfoundland? That is very concerning given the weather ahead, and if something were to happen, there are not enough lifeboats for everyone."

Maggie looked thoughtful. "Now that you mention it, there aren't too many, are there?"

Quinn piped in again. "One day, a ship's safety will be much more regulated than it is today."

"If we do have an accident, you will get right to a lifeboat, won't you, Maggie?" I said. "I could not bear the thought of anything happening to you." A small pit of worry was growing in my stomach that Maggie might do something heroic instead of taking her seat in the boat, now that I'd pointed out the lifeboat shortage.

"Oh, don't you worry about me, missy. I'm made of sturdy stuff."

"Good," I said. "The world needs more women like you—if we are ever going to get the vote."

"Very true," Quinn said, turning on the charm. "I predict women will not only get the vote but will also run for the highest offices someday. But for now, before we decide men are not useful at all, shall we continue our stroll? Perhaps we could get ourselves into some trouble?"

Maggie raised one of her dark eyebrows. "Trouble? Playing shuffleboard?"

"Oh," I said to her, pointing at Quinn, "do not underestimate this one. Mr. Daniels tends to find trouble wherever he goes, even playing shuffleboard."

"Touché," Quinn said. "I will admit shuffleboard can be a dangerous game, if you know how to play it right."

Maggie took his arm. "Then onward, young man," she said, laughing.

# thirteen

Apparently, the *Rubáiyát of Omar Khayyám* had been famous forever, although I'd never heard of it until I got the *Titanic* assignment. It was a collection of short poems attributed to a Persian poet, astronomer, and mathematician who died forever ago, in 1131. Then . . . the extra-special version on the *Titanic* came along. While there were loads of copies of the 1860 Edward FitzGerald translation, what made the one I was supposed to find so theft-worthy was the book-binding. The year before the *Titanic* sailed, a British company created a copy with an ornate cover of Moroccan leather, inlaid with three peacocks with their tail feathers spread out. The cover also had a Persian lute—called an ud—designed of inlaid wood and ivory, with gold embroidery to add shine to the detailing. On top of that, more than a thousand emeralds, rubies, amethysts, and topazes sparkled on the book's cover. Thankfully, if I failed my mission to retrieve it—a distinct possibility—the poetry itself would still exist in other editions.

The Windline collectors were the real deal, and after doing my research, I understood why they'd tasked me with stealing this one-of-a-kind version before it found a home at the bottom of the sea. I'd read it was auctioned about a month before the *Titanic* set sail, with an American buyer winning the bid. The *Titanic* was transporting the book to its new owner in the States. Whether I was successful or not, the buyer would never see his prize.

Technically, Quinn wasn't supposed to help me with any part of my test. He'd made it clear that he wasn't going to actively help with my plan to save the *Titanic*. I hadn't told him all the details, and he hadn't asked. But I was glad to have a sidekick on my quest for the *Rubáiyát*. The two of us had broken so many rules already that it hardly mattered if we added one more to the list. Hopefully he'd be able to squeak through his test on lies and half-truths.

I wondered how he'd feel about me, or me about him, after this was all over. It was hard to imagine going home to my little brother smacking at the dinner table, to Tiana flopping on my bed to chat and listen to music, and to my caring—sometimes annoyingly caring—parents. Of course, Mom and Dad would be all smiles until they realized I'd epically failed every single thing related to my test.

Still, if I changed history, and the ship made it to New York, and Quinn didn't rat me out, then maybe I'd pass. But pass what, exactly? If we did find the *Rubáiyát* and I saved the ship, I'd have to leave the book on the *Titanic* since Windline would never have asked me to retrieve it in the first place. By that logic, would they have ever sent me to the *Titanic* at all?

*Time travel makes my head hurt.*

But if I didn't save the ship, then I'd better have the book in my hands when I went home. So tonight, I'd do my best to find the fancy, jewel-encrusted book for Windline's collection. Better Windline have it than the Atlantic—if it came to that.

Sitting slump-shouldered on my bed, I tucked away my worries and watched Rosalee unpin her curly hair from a simple French knot. I had developed a total friend crush on her. If Tiana were here, she'd have a for-real crush on her. Rosalee was everything I wasn't. Smart enough to be a doctor and committed enough to help people every day of her life. Brave enough to do it in a man's world. Naturally attractive—the kind of glow-from-within beauty that's timeless and definitely jealousy-worthy. And so friggin' friendly. If she lived in my time, she'd probably be one of those doctors who started her day talking medicine on TV morning shows, then delivered twenty babies before lunch.

"You are deep in thought," she said, wiping her face with cream from a perfectly lined-up row of glass jars on the dressing table. "You wouldn't be thinking about a certain first-class passenger, would you?"

"Surprisingly, no." I laughed. "I was actually thinking about how much I admire you. It can't be super easy being a female doctor in 1912. It's probably harder still because you are so pretty. Major props to you for being such a role model."

She pivoted on her stool to look at me. "Charlie, you sometimes use the strangest language. Regardless, you are awfully kind to say such nice things, though I am not usually considered pretty with my untamable locks. And it is hard sometimes, yes. But anything worth having is, especially if you were born into the fairer sex. I fight my battles when I have to, then do my best to leave the anger behind. Otherwise, I would be a bitter woman."

I kicked myself for slipping into contractions and slang. *So—much—work.* I waxed on. "Do you think things will get better for women in the future?" I knew the answer, of course. A mixed bag, for sure.

"I know they will, Charlie, even though it may take a long time. People are afraid of change, but it is change that keeps life interesting. Would you agree?" She stood, tying her robe at the waist.

"I suppose change is good, so long as humanity is actually heading toward a better future. I am not optimistic about that, but mostly I don't think about it much."

"Do you not have an obligation to think about it, as a member of the human race?"

"Probably so," I said, picking at the flowers on the day dress I still wore, "but there are so many people in the world.

I am not optimistic that I can make much of a difference in the grand scheme of things." *Except for saving the Titanic*, I thought.

Rosalee sat on her bed and started brushing out her hair. "Maybe you will, maybe you will not. But if you take responsibility for doing what you can to make the world more livable, less miserable, or maybe just a bit more fair, then you have done your part. I would say you have a lot to work with."

*I do, actually. I'm a time traveler.* But I couldn't say that. "What, like education?"

"Like heart."

"Oh." I would never have described myself as having heart. I liked the sound of it.

"And you are smart and articulate. You saved Rima, so you are brave. You are a natural beauty, which everyone cannot help noticing when you walk in a room. If I were to diagnose your problem," she said, still brushing and looking up and to the right as if dreaming up something important, "I think you may be stuck living somewhere between your mind and your soul. You need to connect the two. It is in that connection where you can find true power, depth, and understanding."

"Gosh," I said. "That was worth the price of my ticket, thank you!"

"I aim to please."

"Turns out you are good at diagnosing all kinds of things."

She laughed, jumping up to put her brush away. "Now, do you not have a date with Quinn?"

I stood to go. Little did she know that my "date" was with a book of poetry somewhere in the cargo hold. "I do, yes. In fact, I suppose I should get going." I stooped to pick up my purse, which happened to harbor a plastic bag I brought from home to keep the *Rubáiyát* safe.

Rosalee gave me a look. "If you were not aware, that boy is head over heels for you."

"Not really, no—I mean we are just old friends. Maybe a little more than that, but only because we are stuck on a ship together."

"You said I was good at diagnosing all kinds of things, right?" She laughed, pulling back her weighty coverlet and grabbing a book. "Listen to the doctor on this one."

~

Quinn and I met in our usual spot to begin "Operation *Rubáiyát*." Quinn was full-tilt 1912. I would've preferred a burglar outfit, like black jeans, a black T-shirt, and some Chucks to crawl around in the cargo hold instead of my constricting and very noticeable day dress. Unfortunately, jeans wouldn't be exactly inconspicuous here, and on this segregated ship, looking like a first-class passenger was the best protection, especially when snooping around areas off-limits to guests.

My research told me that the book was kept in the storage area on the Orlop Deck, close to both the stern and the bottom of the ship. If the *Titanic* were a New Orleans king cake, there'd be a lot of layers for us to cut through in order to find the little plastic baby, or in this case, the *Rubáiyát*. I had studied the plans and tiny drawings I'd found of the *Titanic* down to the placement of the toilets. But figuring out how to wind through the various crew doors to get there would be tough. Luckily, the White Star Line wasn't too worried about passengers sneaking around the ship *because who in their right mind would be sneaking around this ship?* So the worst we would face would be crewmen and locked passageways to enforce immigration rules. In the future, sadly there'd be doors with electronic locks and security cameras to keep everyone from stealing.

Even if we were lucky enough to get to the cargo hold, we might not be able to figure out exactly where the book was stored. Second Officer Charles Lightoller had supervised completion of the *Titanic*'s cargo plan, but we could hardly ask him for directions. Then there was the matter of getting the *Rubáiyát* out of whatever it was stored in.

Our first order of business was to retrace our steps to the third-class General Room on C-Deck, near the rear of the ship.

From there, we'd figure out how to wind our way down five decks to reach the cargo storage area, hopefully without getting desperately lost. I'd never stolen anything before—not even a pack of gum—so this whole theft adventure was a little out of my wheelhouse.

Quinn was all taut energy as I walked up to him. I wondered if his burst of enthusiasm came from finally doing something we were actually supposed to do—or at least, I was supposed to do. As he half walked, half bounced, I said, "Either you've been drinking coffee, mainlining sugar, or you're excited about our little adventure."

"Maybe all of the above," he said as he jumped in front of me and started walking backward.

"Was the shuffleboard not enough excitement for you?" I teased.

"Hardly." He laughed. "I went to the gym after we finished to lift weights."

"Have you tried the pool yet?" I was a little jealous of his pool access—first class only, naturally.

"Oh, yeah. I did that this morning."

"How about the squash court and the Turkish baths—did you do those, too?"

"I didn't have a partner for squash, sadly. And I skipped the Turkish baths since I don't even know what one is—"

"Like a sauna, maybe?" I asked while Quinn literally ran a circle around me.

"I have no idea." He grabbed me at the waist and spun me around, then he took my hand and started running.

This Quinn reminded me of the playful little kid I'd grown up with. There was video evidence of Quinn tossing a ball to me when I was nine months old—which hit me in the head since I hadn't remotely mastered hand-eye coordination. Some of my earliest memories were of playgrounds in the California sun with him going down the slide first, then daring me to follow. When I was old enough to be a competitor, he'd try to outdo me in everything. If I climbed high, he'd climb higher. If I went low, he'd go lower. One time he got stuck trying to shimmy under a fence that I'd made it through with no problem. That was a good day.

Then there was his poking phase, when he'd poke me or fake punch me in the arm every time our moms weren't looking. He'd chase me like prey and then yell, "Tag, you're it!" There was also a building phase, which meant that if we were in the house, he was building forts out of overstuffed cushions and fuzzy blankets—and naturally he'd leave it strewn all over my room when it was time for him to go home. I was pretty fond of the forts, though, and sometimes left them up for days. Outside, he'd stack rocks or try to put up makeshift lean-tos that inevitably flopped over in sad heaps. That was before he became a Boy Scout and starting camping in Joshua Tree and Tahoe.

I didn't see him as much after that, although we'd spent the longest three weeks of my life in the desert together. Our parents had hatched the bright idea to rent campers and hit the road like hippies or retired people. I remembered Quinn covered in Arizona red dirt, standing on a rock above me. We'd looked out over the Painted Desert with its simmering heat and striations of rocks like striped shirts on sleeping giants. He'd kept yelling "badlands" over and over, as if they were a punk band or something. God, I totally remembered plotting how to lose him in the Petrified Forrest. Let him live forever in the fields of wood turned opalized rock.

Obviously, I'd been unsuccessful, and on the way back to California, Quinn had started running circles around everything when we'd stopped for gas—around the parking lot, the gas station, the gas pump, and the Airstreams—until his father had thrown him over his shoulder and dumped him back in his seat. Thankfully, Quinn had mellowed out quite a lot since then, but tonight he was like a kid again.

Soon enough, we were with Rima and our friends in third class for a round of hellos and dancing. We figured we'd want to get to the cargo hold as late as possible so most of the crew would be gone, which meant we had some time to hang out with our friends. Plus, we figured it couldn't hurt to start from the aft section of the ship.

Music filled the room as it had before, upbeat and full of texture. Some passengers were playing cards, others talking in clumps. An older woman sat in the corner knitting, tapping her foot to the music. A guy with biceps the size of small watermelons was literally doing a handstand and moving to the music while his friends cheered him on. Quinn grabbed Rima and started twirling her around, and Rima's brother, Arash, invited me to dance, a poor substitute for Rosalee. Then all four of us grabbed hands for another round of jumping up and down and spinning in circles. Another person broke in, and another, until our circle was pushing everybody else out of the way, and I was holding hands with two Swedish guys in coarse wool vests and caps. Quinn was across from me, all brightness and smiles, light on his feet as we moved.

Maybe this was all too much for him. It certainly was for me. Quinn always seemed so in control, so sure of himself, but I knew him. He could feel something on the inside and never show it on the outside. The *Titanic* had to be weighing on him, too. After all, tonight was the midpoint of our journey. We had one more complete day before the fourteenth, the ill-fated day we were both dreading, even though its arrival meant we'd go home. If my mission to save the ship was successful, we could enjoy another zillion-course meal, take in the moonlight on the promenade, then with everyone sleeping blissfully on the *Titanic* and the

*Rubáiyát* put back somewhere safe, return to Windline to see how history had changed. If our interventions failed to save the ship, we'd leave before it sank, and return home with the book. I couldn't even think about the rest.

When our massive circle in the relatively small room turned into an amoeba, then broke apart, we reluctantly said our goodbyes, made a plan to meet on deck the next day, and set out to wind our way down, down, into the depths of the *Titanic*. Getting to the G-Deck right above the Orlop Deck was easy because there were passenger rooms on G-Deck, though at one point when we were clearly wandering, lost, a crew member stopped us.

"Could I help you, sir?" he asked Quinn in a decidedly Irish accent. "You'll be wanting to take the elevator just down the way"—he pointed—"to get to your class."

A second time, we'd closed a crew-only door behind us when we heard a crewman coming. We didn't have enough time to get back through the door, so, with a quick hip-check and spin move, Quinn maneuvered me into the corner and kissed me, like the kind on TV with lots of movement but nothing really happening. I put my arms around him and moved them up and down his back, so it'd be clear to the approaching crew member exactly what was going on. The feel of Quinn's lips still felt new and strange.

Sure enough, when the crewman got close, he cleared his throat. "Beggin' your pardon, sir, madam," he said, "but me boss'd have me head if I did'na tell ya that this area is not for the passengers, 'specially the first-class ones."

Looking down at me as he spoke, Quinn answered, "Right. We'll just be dashing off, then." He ushered me back through the door and into the passageway, where we doubled over in a fit of soundless laughter. Then we waited until the crewman was gone and went back through, winding our way through a maze of hatches and steel doors.

"Even if we find the cargo area," I whispered, "will we ever find our way out of here?"

"Worst case, we have to spend the night," Quinn said, still energetic despite the late hour. "I wouldn't mind a sleepover with you." He flashed me a cheesy grin.

"If you're gonna invite me to a sleepover, I'd rather you invited me to your super-rich-guy cabin, where at least there'd be a soft mattress and snacks on the veranda in the morning."

"And a steward."

"And him, too."

At last, after five wrong turns and related double-backs, as well as hiding behind a piece of machinery and then in a room full of cigars to dodge more trouble from crewmen, we were getting close. We could hear all kinds of noises. Even though we were near the bottom of the ship, its movement was more pronounced because we were so far away from its center of gravity. We were hit with a blast of heat during an accidental foray into the boiler room, which resembled the biblical depiction of Hell. We passed the refrigerated cargo hold. Finally, after what seemed like an eternity, we entered the storage area we'd been looking for. The light was low, barely enough to see by, and the smell was a combination of newness, milled wood, and stagnant air circulation.

Nothing was certain in my research on the *Titanic*, because who knew every little detail would need to be remembered for this single voyage? Even the passenger list wasn't totally accurate in historical records. I could only hope that the *Rubáiyát* was where my research said it would be.

"Now what?" I whispered.

"I don't know," Quinn said, looking around at the crates stacked high.

My eyes began to adjust to the lighting. "Maybe there's a cargo list in here somewhere, like hanging on a wall or something," I said. "If this were a movie, there'd be a computer we could hack."

From behind a crate, Quinn asked, "Can you hack a computer?"

"Well, no," I said, "but if this were a movie I could. Ouch!" I hit my head on a crate that was sticking out.

"You okay?"

"Yeah—another bump on the head. No big deal."

"We gotta get you a helmet."

"Probably a good idea. Though I wonder if maybe the ship is trying to tell me something. Do you think it could be cursed?" I asked, literally on my knees between a row of crates, squinting at the writing on them to figure out the organizational system.

"I think curses are just bad luck rewritten in hindsight."

I looked up. "Whoa . . . Did you just come up with that off the top of your head?" I struggled to my feet and rubbed my knees.

"Yep. Just now. You like it?"

"Definitely. You know those calendars that have some kind of saying for each day? That'd be perfect." I laughed as I moved to look under the stairs that led to a hatch. "Or maybe it could be the first line of your college admission essays."

"Yeah, if I wanted to go to the University of Transylvania or something."

"I hear it's really coming up the ranks—and has a great football team."

Quinn whistled, motioning me over. "Check this out."

He had hit the jackpot. A bound ledger sat on top of a crate.

"That's gotta be it!" I said, hurrying to see.

He flipped open the ledger, scanning the pages. "Don't get too excited. We have to look through this whole thing, and it's written, not typed."

"And there's so much stuff in here that there's probably more than one ledger. We need to get lucky."

Quinn raised an eyebrow.

Good grief. *One real make-out session and . . . damn.* "One-track mind, much?"

"I'm a guy, Charlie."

I laughed. "Fair point."

In case someone walked in, we tucked ourselves in the corner farthest from any entry, our backs to the wall. We took turns gliding a finger down the rows of lines in the book, looking for either the bookbinder's name or the name of the owner. In the low light, I had to strain my eyes to see the words, written mostly in looping cursive.

We kept thinking we'd found it. "Is this it?" or "This one could be it, but I can't make it out," usually followed by "Don't think so" or "Can't be." Then, about three-quarters of the way through the book, as if a magnifying glass had magically appeared, an entry jumped off the page at me: Sangorski & Sutcliffe. The bookbinders shipping the *Rubáiyát.*

"Got it!" I said, a little too loudly. I cupped my hand over my mouth.

"Oh, thank God. That damn thing was giving me a hell of a headache." Quinn massaged the back of his neck. "Now we have to figure out the system."

"From what I can tell, they're in number order but probably by type of cargo."

Quinn extended a hand. Getting up and down in a tight dress and a corset wasn't the easiest maneuver. If women were considered the weaker sex in history, perhaps it was because they were pressured to immobilize themselves with fashion. I silently vowed to never wear tight clothing again once I got home.

We swept the rows of crates until we narrowed down to the type of cargo, and from there, quickly triangulated the wooden case that matched the ledger entry.

"This is it," I said, bouncing on my toes. "Now, how do we get it open?"

"Don't suppose you brought that crowbar you mentioned?"

I smiled sheepishly. "I'm afraid I'm fresh out of crowbars."

"Then let's look around for anything strong enough to wedge open the box."

The problem with trying to steal things on a brand-new ship was that the place was impeccably clean—no debris in the corner, no mess left by the loading crew. It was probably safe to eat off the floor. So we had to retrace our steps until we lucked out in the refrigerated cargo section, where we found a toolbox near the entry. I guessed it was used to fix the $CO_2$ machines and compressors that cooled this part of the ship.

As I was grabbing a hammer, we heard a metal door creak open, followed by footsteps.

"Oh crap," Quinn whispered softly, "over here!" We scurried like mice on tiptoes behind a large metal box and crouched down, with just enough space to huddle together. Then, horror movie style, the sound of the footsteps got closer and closer, until they were close, so close we could hear the person breathing and rummaging around for something.

Despite having Quinn's warmth pressed along one side of my scrunched-up body, I started to shiver in the refrigerated air, imagining myself as a big ham starting to freeze. I clamped my teeth together so they wouldn't chatter. Quinn looked at me with a question in his eyes, and I gave an uncertain nod. To keep my mind off how cold I was, I started silently counting backward from a hundred. We heard the movement of boxes, then, when I got to sixty-five in my head, a bit of a groan in a male's vocal range, and finally, retreating footsteps. We stayed another couple of minutes to be sure he was gone.

"Are you okay?" Quinn asked as we unwedged ourselves from our hiding place and beelined into the corridor. I unclenched my teeth, which started them chattering like a fast metronome. Quinn rubbed circulation back into my arms and hands, and then he wrapped his arms around me, holding me tight until my teeth slowed down.

I breathed against his chest, warming enough to use my words. "Yeah, I'm good. Thanks."

"Next time you're mad at me, just remember how good I am at warming you up."

I rolled my eyes. "You do have some skills. Now let's see if breaking into a crate is one of them." We headed back toward the cargo hold.

Soon we stood over the box that held the *Rubáiyát* as if we were surgeons about to start open-heart surgery. I handed Quinn the hammer.

"This could make some noise," I said. "I hope no one else is around to hear us."

"Probably not. It's really late by now."

"I wish I had my phone."

"So you could call for a lifeline?" Quinn joked.

"Now that you mention it . . . but no, for the time—and the flashlight. Plus we could take some selfies of our first robbery."

"Let's hope our first and last." Quinn laughed. "Not sure I wanna make a habit out of this."

"But we're like the Bonnie and Clyde of the *Titanic*. We could become time traveling artifact hunters, like my parents, but way cooler."

"Spoken like a true Windline Academy future graduate," he said, starting to wedge the claw of the hammer into the wood.

"That remains to be seen," I said, "but first, let's get this done without winding up in the brig."

Quinn groaned with the effort of wedging off a side of the wooden crate. "Does this ship have a brig?"

"Not that I know of. Maybe the master-at-arms's office."

"Let's not find out." Using his body weight, Quinn tried one last push and the wood gave way. After repeating the exercise on all four sides, the crate was finally open.

Quinn backed up, and I pawed through the crate full of items in paper wrapping, neatly stacking the items that would have to go back in. Nothing matched our prize. I looked through each item again. My heart sank.

"It has to be here," I said. "It has to!"

Raking his hand through his hair, Quinn said, "Shit."

"That about sums it up."

Quinn walked over and picked up the ledger again. I waited while he went back to scanning the rows and held my breath. He came back and looked at the open crate again. Then he held the ledger out. "I think that's a one, not a seven," he said, pointing. "We're off."

I exhaled. "Crap. Let's hope you're right." We continued down the row of cargo and found our new target, and Quinn repeated the whole process with the hammer. Then, I went through the contents, slowly, as if our poetry book might run away if I went too fast.

Near the bottom, I found a wrapped item marked "Gabriel Wells," the man who'd purchased the *Rubáiyát* at auction. My hands shook as I unfolded the paper carefully, almost afraid to find the wrong item inside. But in a moment, my prize appeared. I held it up for Quinn to see like it was the Holy Grail, a triumphant grin on my face.

"I haven't read the poetry, but, damn, that's a piece of art," he said, running a finger over the jewel-encrusted cover.

"It'd be worth a lot in our time," I said. Of course, Windline was not exactly short on cash.

"Let's finish up and get out of here. I'm getting a bad feeling."

I rewrapped the book and stuck it in my two-gallon, waterproof zip-top bag. Quinn repacked both crates and hammered the lids back on, though the seals were no longer perfect.

"Help me," he said as we worked to turn the heavy crates over so the bad sides were facing down. Then, when we managed it without anything falling out, he said, "Time to go."

Just as we turned to make our way out of the cargo hold, we heard another crewman coming and sank down behind the crates.

"Nothing going on down here," he said. For a second, I thought he was talking to us, and my stomach did a somersault. Then I heard a second voice.

"Yeah, all quiet, mate. Let's call it a night."

"Wait a second," said the first. "I left the cargo manifest in here earlier. Where is it?"

The weak light of a 1912 flashlight swept the dimly lit room. I didn't breathe. Quinn shifted his weight. I thought he was preparing to pounce. Instead, he grabbed the ledger and crawled away. I was alone, cursing under my breath and trying to make myself smaller. A floral dress wasn't exactly good camouflage. I was screwed.

Footsteps got closer, and the light grew brighter. Step, sweep, step, sweep. They were way too close.

"Ah, here 'tis!" yelled one.

"Blimey, how'd it get over there?"

"How should I know?"

"Well, bring it here and we'll take it back up to the Purser's Office before I lose me job."

They left, talking all the way out. I could finally breathe.

When Quinn came back around the corner, I fake punched him in the arm.

"You deserted me!" I whispered, securing the *Rubáiyát* in my purse.

"Only in spirit," he said, grinning. "I had to move the manifest, and besides, if they'd found you, I could've jumped them from behind. Much better odds than if I'd been with you."

"Well, next time, tell me first."

He paused. "That's a lot to unpack, Charlie. . . . It assumes there'll be a next time and that I could say anything with two guards breathing down our necks."

He took my hand as we started to wind our way back to the top of the ship.

"Shut up," I said.

"No, you shut up."

"I said it first."

"What are we, twelve?"

"Yes. All this stress is making me age backward. By the time we get home, I'll have to start kindergarten all over again," I said.

"Those were the days—naps and snacks and playtime."

"I actually remember when you started kindergarten better than when I did." At that age, he was like a puppy growing into his feet, except he'd been growing into his big blue eyes and a mop of blond hair that had started to turn a light golden brown.

"How can you possibly remember that?" He opened a hatch and moved me through ahead of him. Then we realized we were going the wrong way and turned around.

I waited for him to catch up. "I lost my best friend that day."

He put his hand on my waist. "What are you talking about? I'm right here."

"It was never the same. Still isn't."

"Maybe not. We had to grow up. But we're here, together, aren't we?"

After several minutes of winding our way in silence, I saw my opening. "Why are you here, Quinn? I mean, as my

Minder?" I bit my lip. Even though I wanted to live in a pretend world, I had to hear him say it. *He thought I'd be easy to manage, especially if he turned on the charm, so he asked for the assignment.*

"I begged anyone who'd listen for the job because I couldn't stand the thought of you somewhere alone with some random senior, maybe getting hurt, or worse. The headmistress finally caved—I think I annoyed her into it. Plus my mom talked to your mom, and they might've put in a call or two."

*Of course they did.* "Got it," I said. "Big brother to the rescue and all that. . . . Then why all the making nice beforehand?"

"Do I really have to spell it out for you?"

"I'm gonna go with . . . yes."

He was silent for a beat, looking down at the inches between us in the cramped junction to the corridor. "Because," he said finally, with a slight break in his voice, "I'm in . . . I mean . . ." He took a deep breath and met my eyes. "Because I'm in love with you, Charlie." He stepped back, shoved his hands in his pockets, and walked ahead, leaving his words ringing in my ears.

I froze and rewound what he'd said in my mind a couple of times to make sure my ears hadn't gone off the deep end. Then I hurried behind him, stunned. "Wait, are you just saying that? Like a junior hazing kind of thing, right?"

He turned back, red faced. "Oh my God. Why would I just say that? Charlie, you proved my point."

"What point?"

"That you're dense, exasperating, and stubborn!"

"For the record, your adjectives keep changing. So you're in love with me? Really?" My mind reeling, I followed him down a long, narrow corridor.

"Charlie, for the last time, yes." We walked up some steps, then stepped through the last forbidden door and spilled into an empty passageway. "And if you say another word, I swear I'll hate you instead . . . or better yet, throw you overboard."

"I'd like to see you try."

"Hating you or throwing you overboard?"

"I don't know. You're impossible."

"I'll give you that," Quinn said, pushing the button for the lift. A passenger walked by, and we fell silent until the lift arrived. We stepped in, and he pulled me close. He breathed into the top of my head.

*He loves me? He LOVES me? He loves ME?* My brain was spinning. *When? Why? And how could I have been so off base?*

"So how would you feel about that sleepover?" he asked while a whole conversation with myself was going on in my head. "We could stash the *Rubáiyát* somewhere in my rooms for safekeeping. And I swear I'll be a gentleman."

I registered his words and stared into those blue eyes, the ones I'd had in front of me for as long as I could remember.

I stifled the urge to laugh at the word "sleepover," partly because it was funny and partly because I was having my "this is a really intimate moment" reaction. And Quinn was doing the asking—actual made-mud-pies-with-him Quinn. I managed, "I suppose I can trust you."

"Then is that a yes?"

"Will I get pastries on the veranda in the morning?"

"Your wish is my command, Miss Landers."

"Then, Mr. Daniels, I accept your invitation," I said, switching into 1912 mode. "However, you simply must do everything in your power to protect my reputation."

He laughed. "I'm not sure I will have much sway over the captain or Mr. Andrews, but I will do my level best."

~

Quinn's suite still took my breath away, but this time it wasn't only the opulence. It was 3:00 a.m., April 13, one day before the *Titanic* would meet its fate. I didn't want to be alone, but I was afraid. Not that Quinn would do anything I wasn't ready for—after all, his mother would murder him if he did—but of Quinn in general. It was like he'd had me off balance our whole lives, whether he was kissing me or ignoring me or carrying me over his shoulder like a sack of potatoes. *Did I love him, too?* I had no idea. But I needed him tonight.

We stashed the *Rubáiyát* in Quinn's trunk, under layers of his things. He handed me a cream-colored cotton undershirt with small buttons at the neckline, and I disappeared into the en suite bathroom to change. I wrestled myself out of my dress and corset, determined not to call for help, then slipped on Quinn's shirt. It smelled like history—musky in a good way. I rested my hands on the cool of the marble and looked at myself in the mirror. My hair, a much deeper brown than Quinn's, was still pinned up, though tendrils had escaped in various places. I took the pins out—carefully around my stitches—and let my hair fall chunk by chunk until it hung like a curtain down my back. My wide-set eyes were bright, the hazel leaning slightly golden in the light of the room. My cheeks were pink, either from the cold night air or the warmth of the suite.

Thankfully, Quinn's shirt was long on me. When I packed for the trip, I'd drawn the line at leaving behind modern underwear. If someone found me dead on the ship, an autopsy would reveal striped microfiber bikinis, and everyone would think I was from outer space. I splashed my face, and after spotting some real toothpaste in Quinn's small bag of toiletries, I swished some in my mouth.

The suite's bedroom had two beds, and Quinn was sitting up in one, with only a single lamp on. In the glow of the light, he looked almost fake, like a painting of the perfect 1912 guy. It could hang in a museum, with a little white card next to it saying "'Young Man on *Titanic*,' by Charlotte Landers." Quinn wore a shirt like the one I had on.

I trotted to my bed, holding my shirt down to make sure it stayed put, which it didn't—at least not when I bent down to pull back the covers.

"You're wearing striped underwear in 1912? How very un-Windline of you."

"I know—couldn't part with them. A girl has to do what a girl has to do," I said sassily, slipping between the sheets. They were cool and soft to my skin. "You try wearing a corset. Not the greatest. Just be glad you're a guy."

"Oh, I am," he said smugly.

"Jerk."

"There you go again."

"Can't help it. Learned behavior." My defensive weapons had been used so often with him that they were nearly automatic.

"But I'm glad you're here."

"I'm glad you're here—on the *Titanic*," I said.

"If I promise to be good, would you come over?" He patted the sliver of an empty spot beside him on the narrow bed.

I thought for a minute. "Nope. But it's okay if you wanna come over here."

I didn't have to ask twice. Quinn squished into my bed

made for one. We hadn't been in the same bed since we were little. I snuggled into his warmth, and we entwined our legs. He kissed me, briefly, lingering nose-to-nose, his warm breath on my face.

"Tell me a bedtime story," I whispered, "maybe about what it's like to be in railroads."

"I hardly have to lift a finger, and the money just rolls in. It's the best job ever," he said into my ear.

"I thought being my Minder was the best job ever?"

"Hmm." His voice was deep and raspy. "I'd say it has its ups and downs. Right now is definitely a highlight."

If I were a kitten, I'd have been purring. "Well, if Minders always provided snuggling services, the JY Test would be a lot more popular."

"And if juniors were always so soft, the seniors wouldn't dread being Minders so much." He kissed my neck. I smiled.

"Quinn, when did you start to love me?" I asked quietly.

Silence again. Then, "A million years ago," he said. "But I had to wait until the right time. When I saw you at your birthday party this summer, I knew."

My reality kept shifting underneath me. "Oh" was all I could say.

We talked quietly for a while after that. Then with our arms around each other, we fell asleep in the lamplight.

# fourteen

As promised, Quinn ordered breakfast for the veranda that Saturday, though the service was what we called a continental breakfast, just rich pastries and morning tea. I was so hungry I ate three scones slathered with butter while I watched the Atlantic pass by, mysterious in the morning mist. Even though I usually avoided tea at home, I sipped from a china cup, my pinky out, temporarily feeling a bit British. The weather was foggy, but the *Titanic*'s daily newspaper, the *Atlantic Daily Bulletin*, said the day would be mostly clear and cool. From my research, I knew the day would be relatively uneventful, except that a fire burning in one of the boiler rooms since the ship's sea trials would finally be put out. After last night, I couldn't imagine extra fire in those boiler rooms.

The morning passed slowly—the good kind of slow. Quinn and I lounged, enjoying being our normal selves alone in his suite. The only time we had to pretend was when Felix knocked or the service was being cleared. We also got into quite the pillow fight, which didn't end well for one of the pillows. Feathers flew everywhere.

"Totally your fault," I said. "What will Felix think? You promised to protect my reputation!" I teased.

"I'll tell him I did something rotten and you beat the crap out of me with a poor, innocent pillow," Quinn said, picking a feather out of his hair.

"That's totally believable." I laughed, picking up a fresh pillow and throwing it at him.

Before any more pillows got hurt, and after peeking down the hall to be sure no staff would walk in on us, we took another look at the *Rubáiyát.* The outside was a work of art, and we both touched the various stones on its cover. It was also a work of art on the inside, full of four-line poems. I'd read that its name came from the Arabic word "rubá," meaning "composed of four." I could see why it was a treasure better off in Windline's hands than on the sea floor.

Eventually, time ticked on by as it always does. I brushed a soft goodbye kiss across Quinn's lips and went to my own room to change. I missed him as soon as he shut the door behind me, so I was glad when I eventually ran into Rosalee in the passageway near our cabin.

"Well," she said, elongating the word, "look who decided to put in an appearance!"

"It is not what it looks like," I said, my cheeks blushing hot.

"Oh, I am not so sure. . . . I would say it looks like a girl who never slept in the bed next to me last night. . . ." I'd only known Rosalee for a few days, so I'd had no idea how she'd react to my impropriety. I was relieved she was teasing me.

"That may be true, but nothing happened. We were talking in his drawing room until all hours, and I slept in his extra bed—that is all. I promise."

"I believe you. Besides, who am I to judge anyway? However, I should tell you for future reference that there can be certain unwanted outcomes of an evening spent with a man." She had gone from teasing to doctoring in a hot second. *Yikes.*

"Are you trying to share the facts of life with me?" I whispered conspiratorially.

Rosalee smiled. "One can never be sure if any given young woman knows all the relevant medical facts."

"Thank you so much, Rosalee. That is very thoughtful. But my mother is the progressive type, so I am well informed." Even if my mother hadn't dragged me to a class when I was twelve, the Internet would've done the job.

"Then I promise not to lecture you any further." She laughed.

"He did tell me that he loves me last night, though. That was kind of a big step in our relationship, I guess. . . ."

"How exciting!" she said. "But you seem less than over the moon about it. Did you tell him you love him?"

"Come to think of it, no." Maybe I was too caught up in our getaway to notice.

"I see."

"I definitely might love him. I mean, I am not totally sure. What does love even mean, really? I have barely even had a . . . a gentleman friend before."

"I am afraid you will have to figure that out on your own," she said, patting my arm. "They failed to teach that course in medical school. Now, I have to dash up to send a message via the wireless. See you later?"

"Sure. Oh wait—I forgot to tell you. We are all meeting at the third-class Promenade area this afternoon at 2:30. Can you join us?"

"Of course! See you there."

~

We were a motley crew, standing in the area on the Bridge Deck meant for third-class passengers. It was less of a promenade and more like a squeezed-in open space surrounded by equipment.

I was back in my second-class day dress, my hair tied back in a simple braid. Rosalee was wearing a deep green. With her red mane billowing, she looked like some sort of romantic sea banshee out of a fantasy novel. Unfortunately, in Gaelic folklore, the appearance of a banshee warns a family that one of them will die soon.

Quinn was suited up, first-class style per usual, and Rima was wearing a striped cotton dress and a scarf covering her head. She'd brought her brother, who couldn't stop eyeing Rosalee, and a few new friends, one of whom was quite pregnant and animatedly talking to my cabinmate.

The afternoon moved along, the warmth of friends around us like a coat on a fall day. We played cards, laughed at stupid jokes, and talked about our very different lives. But as the day grew later, a sense of dread crept into my bones from the deck beneath my feet, making its way up to my head, where it swirled around my brain and settled into a heavy despair. I propped myself on the rail to hold up my weight and looked out at the ocean, magnificent but deadly.

"A 1912 penny for your thoughts," Quinn said, joining me at the railing.

"Oh, it'll take more than a penny." I turned my head toward him with a wry smile. We stood in silence for a few moments, taking in the horizon. "Tomorrow is it," I said.

"Yep," he answered. Then, after a few beats, "You know I disagreed with your plan."

"Yeah, I know."

"I've changed my mind, Charlie."

I stood up straight to face him. "You have?"

"I mean, I wasn't going to say anything to Windline, but it's more than that for me now. We can't let these people die." He gestured with his hand toward our group.

"I still think the rules of time travel are right, but I couldn't live with myself if I didn't help. So what can I do?" Quinn took my hand in his.

I stared at him and his ridiculous blue eyes, trying to figure him out. He kept surprising me, or maybe I was just dense and never saw what was really there. But now I wasn't alone, out on a limb fighting to save the ship by myself. Tears welled up in my eyes, and despite my best efforts to stop them at the source, a couple of runners broke free and started spilling down my face.

Quinn moved in, holding me to him, my head on his chest. He turned to block me from the group behind us. "Talk to me, Charlie," he whispered into the top of my head.

"I'm sorry" was all I could get out. I made a firm point of not apologizing for myself all the time, like girls have been socialized to do, but I couldn't think of anything else to say.

"Sorry for what? Crying? You definitely *should* be sorry," he joked, his voice still quiet. "Hell, if you don't stop, I'll start crying, too, and we can't have a first-class gentleman crying on a third-class passenger deck. It simply isn't done."

Quinn knew just how to get to me. I laughed, and he fished a handkerchief out of his pocket. He had really gotten into the details with his wardrobe. The my-time Quinn probably didn't even own a handkerchief. If I were boohooing back home, he'd have to fish around in his Jeep for an unused drive-through napkin. But this Quinn was a gentleman, through and through.

"Thank you," I said, "for this." I held up the now soggy hanky. "And for being in this with me. I didn't even realize it, but I've been feeling the weight of this whole ship on my shoulders and just having you share that with me is huge. Thank you."

"You said that already." Cue cute smirk.

"I know, but you deserve a double scoop of gratitude," I said, blowing my nose.

"Have I ever told you that you're adorable when you cry?"

"Holy crap—no. Is that why you've been trying to make me cry since the day I was born?"

"Maybe . . ."

"Jerk," I said, smiling.

"I'll own that."

"Well, you could make up for it. . . ."

"How? I'll do anything. Want me to dance?" He stepped back and did a spin and jazz hands. A white-haired man with a long beard was strolling by, and he looked at Quinn in horror.

"You're a geek in a hot jock's body, did you know that?"

"Uh, no, but thanks?"

"Anyway, here's the thing. At the risk of my roommate never speaking to me again after the *Titanic*—which is pretty likely in any case for a variety of reasons—would you consider inviting me for another sleepover? I won't sleep a wink anyway, and we could put together our plan of action for tomorrow?" I blushed, which I thought was reasonable, considering I'd never invited myself to spend the night with a guy before. *Go me.*

"On one condition," he said.

"What's that?"

"You don't eat all the scones in the morning."

"Oh, I'm eating the scones."

"Damn. Well, I'd lose my man card if I turned down a night with a hot chick over some scones." He laughed. "You've got a deal."

~

Most of my second night with Quinn was decidedly unromantic. I pulled out a few notes from my research at the library in New York, refreshing my memory and sharing the details with Quinn. Then we carefully sketched out our timeline for the next day and ran through various scenarios.

April 14, 1912, crept quietly into existence while we sat up talking and planning. The day was here. I felt like I'd been in 1912 for an eternity, yet only for a blink of an eye at the same time. My mom always said that certain intense memories—great ones or awful ones—stand out like bright spots painted on the dark canvas of the mind. My time on the *Titanic* would always be a standout for me. I only hoped that our plan would work, and the ship would pass by April 14 in a remarkably unremarkable way, in a blur of food and sea and music and card games that led to a blissful night of sleep, with passengers and crew waking in their beds to a new day on April 15.

We forced ourselves to crawl into our separate beds around 2:00 a.m. so we could get enough sleep to carry out our plans with a clear head, like two generals readying for battle. But as soon as Quinn turned out the light, I stared into the dark, alone with the slight movement of the ship.

In under sixty seconds, I slid back out of my sheets and snuck into Quinn's bed. He didn't say a word. He just pulled me in close and held me there until we fell asleep. We'd have the rest of our lives to talk and tease each other. For now, we were about to try saving more than fifteen hundred souls from death in the frigid Atlantic.

Light streamed into the room too soon the next morning, and butterflies started flying in my stomach the second my eyes opened. Part of me didn't want to get up at all. Like a turtle, I wanted to withdraw into my trusty shell until I could go home. But lives were on the line.

I remembered another of my mom's pithy sayings, which was "When things get hard, get calmer." I never really understood what she meant until the *Titanic*. So I took a deep breath and allowed my inner voice to say what she might've: *Get up, stay calm, and hold yourself together, Charlie. It's now or never.*

Our plan began when the first ice warning reached the *Titanic* at 9:00 a.m. from the *Caronia*. About that time, Quinn called in his steward.

"Felix, I need a favor," he said.

"Of course, sir. How can I be of service?" His accent was decidedly British.

"I need a good pair of binoculars." He slipped a wad of bills into Felix's hand.

"Yes, sir. Binoculars. Of the opera glass variety or the hunting variety?" Felix asked, his eyes growing wide as he looked at the bills and then pocketed them.

"The hunting variety would be best—you know, like the kind the crew might use. But I will settle for opera glasses if that is all you can drum up."

"I will do my best, sir," Felix said.

"Very good. I will need them left in my suite before dinner, please."

"Yes, sir."

Check. Step one, complete.

I went to my cabin to change into my first outfit for the day. April 14 happened to be a Sunday, and I had to look my first-class best to attend the church service with Quinn. We had debated on whether I should go, since the captain would also be attending. There was a definite chance he'd do something drastic if he saw me again. Eventually, we decided it was worth the risk, given that Mr. Andrews, Maggie Brown, and other dignitaries would be there as well.

Church convened at 10:30 a.m. in the first-class Dining Room on D-Deck. We arrived early, hoping to catch our targets before everyone crowded in. Maggie was one of the first to arrive. She was with Emma Bucknell, a wealthy widow from Pennsylvania.

"Well, a good morning to you, Charlotte, Quinn." Polite introductions followed. Then, "How are you two faring?"

"Quite well, thank you, though I did overhear a crewman saying the ship has received an iceberg warning," I said dramatically. "The weather is supposed to cool off as well. I think we should ask the captain whether we will be quite safe!"

"My dear, the *Titanic* surely is strong enough to protect us through any weather, and, if not, I understand the captain to be quite capable," Mrs. Bucknell assured me.

Quinn added his rehearsed lines. "I have heard it said that it is the hubris of men to assume Mother Nature is the weaker of the two. I think it is up to us to remind the good captain that we would rather reach New York a bit later than risk running this ship into an iceberg. Do you not agree?"

Maggie piped up. "I'm as anxious to see Lady Liberty as the next gal, but I'm not too proud to put in the request. Emma, how about you?"

"Absolutely. You say there was already an ice warning?"

"Indeed, yes," I said, casting a glance at Quinn since I'd stolen his favorite 1912 word. "Just this morning from the *Caronia*. I imagine the crew would be able to see ice ahead well enough in the daytime, but this evening has me most worried."

After more pleasantries, the ladies moved in to take their places for the service. Quinn and I spotted the captain and Mr. Andrews at the same time.

"You got the captain?" I asked.

"Yep. And you've got Andrews."

We split up, Quinn beelining for the captain, who was still our best shot at success, despite how angry I'd made him. I wished I could hear them, but I had to focus on doubling down with Mr. Andrews.

"Good morning, sir," I said brightly when he approached the doors to the dining saloon.

Mr. Andrews said, "Good morning." Then his face went from friendly to flat as he recognized me. "Miss Landers."

I hooked my hand around his arm. To anyone else, he looked like a gentleman walking a young lady into the service. To him, he'd been captured.

"I am very sorry to bother you this morning, Mr. Andrews, but I have just heard that we have received our first iceberg warning. Do you remember what we talked about the other day?"

He nodded, his lips pursed. "I do, yes."

"Then do you think you might speak to the captain and the Bridge crew? Late this evening promises to be very dangerous, with a cold front setting in as well."

He stopped and gently removed my hand. "Miss Landers, you are nothing if not persistent. I built this ship to last, but I will do as you ask. There is no reason not to take precautions when they are warranted. Enjoy your day."

"Thank you so much, Mr. Andrews. You will be saving lives."

He nodded and walked away again. I had a sense that he was a man of his word. I hoped it would be enough.

I tucked myself in next to Mr. Guggenheim for the service, wishing him and Ms. Aubart a good morning. "I'm praying for our safety today," I whispered as the crowd began to quiet for the service, led by none other than the captain. "We have had an iceberg warning and tonight looks to be treacherous, especially after dark."

"Mon dieu!" Ms. Aubart whispered.

"Mr. Guggenheim, perhaps you should mention to the captain to slow the ship tonight when visibility becomes poor. He will listen to someone as smart and highly regarded as you are!" I did my best impression of hero-worshiping puppy-dog eyes. He smiled, then I locked eyes with Ms. Aubart, silently communicating my request to her. She nodded.

After the service, I excused myself and hurried away while Quinn lingered in the hopes of spotting Americans George or Eleanor Widener. We had no idea what they looked like, but I knew they would be hosting a dinner party that evening with the captain, which made them the perfect pair to intercede with him at the exact right time. Quinn's job was to spot the couple, then we would find them sometime later in the day, after the second and third iceberg warnings were received.

We rendezvoused back in Quinn's suite.

"Any luck finding the Wideners?" I asked as soon as the door shut behind him.

"None. We may have to get them at lunch."

"And the captain?"

"Well, thankfully, he didn't recognize me. Let's just say he's a friendly man until you get into his business. I introduced myself and made small talk, which went fine. Then I told him that word was getting around about ice in the area—even a warning this morning from another ship—and that while the first-class passengers were marveling at our speed, we'd rather go a little slower to be on the safe side through Iceberg Alley."

"Perfect. What did he say?"

"He just pasted that 'I'm humoring you' look on his face and assured me that we were in the hands of a 'capable and experienced crew.'"

"That was it?"

"Not quite. Then I told him there was no need to humor me, that my family had built its wealth in transportation, and even a ship as great as this one was no match for an iceberg. I said that an accident—even a minor one—on the *Titanic*'s first passage would be a disaster for the White Star Line."

"Oof. I bet that didn't go over well. . . ."

"Bingo."

"Let me guess, his face turned red and he huffed and puffed?"

"He said something like 'You, young man, are presumptuous to speak to me that way,' blah, blah. . . ."

"I get the gist." *Guys are so bad at sharing details.*

"I think he wanted to toss me overboard but figured I might win that battle."

Something—something about his statement flipped a switch in my mind. I stared at him, my eyes wide, and my mouth dropping open.

"Charlie, are you having a stroke?"

"No, genius, I'm having an *idea*!"

"Well, spit it out, then. Let's hear it."

"I can't believe I didn't think of this before!" I started pacing around the room.

"Tell me the idea, Charlie." He put himself in my path to stop my pacing.

"Quinn—it's so simple. All we need is to delay the ship for a few minutes, right?"

"Um, maybe. What did you have in mind?"

"So I started thinking during the church service about how we could delay the ship. Maybe we could break a boiler or something. But what you said just now might be the perfect solution. . . . Quinn, I could *throw myself overboard!*"

Quinn scrunched up his face like he'd just eaten English peas, the kind he despised.

"Just think about it," I continued. "I 'accidentally' fall overboard, and you start screaming. The ship will have to stop so the crew can try to find me in the water. They won't give up the search for, say, an hour or more. Then the iceberg . . ."

Quinn was jiggling his foot.

"Oh, wait. . . ." I said.

"Yeah. Good try. . . ."

"The iceberg could still be on the same path, we'd just hit it later."

"I thought you were great at geometry."

"I got an A, but I always bombed the word problems." This was a helluva word problem. *A ship is traveling at twenty-two knots westbound, with an iceberg floating at some sort of speed, and a girl jumps off the ship, etc.*

"The iceberg might be moving, but we don't know if it is or in which direction or how fast," Quinn said. "We only know the facts from history, so we have to work with those. You also might get yourself killed jumping off the *Titanic*. You know it's, like, seventeen stories high, right?"

"That's with the smokestacks, and I was thinking about jumping off a lower deck. Besides, I could take myself home before I hit the water."

Quinn put his arms around me. "We've got to stay the course, Charlie. Our plan is solid. We just need to change one of the primary factors that led to the collision in the first place."

"And breaking a boiler wouldn't do much either, huh?" I knew I was grasping at straws, but most of our plan hinged on whispering in people's ears.

"Do you know how to break a boiler, or do it without twenty crewmen seeing you? And then maybe they'd fix it in time. Or maybe one boiler can go down and it doesn't matter. Didn't you say there was some fire in one of them already?"

"Uh-huh." I pouted. "You're such a downer sometimes."

"I'm a downer? I had to follow *you* onto the friggin' *Titanic*."

"Yeah, sorry about that. It's just too bad we can't tell everyone to be on the Boat Deck tonight."

"We'd need a lot more lifeboats for that."

"I know. This really sucks."

"It's not over 'til it's over."

I plopped down in a chair and started wringing my hands. "If our plans don't work, it'll never be over for us. We're going to live with the *Titanic* every day for the rest of our lives."

"If our plan doesn't work, we'll know we did everything we could." Quinn squatted in front of me and took my hands, his blue eyes mesmerizing. "And we'll take what we learned here and turn it into something good."

~

The line between not doing enough and doing too much was razor thin. I could talk to my friends in third class to let them know what might be coming, but to what end? I could jump on a table at lunch in first class and start screaming about the captain and the iceberg, but the ship's surgeon would probably sedate me and I'd drown along with everyone else. I was beginning to understand that for time travelers, time was a mystical living creature, like a mercurial dinosaur with big teeth that never went extinct. And one that could whip its tail in your direction and knock you off course when you least expected it.

Walking into the buzzing first-class Dining Room on the Saloon Deck, I wondered whether we would see George or

Eleanor Widener, or J. Bruce Ismay, the British chairman and managing director of the White Star Line. He would survive the *Titanic* by jumping in a lifeboat while women and children remained on the ship. Then, when that lifeboat was rescued from the Atlantic the morning of April 15, he'd ask for a private room on the *Carpathia* away from the other survivors. He'd get crucified for both in the press. Other *Titanic* survivors would recount that he'd pressed the captain to keep the ship at or near top speed before the crash. If that was true, we hoped to change his mind.

Lunch was as grand as ever, a vegetarian's nightmare buffet with fare such as potted shrimps, soused herrings, roast beef, veal and ham pie, Bologna sausage, galantine of chicken—which I misread as guillotine of chicken—and corned ox tongue. Even if I'd been excited about super-fishy-tasting soused herrings, I wasn't remotely hungry. I forced myself to pick at the meal in front of me, managing some Cheshire and Stilton cheeses and some bread and tomatoes to keep my energy up for the work ahead. Quinn said he wasn't hungry either, but he ate as much as ever, muttering "fuel" a couple of times as he packed down a pile of chicken and roast beef from White Star Line–crested china. As he ate, I watched the clock on the wall. I knew two more iceberg warnings had just come in, one at 1:42 p.m. from the *Baltic* and another at 1:45 p.m. from the *Amerika*.

Still no luck on the elusive Wideners, but we were able to spot Mr. Ismay in the 532-seat dining saloon. He sat with a group that appeared to be in deep discussion at a table for six. With his heavy mustache that disappeared his upper lip and presided over a pointy chin, he was a man on top of the world, leading the White Star Line into glory on its man-made marvel. Sadly, he would live a life plagued by his own cowardice if the *Titanic* continued its course.

"How are we gonna get to him?" I asked, as much to myself as to Quinn. "Wait outside until he's finished?"

"I have a better idea," Quinn said, downing some custard pudding.

"Do tell."

"He's sitting on the inside, next to the aisle. Why don't you trip into him? We'll apologize profusely while introducing ourselves and mentioning the iceberg warnings. Maybe the group he's with will catch on and help persuade him."

"Not bad. I just hope I can fake-trip properly in these 'country clothes'—also known as this long, fancy dress. I might actually bite the dust."

"If you can't fake-trip, I could trip you myself." He smiled, like a cat that ate the canary.

"You are still eight years old."

"It's 1912, so I'm actually into negative years, like negative a hundred."

I rolled my eyes. "Okay, old man, let's do this."

I patted the edges of my mouth with my white linen napkin, then placed it on the table and stood up. We walked toward Mr. Ismay's all-male group. My palms got sweaty, like when I played basketball in gym class. I was great on a court by myself, swishing shots from every angle and distance, but when someone guarded me in an actual game, I couldn't sink a shot to save my life. I think that was why surfing became my sport. The only person I could disappoint was myself, and the ocean would let me try again and again and again.

"Go," Quinn said under his breath as we got close.

*Don't mess up*, I thought as I stutter-stepped my toe on the lush, patterned carpet and pitched forward toward Mr. Ismay's seat. But I overestimated the distance between me and him, and I lost my balance for real. I careened into the man broadside and caught myself on his shoulder, a handful of wool suit fabric in my grip and my face way too close to his. To make matters worse, he'd been holding a glass and the liquid launched up and out like gravity had reversed, catching his other shoulder and the sleeve of the man next to him.

I felt Quinn's hand on my upper arm, pulling me back toward an upright position. But even with his help, it took me a second to get my feet back under me and regain my balance. When I did, I'd forgotten everything I wanted to say and just stood there, mute, until Quinn stepped in.

"Indeed, our profound apologies, gentlemen," he said. Then, addressing Mr. Ismay specifically, he added, "And to you, Mr., uh . . ."

"Ismay, Bruce Ismay." Mr. Ismay reached for his napkin, attempting to clean up the mess I'd made, his face screwed up in clear annoyance and disapproval. I suppose a lady tripping into a man just wasn't done in first class in 1912.

"Mr. Ismay," I said, finding my voice at last, "please forgive my clumsiness and the interruption. I got a bit dizzy for a brief moment."

"It is quite all right," he said, regaining a semblance of his gentlemanly composure. "Could not be avoided, certainly."

Quinn gave a knowing "guy" look and said, "I am afraid she is in something of a state because of the multiple iceberg warnings we have been hearing about today."

"Yes," I said, faux-fanning myself and looking around the table, "I am sure these good gentlemen are resting easy on the *Titanic* knowing you are the man in charge."

"Well, I—" said Mr. Ismay.

"I mean, I have heard your name, and I know how powerful you are." *Hurl. Male ego appeal—revolting, but always a safe bet.*

"You are too kind."

Quinn jumped in. "Indeed, my friend would rest easier if you would assure her you will speak to the captain about slowing the ship. Given the iceberg warnings and cold temperatures, we would be greatly disturbed if an errant iceberg were to impose itself on the *Titanic* in the dark of this evening. Speed is grand, but the ladies might prefer a slower, safer pace, just for tonight."

*Well done, Quinn. But if you say "indeed" one more time. . . .* I swear, Mr. Ismay was on the verge of nodding, or committing, or something positive, but a grim-faced crew member interrupted us at that precise moment.

"Miss Landers," he said. He turned to the group. "Pardon the intrusion." Then he turned back to me. "But the captain asked that I escort you to your cabin in second class, where I am sure you will be comfortable for the remainder of our journey."

My heart sank to my ankles. I'd been crisscrossing the ship with ease, thanks to my wardrobe and Quinn's nearly constant escort. My luck had apparently run out, and in front of a table of men I needed on my side. It was almost like we were in a real-life version of the game Clue, my dad's favorite, and I'd been busted for murdering the wealthy man in the conservatory with a candlestick.

Thankfully, Quinn spoke up. "There is clearly some misunderstanding here, but come, let us sort this out in the foyer and leave these good people to their meals. Good afternoon, gentlemen, and thank you in advance, Mr. Ismay."

Quinn nodded to Mr. Ismay and offered me his arm, which I took gratefully. We were closely followed out of the dining saloon by our burly escort, as if we might make a run for it on a friggin' ship. In my time, the guy probably would've been a bouncer for some trendy West Hollywood bar—the kind of person who'd take pleasure in throwing the "wrong sort" right out on their butts.

Outside, my wits returned, and I quickly formulated arguments in my mind. Quinn's hands were balled into fists. I was afraid he'd try to punch the guy, and where exactly would we hide if he belted a member of the crew in a crowded lobby? The cargo room, maybe?

"We—"

"I—" We both started to speak at the same time.

The crewman held up his hand to stop us. "I've been instructed to give you this." He pulled a note from a pocket of his perfectly pressed uniform.

*Dear Miss Landers,*

*I understand you joined church services this morning with our first-class passengers, raising concerns among them regarding this ship's safety. While the White Star Line aims to please each passenger aboard this ship, the classes must remain segregated on every transatlantic passenger vessel in order to satisfy US Customs requirements.*

*Given that you hold a second-class ticket, we ask that you kindly remain in the second-class section of the ship for the remainder of the voyage. If you disregard this request, the master-at-arms will be summoned. I trust you will comply, and, in the future, will enjoy traveling with one of the other fine companies whose vessels make the crossing.*

*Yours truly,*
*Captain E. Smith*

The looping cursive was a disguise for the steely message between the lines of his note—*"You are banned from polite society on the Titanic."*

I might be a future girl who shouldn't care about being admonished by the captain of the most famous ship that ever sailed, but in that moment, I felt about twelve inches tall. Clearly I had not persuaded the captain at all. I'd made a terrible impression on him, and he obviously didn't appreciate young women confronting him or enlisting others to make requests about the running of his ship.

Now, Mr. Ismay was probably back in the dining saloon, feeling superior and laughing with his well-to-do buddies about how silly women could be. He'd probably press the captain to speed up, just to make the point with his peers.

The Saloon Deck was the highest continuous deck on the *Titanic*, a microcosm of the entire ship. The first- and second-class dining rooms were there, along with third-class open space near the bow, so we didn't have to go far to put me in my proper place. I noticed the temperature was dropping as expected. I shivered. Quinn walked with me, my arm in his, as if we were strolling, but once we crossed into second-class territory, the bouncer guy called from several paces behind us.

"Excuse me, sir," he said loudly to Quinn, "but we will say goodbye to you here."

"That is quite all right," said Quinn, still moving forward.

"I am afraid I must insist. We have exited the first-class section of the ship, and you will want to return to the section for which you are ticketed."

Quinn stopped. "Very well," he said, "please step away to allow me to say my goodbyes with Miss Landers." He gave a haughty look back at the crewman. After all, he was still a first-class passenger, and a stateroom passenger at that. The crewman obeyed.

Quinn angled himself away, just in case our escort could read lips. "They can't keep us off the Boat Deck," he said, sotto voce. "It's got areas for both first and second class. Meet me there at 5:30?"

"Of course," I said. "But you know we're going through with the plan, master-at-arms be damned, right?"

"Absolutely. But promise if things go south, and we get separated, you'll go back to Windline before this ship goes down."

I looked at him with a blank stare.

"Charlie?" he prodded, elongating the "eeeeee" sound in my name.

"Of course," I said, considering all angles. "There's no point in my going down with the ship."

Quinn exhaled like he'd been holding his breath. "Good," he said in a loud voice. "Miss Landers, I'll say goodbye and bon voyage, then."

"Thank you, Mr. Daniels. I will look forward to seeing you in New York."

Quinn stepped away as the crewman approached to lead me forward, like I couldn't find my own cabin. As we walked away, I turned. "Oh, and Mr. Daniels?"

Quinn was still standing there, watching us leave. "Yes, Miss Landers?"

"Do have safe travels."

"And you as well," Quinn answered with a wry smile as I turned away.

# fifteen

The bouncer walked me all the way to my cabin in silence, and for a second, he looked like he might step in my door. I blocked it, my hands on either side of the doorframe. "Thank you for the escort," I said, sugary sweet, "but you may go now. I do not think it is appropriate or necessary for you to stand guard."

He remained stone-faced for a moment as if weighing his options. Then, with a parting shot, he warned, "The captain is a generous man until he is tested, Miss Landers. I suggest you follow his orders."

I straightened my back. "Sir, please give the captain my regards. He is absolutely responsible for all that happens on this ship, and I suggest he heed my warning, just as I have heeded his." *Well, I'll heed it for a few minutes. I didn't say I'd keep heeding it.*

The brute knitted his bushy eyebrows and nodded.

I shut the door behind me, closing my eyes and leaning back on it in case the crewman had a change of heart about leaving. My plan was getting harder, like I was running an obstacle course made of cotton candy with a finish line that kept moving farther away from me.

When I opened my eyes, I spotted Rosalee and jumped.

"Well, *that* sounded interesting," she said, putting her book down and swinging her legs off her bed. "I'm all ears."

"I was just banished to second class for the rest of the trip because I stirred up some trouble with the captain."

"Oh, I see."

I looked at Rosalee, with her kind eyes and her wild red head of hair, and something snapped inside of me. I'd protected her from the truth this whole trip because there was nothing she could do until tonight. Now was the time, and if I couldn't save anyone else on the *Titanic*, by God I would save her.

"Rosalee, I said, slipping off my satin shoes, "I have to tell you something."

She nodded.

"And I have to trust you to keep it a secret, no matter what. Well, at least for a while."

"I am a doctor," she said, her voice lowering conspiratorially. "I keep secrets all the time." She grinned.

I sat down on my bed so we were facing each other. I took a deep breath. "For reasons that I cannot explain—and that would definitely freak you out—"

"Wait, what does 'freak you out' mean?"

*Oh, crap. I did it again.* I'd started to think of Rosalee as a friend and had forgotten to speak like I was at an uptight 1900s finishing school. "Sorry," I went on, "I mean, for reasons that would be very difficult for me to explain and for you to understand, I have reason to believe that the *Titanic* will hit an iceberg tonight at 11:40 and will sink about two hours after that." I paused.

Rosalee stared at me as if she expected a punch line, like I was a little late with my April Fools' Day joke. Then she started laughing. "You had me there for a second, Charlie," she said. "You are too funny!"

I watched her, stone-faced. "I am afraid, Rosalee, that I am not joking at all. The ship has already received three of a long list of iceberg warnings it will get today from other ships. We are going too fast. . . . I tried to tell the captain, and that is why I was escorted out of first class. You need to listen to me. We will turn when the ice is spotted but not enough, and the iceberg will slash the side of the ship, flooding too many of the watertight compartments. The *Titanic* will take on water, then sink. And there are not enough lifeboats on this ship. More people will die than will survive."

Rosalee sat quietly, looking at her hands clasped in her lap. Then she said, "Charlie, when you hit your head—"

I should've known my head injury wouldn't make me a convincing clairvoyant. "When I hit my head," I interrupted, jumping up and pacing around the room, "I got stitches and that was it. I am not mentally impaired, Rosalee."

"Then how could you possibly know what is going to happen at 11:40 tonight on a ship in the middle of the ocean?"

"I just do." I stopped pacing for emphasis.

"That is not really an answer."

"I know, but I told you. . . . You would not believe me, and it is big-time against the rules for me to say."

"I see."

I needed another tack. She had a "my roommate is insane" look on her face. "Rosalee, do you believe in things you cannot know, like in God?"

"Yes, of course."

"And are there people in your circle who believe in God, not because they have experienced the divine, but because they think it is in their best interest to do so—to save their eternal souls or maybe look good to their neighbors?"

"I suppose so, yes. But, if you think you are God, Charlie—"

"No, no, of course not. What I am saying is that if I am right, and this ship will sink tonight, then perhaps you should just believe me—have a little faith—not because you know me, not because you trust me, but because the cost of not believing me could be your life.

"All you have to do is humor me until tonight. If I am mistaken, no one will be happier than I will be, and I promise I will completely own being crazy. But if I am right, I want you to be in one of those lifeboats on the Boat Deck."

We sat in silence, the kind that made me antsy to double down on my point until the other person gave in. Tiana called it "word vomit-itis." I pressed my lips firmly together to keep myself quiet.

Finally, Rosalee spoke up. "I understand what you are saying, Charlie, and, if we hit an iceberg tonight, I will be on the Boat Deck."

I breathed an audible sigh of relief. Based on her lack of expression, I assumed she was trying to look like she believed me. I didn't care—as long as she followed the plan. "Thank you," I said.

"But I think you may have hurt your head more than we realized."

"Fine. I have a head injury that is giving me delusions of icebergs. Just get on a boat."

"I said I will," she responded, slowly moving to the dressing table, her eyes still on me. "Are you planning to explain all of this to Rima?"

I couldn't tell if she was probing further to see just how crazy I was. I'd have bet everything I owned that she was. In her shoes, I'd do the same. "Not exactly."

"So do you not think she and her family need to know about this iceberg you are so worried about?"

I looked at the floor, my hands on my hips. "Unfortunately, what I know is that only twenty-five percent of the passengers in third class will survive the night." I raised my gaze to meet Rosalee's.

The color drained out of her freckled cheeks. "So if this ship were to sink, seventy-five percent of the passengers in third class would drown?"

I nodded. "Or freeze. And only forty-two percent will survive in second class. Sixty-two percent in first. Women and children fare the best, so you and Rima have that going for you."

"Now you are starting to 'freak me out,'" Rosalee said.

"I am sorry. I am *so* sorry. But I do have a plan for saving Rima. I will need your help to do it, though."

"My help?"

"Sometime between now and dinner, I will sneak down to third class to invite Rima for a fun night with us. I will take an outfit for her, so she can dress like a second-class passenger. We will meet you here. She can go with you to dinner, as if she were me, then she can stay with you until 11:40."

"And after that?"

"If we hit the iceberg, you two have to get to the Boat Deck with warm clothes and life jackets at midnight on the dot. The order to muster the lifeboats will happen at 12:05."

"What about Arash and the rest of her family?"

"I can tell the others to make their way to the Boat Deck if they hear the engines shut off—that there have been iceberg warnings in the area—and for the guys to stay in the women's section of the ship. They'll have a better chance from there."

"To get to the boats."

"Exactly. But it might be worse than saying nothing if I panic everyone in third class. Unfortunately, with the lifeboat situation, the men do not stand much of a chance."

"I agree. There is no need to panic hundreds of people by telling them about your hunch." She shook her head like she couldn't believe she was elevating my delusion to a hunch.

"Yes."

"Where will you be during all of this if not with us? I thought you were ordered to stay in the second-class section."

"If there is any hope of stopping this tragedy from happening in the first place, I will have to break a few rules." I smiled, but it felt like moving my facial muscles took an epic amount of energy. As the minutes ticked by, and without Quinn by my side, the weight on my shoulders was growing heavier and heavier.

Rosalee stood up, her energy increasing while mine waned. "Well, I still think you may have a head injury, Charlie, but your delusion is just clear enough that you have convinced me to take a leap of faith. If nothing else, I will enjoy having my friend Rima up here. So, come on, let us figure out what she can wear."

~

Rosalee insisted on coming with me to find Rima, saying I would be less conspicuous if I weren't alone. She loaned me a hat with a wide brim. With a slight dip of my head, I could shield my face from the view of anyone passing by. Rosalee carried a small piece of luggage, a needlepoint-covered bag with leather handles, that contained one of my second-class day dresses and hair accessories. I'd come a long way from my gummy flat iron on the first day of school.

When we arrived at Rima's cabin, the door was wide open and there was no sign of anyone. We poked our heads in to see if we might find a clue, but one arrived in the form of a low moan coming from down the passageway and around the corner. We trotted in that direction and found Rima and her mother standing there, along with quite a few other women, all clumped outside an open cabin door.

Rima saw us, and her face lit up. "Charlie, Rosalee!" She wiggled through the crowd to reach us.

"What is happening, Rima?" I asked.

Rima clapped her hands together. "My friend is in—how do you say—labor! The one you met on the deck!"

Instead of feeling joyful, I took Rosalee's arm to steady myself. I'd never read about a woman in labor on the *Titanic*. . . . "Excuse me," I said, covering my mouth with my hand, my other hand on my stomach. I ran back to Rima's cabin, barely making it to the washbasin before I emptied the contents of my lunch. I held my head in my hands. *A newborn on April 14? Just how cruel could history be?*

As soon as my queasiness subsided, it was replaced with guilt over soiling the family's washbasin on top of everything else. By the time I'd figured out how best to clean it and went back to the gathering, Rosalee had disappeared from the passageway.

"Are you all right?" Rima asked, rubbing my back.

"Yes, I am so sorry. I think I have a touch of seasickness. Where is Rosalee?"

"She is with my friend, helping her. The ship's surgeon came here about an hour ago, but he said all was fine and that we should call him when the pains are closer together."

"The contractions?" The surgeon had probably run off to see to a first-class passenger with a hangnail. I hoped he'd come back soon.

"Yes, that is it."

~

The time passed at a snail's pace in that hallway, listening to the moaning sounds of the laboring woman for what seemed like an eternity. I began to worry about the time, so I made my way to the door of the cabin. Rosalee was crouched beside the pregnant woman, who was on her hands and knees in the small amount of space between the bunks. Rosalee was massaging her back.

"Rosalee, I am sorry to bother you, but . . ."

Rosalee stood up, rubbing her own back as if she were having sympathy pains.

"Charlie," she said, "I am afraid this baby is in an occiput posterior position."

"What is that?" I asked, looking at the poor woman on the salmon-pink-colored linoleum floor.

Rosalee wiped her hands on her skirt. "It is when a baby is facing the mother's abdomen. The baby's head pushes on her sacrum, which causes a lot of pain, and often, the baby has trouble getting through the birth canal in these cases. Charlie, her labor is likely going to be a long one and potentially difficult."

My eyes grew wide, like an actress in a horror film, except this was real. "Rosalee—no. You have to speed it up. I—you know why." *This is not happening.*

Rosalee smiled. "I hear you, Charlie, but nature will take its course. You know I am a doctor, and I cannot leave this woman. Her name, by the way, is Astrid."

"What about the Hospital—the ship's surgeon? Can he not help Astrid instead of you?"

Rosalee put her hands on her hips. "I'm afraid Astrid would not be able to make it to the Hospital in her condition. I will stay here with her until the baby is safely delivered. If the ship's surgeon comes back, he can take over or consult with me on the birth, though I dare say I know more on this subject than he does."

My head was starting to throb. "Rosalee, just remember. If you are down here at 11:40—"

"Charlie, I just cannot discuss this right now." I'd suspected she'd been humoring me, but now it was evident. She put her hands on my upper arms. "Everything will be okay, Charlie. Go back to the cabin. I *will* see you later." She kissed my cheek. "All right?"

I looked at Astrid, her head down between her arms as she swayed on her hands and knees. "All right." I made my way back to Rima, who stood with her younger brother in her arms. He was all rosy cheeks and irresistible baby fat. I felt my stomach churn again.

"Rima, Rosalee is going to stay here with Astrid. Would you like to come with me to our cabin? We actually brought you some clothes. . . ."

"Oh, that is so nice of you, Charlie. I would love to see your part of the ship, but I should not leave my friend."

"Really, she is in good hands with Rosalee, and there is not much you can do. Why not have a nice evening together?"

"You are a very sweet friend, but I have to stay here. Maybe tomorrow evening?"

I muttered under my breath, "I was afraid you'd say that."

"What was that?"

"Sorry. I just said, 'Of course you should stay here.' But Rima," I said, pulling her away from the group and lowering my voice, "I need you to know that there have been iceberg warnings in the area, and the part of the ocean we are in tonight is dangerous because of all the ice. You and your family should stay dressed until midnight, and if you feel anything happen with this ship, like a shuddering or shaking or the engines stopping, you must go up on deck as quickly as you can, with your life jackets on.

"Tell Arash—he should stay with you and not in his cabin in the front of the ship. It is almost impossible to get to the Boat Deck quickly from there if you do not know the way. No matter what, get to the Boat Deck—especially the women and children." I patted the soft, dark hair on her little brother's head. "Promise me?"

Rima knit her eyebrows together until they nearly formed one long line. "What an unusual thing to say, Charlie, but I will remember."

"Rima, I am begging you to listen to me. The *Titanic* is a great ship—the greatest ship, in fact—but it is still man-made and nothing in the face of Mother Nature. The *Titanic* can sink like any other ship, and this ship does not have enough lifeboats for all the passengers—not by half. Stay awake and be ready. Please?"

Rima nodded slowly. "You saved me once, perhaps you will save me again." She smiled, clearly humoring me, like she might the small child in her arms.

"One of my dresses is in this bag." I put it down at her feet. "It is yours now. Perhaps you could wear it tonight. . . ."

"What a wonderful surprise," she said. "I promise to take good care of it."

"And of yourself?"

"Yes, of course. And of myself."

Turning to go, I felt like Sisyphus, the Greek king who cheated death. For his trouble, he got the pleasure of rolling a big boulder up a hill, only to watch it roll back down, over and over and over again. Except, in this case, I wasn't a king, I hadn't cheated death for anyone, and the boulder I was working against was time.

# sixteen

With my coat wrapped tightly around me, as much to guard against the dropping temperature as against the chill in my bones, I made my way to the Boat Deck to meet Quinn. I'd changed into the fanciest evening dress in my suitcase—a heavily beaded silk and chiffon gown, rose colored with a square neckline and a fitted bodice that led to a skirt layered with folds of fabric. A fan dangled from my wrist, ready to open and hide my face when needed. My hair was up, of course, though I hadn't taken the time to secure it well, so tendrils were already escaping around my face and down my neck. Playing dress-up hardly seemed fitting for the evening to come, but even though I was banned from first class, I would still need to take advantage of the bias that favored the highest-paying passengers.

Quinn was dressed for dinner, his overcoat open. He leaned against an interior railing with his arms and ankles crossed. Anyone else would've seen his posture as relaxed, but I knew better. He was staring at a lifeboat, his mouth set in a straight line.

I looked at him, my handsome Malibu swimmer turned 1912 aristocrat, and a feeling swept over me. It was the kind of feeling I got when the family gathered around the fire pit on a cool evening, the sun dropping low on the horizon. Or when Mom made her ridiculously rich macaroni and cheese with bread crumbs on top, or when I turned on my heated blanket before slipping between the sheets on a chilly, fog-rolling-in kind of evening.

Quinn had become my comfort. He represented *my* history. He'd been witness to every stupid piñata-busting, pool-jumping, cake-smearing, pony-riding birthday I'd ever had. He annoyed me on the drive to and from school. But he held me through the night on the *Titanic*. He'd actually asked to be in this nightmare with me. And now he'd said he loved me. I wondered if comfort and love were the same thing.

As I approached him, I asked, "What's going on in that good-looking head of yours?" He stood up straight and opened his arms. I stepped into them.

"I'd like to say I was thinking up some new miracle plan," he said into my hair, "but I'm just angry. How could a ship like this sail with so few lifeboats?"

"Aesthetics," I mumbled into his chest. I could feel his heart beating. So much pressure on that one muscle, the heart. I went from thinking about Quinn's heart to thinking of all the ones beating on the *Titanic*. *So many hearts.*

We stood pressed together in silence for a while. "I'm not gonna give up," I said finally, standing back and feeling a void where my chest had been against his body. "It just takes one pebble in the water. . . . There's still hope, Quinn."

"Definitely. Felix scored some binoculars—that's a positive. Oh, and I brought the *Rubáiyát*." He nodded his head toward a small bag with a shoulder strap at his feet.

"Great," I said. We needed the binoculars, but as beautiful and unique as it was, the *Rubáiyát* was this journey's red herring, a check-the-box item for a high school test. I was focused on bigger things.

I filled him in on the drama with Rosalee and Rima. "It's like history is a current, and we're swimming upstream against it," I said. "Nothing seems to be working right."

"Feels that way," he agreed. "But so far, we've been playing the long game—dropping hints hoping someone will listen and change things. Tonight, we can change them ourselves, and then it won't matter that Rosalee and Rima are stuck in third class. We can do this."

"We can—I mean, we will," I said. "So what time is it now?"

Quinn pulled out a gold pocket watch. "It's about 5:40."

"In ten minutes, the captain orders the ship to adjust its course slightly south."

"But he doesn't slow the ship's speed."

"Well, he didn't before, but maybe Mr. Andrews, Mr. Guggenheim, or Maggie got to him, and he will this time."

"Let's hope."

Quinn and I stayed huddled together in a pair of out-of-the-way chairs until after 7:00 p.m., jumping up occasionally to get our blood moving in the dropping temperatures. I was reminded of a joint family ski vacation, the one where Quinn and I had our first little-kid snowboarding lessons on the bunny slope. He'd wanted to stay on that hill all day, practicing the short run over and over again. I'd gotten so cold that I'd started crying.

"Quinn, my nose!" I'd whined at the time.

"What about it? Looks fine to me," he'd said.

"It's frozen."

"No, it's not. C'mon, one more run. Don't be a wuss."

"I'm going inside."

"One more run."

And so on. We'd wound up staying on that hill until our parents had come for us in the late afternoon.

On the deck of the *Titanic*, I totally could've gone for a cozy ski jacket instead of a fancy wool coat. The sun had dipped just below the horizon. We found ourselves practically alone in our tucked-away corner, thanks to the cold and the impending dinner rush on the Bridge and Saloon Decks below.

"Well—" Quinn stood and put on his top hat. "Ready?" he asked.

I stood, too, and opened my accordion fan. "Yep. Or . . . actually, no," I said, my cold feet suddenly getting cold feet. "What if we get caught tonight?"

"We play it by ear. Worst case, you go back to Windline. You can't do any good here if you're locked up somewhere. If I'm not taken, I'll try to carry out the plan."

I stared up at him in the twilight.

"What is it?"

"Just . . . Quinn, thank you."

"For what?"

"For being here with me. For trying."

He offered me his arm, like a proper gentleman, then put his hand over mine when I rested it there. "Why, Miss Landers, I would not dream of being anywhere else," he said with a flourish. He smiled down at me reassuringly. I tried to smile back, but I don't think I managed it.

As we strolled down the deck, I worried that my fear would give me away, like when I rode horses at camp when I was little. Those horses had sensed I was scared and took advantage, veering off the trail to eat grass or brush against a tree to scrape me off. Tonight, I was afraid of the master-at-arms. And time. And the North Atlantic.

As we approached the Boat Deck's first-class entrance, I took a deep calming breath. If only I could shrink a few inches and be a short, wispy 1912 girl instead of a tall, athletic future girl. Since I couldn't, I tucked myself behind Quinn as much as I could without tripping into him. We walked inside to the sounds of the piano echoing from the corner of the opulent area surrounding the grand staircase.

A uniformed crew member nodded as we entered. "Good evening, sir," he said to Quinn. "You may take either the lifts or the stairs down to reception and dinner."

Quinn was just about to reply that we'd be doing neither, when the door in front of us—the door that led to the Marconi Room and the Officers' Quarters beyond—opened in what seemed liked slow motion. I glimpsed an older officer and behind him . . . the bouncer. I tugged on Quinn's sleeve. Fan or no fan, it wouldn't take a rocket scientist to recognize me and Quinn together.

Quick on his feet, Quinn managed a formal "Very good," even as he spun me toward the stairs. We took the first two at a normal pace, then Quinn grabbed my hand and we practically hurled ourselves down to the Promenade Deck. I didn't dare turn around to see if we were being followed.

"This way!" Quinn said, pulling me through a doorway, away from the gathering crowd and into the hall leading to the first-class cabins.

I spotted a ladies' lavatory. "You won't like this, but come with me," I said. I ran in to check for occupants, then pulled Quinn in, ignoring him as he mouthed "no way" a few times.

Exposed pipes were visible, just as they were in the bathroom we used in second class. There were three sinks and as many stalls. We crowded into one, Quinn's bag wedged between us. First class or not, the bathroom smelled like any bathroom, except this one had an added saltwater scent.

"You take me to the nicest places," Quinn whispered, wrinkling his nose.

"You're welcome," I whispered back. "Best I could do under the circumstances." My face was just inches below Quinn's. *Guys definitely shouldn't be allowed to have those cheekbones.* "Do you think they saw us?"

"I don't know. We should stay here for a few minutes just in case." Quinn shifted uncomfortably.

"But we've got to get up to that radio room."

"We had some extra time built in. As long as we get there by 7:25, we're fine."

"By the way," I said, "have I ever told you how much I hate public restrooms?"

"I think I missed that important detail about you." Quinn smirked.

"It's true. Especially the ones at airports where the toilets flush automatically."

"What's wrong with automatic flushing?"

"Oh my God, you're such a dude," I complained. "Here's the drill. . . . You stand there and clean the seat, then put paper down so no actual skin will touch anything.

Just when you get the papering done, the stupid thing flushes automatically, and you have to jump back not to get sprayed in the face. Then you have to start the process all over again. It's ridiculous."

"Gross."

"Yeah—and then sometimes you sit down and it randomly flushes while you're siting there."

"Ooooh . . ."

"So you jump up like your butt's on fire."

"No wonder it takes women so long to go to the bathroom. Must suck being you."

If I'd had enough room, I would've smacked him. "You have no idea."

Just then, we heard the door open, so we zipped it. Water ran in the sink. A few seconds later, someone tried to open the door to our stall.

"Taken," I called in a singsong voice.

"Oh, I beg your pardon" came the reply from the other side of the door.

More banging, followed by the sounds of her using the toilet in the neighboring stall. *Lovely.*

When she left, we stood quietly, the silence punctuated by my looking for my smartwatch, not finding it on my wrist, and asking Quinn for the time.

I asked in a whisper again, "Quinn—time?"

"It's one minute after you asked the last time."

And so it went until just after 7:20, when I crept out to check the hall and called to Quinn to come out.

"Take the lift?" Quinn asked as soon as we reentered the open landing area.

I nodded behind my fan. He was right. Better not to be on the open staircase where anyone could spot us. We'd have to chance it on the lift.

The lifts were just behind the grand staircase. Brand-new sofas invited passengers to rest in the lift lobby while waiting. Thankfully, one of the lifts was just opening, and we hustled straight in, Quinn blocking me from full view of the attendant while I tucked myself into the back corner.

When the lift doors opened on the Boat Deck, I held my breath as we stepped out. The coast was clear. We quickly slipped around the corner and through the door. And a few steps in, behind the elevator banks, there it was . . . the Marconi Room. Quinn held out his watch—7:26. I knocked, waited a beat, and opened the door.

The two wireless operators looked up as we walked in, mouths ajar. They didn't get many visitors, just lots of passenger messages via pneumatic tube for them to transmit. It was considered a novelty to send messages via the relatively new Marconi technology, so of course the first-class passengers sent a lot of them. Even Rosalee had sent one.

Unfortunately, in 1912 there was no emergency channel that was kept clear for distress calls. Without those passenger messages clogging all the channels—and the operators focused on them—things might have been different altogether for the *Titanic*.

"Mr. Bride, we meet again," I said brightly. "I visited before with Mr. Bean but was dressed very differently and was without my brother here, Mr. Quinn Daniels. And you must be the man in charge, Mr. Phillips."

"I am indeed, miss. What can we do for you? I dare say, we are rather busy. . . ."

"Of course. I will be brief. I am interested in transmissions to and from the *Californian*. In fact," I said, pointing to the wall clock that said 7:29 p.m., "you should receive a report about ice from the *Californian* in about sixty seconds."

The clock ticked over to 7:30, and like I'd scripted it, the message came through.

Jack Phillips read it out loud. "'Ice latitude forty-two degrees, three minutes north, longitude forty-nine degrees, nine minutes west.'"

The two operators stared at the message like I might have conjured it, then at me.

"My sister is a clairvoyant," Quinn said, as if it were the most normal thing in the world. "It is rather tiresome, but it can come in handy."

"Gentlemen, I sense we are traveling into a disaster this evening, and you two can stop it." I wasn't sure whether "clairvoyant" or "disaster" had the two more off-balance.

"We can? How?" Harold Bride asked, his eyes wide, his face having gone from pale to paler.

"Respond to the *Californian*. Ask her to keep you updated and to leave her wireless on tonight in case the *Titanic* runs into trouble," I said. "Then, when she reaches out again at eleven o'clock tonight with another ice warning, do not cut her off. Our lives may depend on it."

"And make sure the Bridge gets all the ice warnings," Quinn added.

"That is right," I said. "I know the *Titanic* has received ice warnings already today, from the *Caronia*, the *Baltic*, and the *Amerika*, but the captain has not slowed down. If we hit an iceberg at our speed, this ship is doomed, no matter how great a marvel it is."

Jack looked at Harold. "Well, what are you waiting for? Send a reply to the *Californian*."

I reached for Jack's hand to shake it. "Thank you, Mr. Phillips. Mr. Bride. Remember, stay in touch with the *Californian*."

"We will, miss," Jack said. Harold was busy transmitting.

We hustled out, leaving Jack staring after us. If the *Titanic* sank that night, those two would transmit distress calls until the very end. Jack would die, possibly in that very room, but Harold would make it out alive. Both would be heroes.

"Where to now?" I asked Quinn when we were safely around the corner from the Marconi Room.

"We have a few hours to kill."

"Bad choice of words."

"Oh—yeah. Right."

"We could go back outside—either stay on this deck or head back down to the Promenade Deck," I suggested. "Nobody'll be outside. The temperature should be in the high thirties by now."

"We didn't think this part through last night, did we?"

"No, but we didn't know I'd be an outlaw at this point, either."

"True," he said. "I think it's too cold for us to wait outside again."

"Then we've gotta go to your cabin. We can't risk going to mine and trying to get back to first class."

"Agreed," Quinn said. "Let's go."

We took the elevator down to the Bridge Deck without incident and ducked into the passageway that led to Quinn's stateroom. We ran into the valet in the hallway around the corner from the suite.

"Mr. Daniels!"

"You *did not* see us, Felix," Quinn said, patting Felix on the back as we hustled by.

"Wait!" Felix called, moving toward us as we hurried down the passageway. "Mr. Daniels, there is—"

As we turned the corner, we understood what Felix was trying to tell us. The bouncer and another large man, presumably the master-at-arms, stood in front of Quinn's door. We were busted.

They saw us at the same time we saw them. "Holy crap!" I yelled reflexively. Quinn grabbed my hand. We turned to run, and Felix plastered himself to the wall as we careened by him. I glanced over my shoulder. Felix had stepped back into the middle of the passageway, deliberately dropping whatever he was holding and crouching to pick it up, just as the bouncer and the master-at-arms were trying to run past him. He'd gained us a few critical seconds.

"Stop!" yelled the bouncer behind us. Footsteps thundered, sounding as if we were being chased by a pack of men instead of just two. While I ran, it occurred to me that if we were caught, we'd be in trouble for much more than disobeying the captain's orders. Quinn had the *Rubáiyát* in his bag. First-class passenger or not, he'd be arrested as a thief.

We kept running and ducking and dodging passengers until we had to slow to a trot to pick our way through a clump of chatting first-class passengers. When we made it through, the group huddled back up behind us, blocking our pursuers. After a few more minutes and two more passageways, we ducked into a room marked "Linen."

"Quinn," I panted, my dress suddenly feeling at least a size too small and my stitches starting to itch, "you have to give me the *Rubáiyát*. If we get caught, you can claim you had no idea I'd stolen it."

"Damn. I hadn't even thought about that." He handed it over. I shucked out of one arm of my coat and slung the bag with the *Rubáiyát* in it over my shoulder like a crossbody before putting my coat back on. Quinn looked around at the room full of towels, sheets, and cleaning supplies. It smelled of flowers and disinfectant at the same time. "We can't stay in here."

I bit my lip, thinking. "We have to be able to get to the Forecastle Deck, so we'd better stay forward."

"Agreed."

"Why is it so hard to hide on a ship nearly the length of three football fields and with ten decks?" I pictured the master-at-arms opening the door to the closet at any second.

"Probably because it's more like four different ships—one for each class of passenger and the fourth for the crew. But, Charlie, we can do this. We were able to get to the cargo hold."

"That was aft."

"I know, but the squash court spectator area is forward on F-Deck, or the court is on G-Deck. Maybe there'll be a place to hide there. If not, third class is close by."

"Okay, c'mon. Let's get to the staircase."

I took Quinn's hand, and off we went, trying to act casual but not feeling that way at all. When we arrived at the squash court, we ducked into the changing room.

No one would be using it at the dinner hour, and we were able to find a nook where we could tuck ourselves away, out of sight. I silently clapped, and Quinn pulled me into a hug, our breathing slowing.

"We made it," I said quietly into his chest, relaxing a bit now that we were temporarily safe.

"We make a pretty good team."

"We sure do. If we ever do decide to go all Bonnie and Clyde, I think we could be legendary."

"Except we'd be Clyde and Bonnie. Never understood why her name had to be first." He wrapped his arms around me tightly and lifted me off the ground, mock-laughing.

"Chivalry much? How about alphabetical order, like Charlie and Quinn?"

"Or Daniels and Landers." He put me down, and I rolled my eyes at him. We sat on the floor, our backs against the wall, reality sliding back into focus. Now we had to wait.

"Before you ask," Quinn whispered, "it's 8:15."

I sighed. We still had hours to go before our next move. "I'm hungry now that we're sitting still."

"Same. Too bad Felix isn't here. I'd planned to ask him to forage some food for us."

"Yeah."

"But this'll be over soon, one way or the other." Quinn stretched his legs out in front of him and reached to touch his toes.

"That's what I'm afraid of—that it won't end the way we want it to."

"Keep the faith," he said. "We have to get back to Windline by midnight, right?" Quinn sat back up and took off his bowtie. He unbuttoned the collar of his stiff white tuxedo shirt.

"'On or around' . . ." I answered, suddenly mesmerized by the indentation between his collarbones, ". . . but I'm not leaving if I can save one person."

"I guess the master-at-arms won't care about us so much if the ship starts to sink."

I nodded. In the low light of the empty room, Quinn almost looked golden, the nearby bulb warming his Malibu-tanned skin. "I suppose not."

I reached out and touched his face with my fingertips, then traced his jawline. He stared back at me, his eyes shining blue like the California sky.

"You're beautiful," I said softly.

"Mmmmm," he said, his voice low. "Thanks, but that's my line." He took my hand away from his face and put it on his thigh, then reached for me, pulling me close as he brushed my lips with a kiss. It was so light it felt like he'd swiped a feather across them. "When we're back home . . ."

"Speaking of home," I said before he could finish. I kissed him on the neck. "Why didn't you invite me to that party at your house?"

"You mean the one you crashed with Gustavo?"

"I don't know about 'crashed,' but, yes, that one."

"Just to double-check, the one where you puked in our guest bathroom?" He flashed me a one-sided grin.

"For the record, ladies do not puke."

"So what do you call it when a lady blows chunks?"

"I'd say she was 'sick to her stomach.' In my case, I would've been fine if I hadn't been bouncing on your shoulder all the way up to the house."

"Let me be sure I'm following. . . . You crashed my party with my friend, did a striptease in front of half the senior class on my diving board, got plastered, and puked, but I owe you an apology for carrying you to the house?"

"I was your friend's date, I had on a bathing suit, and you didn't carry me . . . you slung me over your shoulder in front of everybody."

"That bathing suit hardly qualified."

"What does that mean?"

"It means the top was a little small."

"So you were looking at my top?"

"I wasn't looking at your top exactly." He laughed.

"All right," I said, blushing, "but you never answered my question. Why didn't you invite me in the first place?"

"'Cause you always said my parties were stupid," he said, the joking tone gone.

I thought for a second. "I think I said that because you weren't inviting me."

"Hmm. I guess we could both use a little work on our communication skills."

"Yeah—that's fair."

He kissed me again, softly, a kiss full of promise to do better. "Charlie?"

I kissed him back before he could finish. "Yes," I murmured, in answer to whatever his question was.

"When we get back home, I want to be with you."

I smiled up at him. "That's good, because if you didn't, I'd have to stalk you . . . and then you'd get a restraining order . . . and our moms would stop speaking to each other. . . ."

"You are such a goof."

"Goof or not, you're stuck with me. I can't wait 'til we're back home."

*Back home.* Home was right in front of me in Quinn's kisses, but as much as I wanted to get lost in him at that moment, I couldn't help feeling like a soldier in the trenches. I was taking a smoke break, joking around, all to postpone the inevitable. Soon the whistle would blow, and we'd go over the trench wall to face whatever came our way on the battlefield. I could only hope that the two lone soldiers in this fight—me and Quinn—could win the battle for the *Titanic*.

# seventeen

Exactly as planned, Quinn and I ran onto the Forecastle Deck and into the bitter cold. The air stung my nose. The water was calm, like glass, the clear, moonless sky above us. The crow's nest rose up about forty feet off the deck. The time was 11:20 p.m.

I pulled the binoculars out of the bag over my shoulder and handed them to Quinn. "Be careful," I said. He kissed my cheek and took off at a run. I tucked myself away so I could see but not be seen.

A ladder provided access to the crow's nest, and Quinn dashed up, hand over hand, as if he'd done it a thousand times. One of his dress shoes slipped off a rung, and I held my breath. He caught himself and kept going. The plan was for Quinn to hand the binoculars to the lookouts, Frederick Fleet and Reginald Lee, with enough time for them to get over the shock of seeing a first-class passenger at their post. They would be keeping watch that night with their naked eyes since the binoculars they normally used had been lost. Quinn would tell them to look sharp—likely straight ahead—for an iceberg starting no later than 11:38. "Be ready to alert the Bridge—seconds could make the difference," he would say.

My hands were tingling. I wasn't sure if the cold was the cause or nerves, but I let out my breath when I saw Quinn coming back down the ladder. He ran to my hiding spot.

"How'd it go?" I asked, noticing how my words lingered in the cold air like a cloud.

"They obviously thought I was drunk or delusional—a passenger climbing up there and telling them to look for an iceberg ahead," he said, blowing into his hands and rubbing them together, "but they took the binoculars. Let's hope the Bridge slowed to below twenty-two knots so the extra time will make the difference."

"Well, let's be sure of it. Come on!" We started running again. We needed a few minutes to get to the Bridge on the Boat Deck.

Then we heard, "Stop, there!" My stomach dropped. We'd never make it now.

But the voice wasn't the bouncer's or the master-at-arms's. It was Russ Bean's, the crewman I'd hugged outside the Marconi Room.

We skidded to a halt in front of him. He didn't seem to recognize me.

"I beg your pardon for the intrusion," he started, "but we have been asked to check for a couple who fits your description entering the first-class areas this evening. Seems we have a bit of a security issue. May I have your names and cabin numbers, please?"

Quinn started to speak, but I stepped in front of him.

"Mr. Bean—Russ," I said, "it is me, Charlotte. We met the other day, and you were so kind to me. I did not have my brother with me then, of course." I gave Russ a knowing smile, hoping he would recall our moment together.

"Miss Charlotte?" he asked to himself. "You look very . . ."

"I know," I said, taking his gloved hand in my own. "It is amazing what a change of attire will do for a girl."

"Then you must be the pair the master-at-arms is looking for. He said it was a second-class passenger with a first-class gentleman." He looked at Quinn.

"Mr. Bean," I started, moving a step closer, "I am afraid I do need your help again. You see, we are simply heading for the Boat Deck, where we both belong. It is a terribly long story, but perhaps you could meet me there at midnight so I could fill you in? Until then, I wonder if you might just forget that you have seen us? I would be truly grateful." I squeezed his hand.

"I—"

Quinn spoke up. "I am sure you can see that we are not hurting anyone here," he said, "and as my sister said, we would be grateful for your discretion." He held out a wad of bills. "Rest assured that we can be found on the Boat Deck for the rest of the evening."

Russ looked from Quinn and his wad of bills back to me. I summoned the sweetest face I could muster. He stepped back, opening the door that stood between us and our destination. He reached out his hand, and Quinn planted the bills there.

"Enjoy your evening," he said. "Miss Charlotte, I look forward to seeing you on the Boat Deck at midnight."

"Do not be late, or I will be sorely disappointed," I said as Quinn's hand pressed on the small of my back to urge me forward. I turned back. "And thank you again for your kindness."

We ran for the stairs, and I cursed my dress, which only allowed for me to take the steps one at a time. We received a few dirty looks for our unseemly dash, but we soon arrived on the Boat Deck above us, and ran forward toward the Bridge.

"Time?" I yelled to Quinn, who had his pocket watch in his hand.

"11:35," he responded, not breaking stride as we ran down the Officer's Promenade.

We were stopped before we reached the entrance to the Bridge area.

An officer put up his hand. "You will need to turn around here, if you please," he said.

Like a coiled snake, Quinn unleashed his fist, connecting with the officer's chin. The man crumpled to the ground, and we leapt over him and ran ahead. We were close.

"Iceberg right ahead!" we yelled in unison. We looked at each other and yelled again, "Iceberg right ahead!"

Chaos ensued for the next few minutes as First Officer William Murdoch came out to see what was going on. Captain Smith emerged from his cabin near the Bridge.

"11:38!" yelled Quinn as they all approached us.

"Get to the Wheelhouse," I demanded to First Officer Murdoch, pointing. "There's an iceberg—ram it straight on so we don't broadside and slash the watertight compartments!" Even seconds of time for him to think could make the difference.

"What is the meaning of this?" Captain Smith hissed at us.

We heard the phone ringing on the Bridge. "That's the crow's nest—hurry!"

First Officer Murdoch ran back to the Bridge. The captain, Quinn, and I followed quickly behind.

The officer Quinn had punched, who I now recognized as Fourth Officer Boxhall, entered the Bridge right after we did. "These two—"

"Shut up!" I yelled at him. "There's an *iceberg*!"

"I understand," Murdoch said. He hung up the phone and pulled the engine-room telegraph handle to stop. Then, "Turn the wheel hard a-starboard!" The engine room telegraph was moved to full-speed astern. Murdoch pulled the lever to close the watertight doors.

I wanted to yell out again to ram the iceberg, but I had no way of knowing what its position was, since we could have changed course slightly or seen it early enough to make a slight difference. I held my breath.

Then, as if time stood still . . . nothing. Silence. The feeling of gliding on ice, smooth and silky, cold but calming. The seconds ticked by in frozen silence, a movie freeze-frame but in real life. I sent up a silent prayer that some change in the timeline had saved the ship, that we'd had the few seconds needed to avoid the deadly collision.

Then we saw it. The iceberg rose out of the water like a one-hundred-foot mountain against the black sky. As if we were frozen in place, the iceberg appeared to move, first in front of us, then drifting astern. My heart beat the seconds out in my chest.

Then we felt it. A shudder. A movement under our feet, like the tremor of a small earthquake back home. Quinn took my hand, squeezing hard, transmitting questions without words—*Did we do enough? Did we accomplish anything?* All we knew was that we'd hit. That the first officer hadn't navigated straight on. When presented with a crisis, he'd done just what history said he would. He reversed the engines and tried to steer clear, exposing the *Titanic*'s Achilles' heel.

Lights would be flashing as the watertight doors snapped shut down deep below our feet. I pictured the boiler rooms. Some would be flooding, the water pouring in from gashes in the side of the hull. Men trying to escape before they were sealed in a flooding compartment. Soon rooms on the starboard side, down in third class, would start to fill with water. I noticed that in the ship's lights on that side, a halo appeared, thanks to the ice shards in the air. Somewhere in the distance, the *Californian* would have seen us race past, as it stood still, surrounded by ice.

Captain Smith took charge. He walked to the starboard side of the Bridge to look. The first officer and the officer Quinn had punched trailed behind him. Quinn and I looked at each other, unsure of what to do next. If anything had changed, it was possible that enough of the *Titanic*'s watertight compartments had remained unfilled that the ship could still float.

We followed and heard the captain order Fourth Officer Joseph Boxhall to survey the ship. As the officer stepped away, I jumped in.

"Captain, unless you heeded my warnings—unless you did *something* other than that minor turn to the south—the *Titanic* is going to sink to the bottom of the ocean. You know there are not enough lifeboats. The best hope to save lives is to raise the *Californian*. She's nearby and could get here before the ship founders at 2:20 a.m."

Captain Smith turned, and I expected him to unleash the hounds of Hell. Instead, he spoke calmly, looking directly at me. "Mr. Murdoch, contact the wireless room with instructions to raise the *Californian.* We've struck an iceberg and are assessing the damage. Immediate assistance is requested." Murdoch ran back to the Bridge.

To me, he said, "Is there anything else?"

Quinn spoke up. "Muster the lifeboats now. Do not wait. And fill each of them to capacity, even if it means pulling in men from the deck when no women or children are nearby."

"And," I added, "for God's sake, order your crew to allow third-class passengers to move about the ship freely. If the *Californian* arrives in time, they could be saved, even from the water."

"Mr. Murdoch," the captain said as the first officer returned, "get me Andrews, but first give the order to muster the boats, women and children first but filled to capacity with any soul on board. Make sure third-class exits are clear."

The two of them returned to the Bridge, with only a nod our way from the captain. Quinn and I stood planted where we were, with nothing more to be done at the moment. After a few minutes, we spotted Mr. Andrews hurrying in our direction, his distress clear from his slightly hunched posture. He saw me and paused.

"I want you to know that I tried, young Charlotte. I did try." He nodded, as if he could convince me that way.

"You're a good man, Mr. Andrews," I answered. "Thank you."

We also saw Mr. Ismay, with a coat and slippers. He ignored us entirely.

"Time?" I asked Quinn.

"11:53."

"Should we get to the boats? See if we can help?"

"Yeah, I think so," he said, turning for the railing and putting his head in his hands. "But I need a minute." Before the *Titanic*, I'd always thought of Quinn as someone with a natural-born calm and a little pinch of indifference. I'd been wrong, at least on the indifference part.

I hugged him from behind, wrapping my arms around his stomach.

"This is a lot," I said.

"Yeah—a lot. I really thought we'd done it—that you'd done it."

"That *we'd* done it, Quinn. And the *Californian* might still save the day."

"You're right. It isn't over 'til it's over. Let's go see how we can help." He stood up straight, turning until he faced me. "Charlie, in case I forget to say it later, I'm proud of you."

I drank in his words. They meant more than he could know. "I'm proud of you, too, Quinn."

We ran back toward the middle of the Boat Deck, where the crew was beginning to assemble. I spotted Russ Bean standing on the periphery of the group, looking around.

"Be right back," I said to Quinn.

"Mr. Bean," I called and waved. He moved toward me and I toward him. "You made it," I said when we came together.

"Yes, what is going on up here?" he asked as if I'd know.

"The captain has ordered the crew to muster the lifeboats," I answered. "We have struck an iceberg, and the ship will founder, Russ. You have to make sure you are manning one of those boats. Your life depends on it. And make sure it is filled to capacity."

Russ looked down at me. "This is why you told me to come up here." It was a statement, not a question.

"Yes, it is."

"Not to see you."

"No—to say goodbye to me. In another life, it might have been to see me. But tonight, your safety is what matters."

"Well, I suppose I owe you a debt of gratitude, then, miss."

"We owe each other one." I stood on tippy toes and kissed his cheek. "Be safe, Mr. Bean." With that, he turned into the crowd of crewmen receiving orders, looking back only once as I stood watching him.

Quinn came up behind me and draped his arm over my shoulder. "I think I might be jealous."

"If you weren't my brother, I'd prove you have nothing

to be jealous about." A reprieve of nervous laughter was short-lived, as the deck began to fill with crew and the covers were removed from the boats. A few passengers with life vests began to appear in all stages of dress. The band had arrived, setting up to serenade the passengers. I dragged Quinn over.

"You men are heroes," I said. "Thank you for playing out here tonight. You will make a difference, and history will remember you."

I received a few grateful nods as they lifted their instruments.

According to Quinn, the time was 12:03, and the first lifeboat, Lifeboat No. 7, was being filled.

"Women and children only!" yelled the officer in charge, with his commanding British accent. "Orderly, please. Step here!" Quinn and I separated, each moving passengers toward the boat.

"But it is dangerous—we are so high up!" one passenger said.

"I am waiting on my husband," said another.

One young woman had lost her child in the crowd. "What does he look like?" I asked. She told me as she inched toward the boat. I ran around the deck, scanning until I spotted the little boy in a corner.

"Are you Philip?" I asked gently. He nodded. "Everything is just fine, Philip. I'm going to take you to your mommy, okay?" I lifted the boy and ran, catching his mother just as she was going into the boat.

"Bless you," she said as I passed the boy into the boat.

Suddenly, I felt hands on my arms, as two crewmen lifted me into the boat, too. I had almost forgotten that I was part of the call for women and children. Plus I looked like a first-class passenger. "Thank you, but no," I yelled. "I'll take the next boat."

I underestimated the will of the crew, especially since, thanks to me, they'd been told to pack the boats. Not only did they not hear or heed my protests, but the next person was coming in right behind me, pushing me farther into the boat and away from the deck side. I was trapped, with only a handful of seats left. I tried to scramble out, but the woman next to me grabbed my hands, telling me to be brave and asking me to pray with her. I'd already prayed. I couldn't live with myself for taking a seat on a lifeboat—the first lifeboat launched—from the *Titanic*.

"Lower the boat!" came the call. Just then, the first rocket was fired, like fireworks against a sky so perfect that it didn't seem real.

I looked around desperately. I saw Quinn appear at the railing. He looked down as the boat was lowered, and our eyes met. His grew wide. He knew I wasn't on that boat by choice. I looked around wildly, then pointed down at the Promenade Deck.

Quickly, but carefully, not wanting to tip the whole boat on its descent, I moved toward the side closest to the ship, others turning sideways to let me pass. As we reached the next deck, I took a deep breath, and using all the strength in my legs, I jumped, barely grabbing the ship's railing. The women in the boat screamed, and one or two even tried to grab the hem of my dress, pulling me down as I clung to the railing.

Quinn came barreling down the promenade, now filling with passengers. I was strong, but not strong enough to hoist myself up and over, especially wearing a dress, a coat, and those 1912 restrictive undergarments. Quinn grabbed me under my arms and, with an epic bicep curl, hurled me upward until he could get his arms around my whole body. He pulled me over the railing. We fell together onto the deck, me on top of him.

"Quinn, are you okay?" I asked, hoping he hadn't hurt his head like I had that first night.

"Am *I* okay?" Quinn laughed. "You realize you were just hanging off the side of the *Titanic*, right?"

We got to our feet, straightening ourselves out. "I didn't want to get on that lifeboat! I can't believe I took someone's spot."

"Did you see how full that boat was? That's *because* of you. Now, come on. Let's get back up top—and try to avoid getting into any more boats, okay?" He pulled me to him for a reassuring hug, then we were off at a run.

As we reached the grand staircase, we spotted Felix. He was holding two life jackets.

"Felix!" Quinn yelled. "Over here!"

Felix lifted his head up and spotted us. He dutifully hurried over with the life jackets. "There you are, sir, miss. Please put these on. Captain's orders."

Quinn took the life jackets while I took Felix's arm. "Thank you, Felix. You have saved us more than once tonight. Please try to get to a lifeboat. If you cannot, stay on the ship as long as you can. The front will go down, then the ship will break in half before the stern rises up and goes straight in. The *Californian* is only a few miles away, and it might be able to reach us."

Felix nodded and gave me a weak smile, ever the professional, even as fear showed in his eyes. Quinn reached into his pocket and gave Felix some bills—not that they'd help him if the *Californian* didn't arrive in time. I took off my coat and put on my life jacket, even though I wouldn't need it. I put my coat back on, but it barely fit over my shoulders with the addition of the life jacket underneath.

We turned to sprint back up the grand staircase and got to the landing under the big clock, when we spotted the master-at-arms and the bouncer, still together.

"Really? They're still f'ing looking for us?" Those two were like dogs with a bone.

"Nowhere to run this time," Quinn said.

The bouncer got to us first. "At last. We have you."

"The reason the captain wanted her silenced," Quinn said, nodding my way, "is that she was trying to stop the ship from the disaster that is happening right now. So what is the point of detaining us?"

The master-at-arms arrived to stand next to the bouncer. "The point is that you are under arrest."

"This is ridiculous," Quinn said. "We are SINKING!"

Seemingly impervious to that fact, the master-at-arms pulled handcuffs out of his coat.

But just as he grabbed Quinn's wrists to put them on, Mr. Andrews bounded up the steps two at a time to where we stood.

"What is the meaning of this?" he demanded.

"Captain's orders, Mr. Andrews."

"Well, I have just left the captain, and I have told him that the *Titanic* will founder. You may release these two on my authority, or, if you choose not to, then I will speak with one of the officers and have you locked up instead!"

The bouncer opened his mouth as if to argue with Mr. Andrews, but the master-at-arms pulled the cuffs back. "Very good, Mr. Andrews," he said. "Forgive the inconvenience." He nodded to us both. The bouncer narrowed his eyes and glared, then turned on his heel.

"Mr. Andrews, thank you again," I said, putting both hands on his arm.

"It is my small way of saying that I am sorry I doubted you."

"Will you get to a boat?" I asked, not knowing what else to say.

Mr. Andrews smiled wistfully. "As you know, there are not enough boats, Miss Charlotte. I built the *Titanic*, and I suppose my fate lies with her now."

"But the *Californian* is only six miles away. Have faith, Mr. Andrews." I tried to sound upbeat.

"I am afraid they have not been able to raise her."

"Are you sure?" Quinn asked. "It has only been a short while."

"I just came from the Bridge. But maybe there is hope yet." Then, turning to go back down the stairs, away from the boats, he added, "My best to you both." A gentleman to the end.

I backed up, then sat down, hard, on the nearest stair. How could the *Californian* not be responding? We'd made sure they would. Was time immovable after all, and no matter what we did, the same ill-fated conclusion would be reached? Was there some cosmic rule we'd never been taught?

"It's okay, Charlie," Quinn was saying. "They'll see the rockets even if they didn't get the messages."

"No, no, they won't do anything. They didn't before, Quinn. The captain of the *Californian* thought the rockets were some kind of White Star Line ship-to-ship communication or something. It's all happening, just like it did before." I was suddenly spent. Hungry, cold, tired, discouraged. This was the *Titanic*'s fate. Like in the tale of Sisyphus, the boulder just kept rolling back down the hill.

Quinn was silent for a moment, looking at his feet. "We could go home," he said softly.

"Not yet," I said. I reached for his hand and stood. I had to do what I could. Had to see this through. "Not yet."

# eighteen

One after the other, lifeboats were filling on the Boat Deck, which had started to become crowded with passengers. I spotted Maggie Brown, bundled in fur, awaiting Lifeboat No. 6. "Maggie," I yelled, waving. She motioned for me to join her. I shook my head no, pointing to Quinn, then blew her a kiss with both hands. She put her right hand over her heart and smiled. Then she turned to step in.

I noticed the boat wasn't full but didn't dare get closer in case I was put on board. Besides, what made Maggie so famous was her argument to row back to save others from the water. She would be overruled by the crewman in charge. I watched the boat lower until it was out of sight.

"Quinn, we have to go to third class to get Rosalee and Rima," I said, tugging his sleeve. "I don't see them anywhere, and they might be trapped." The ship was already listing forward, with water pouring in through the breaches in the front of the ship. Water was spilling over the bulkheads. Rockets were still being fired overhead, lighting the faces of the passengers, who were in shock, or denial, or were fighting for their spots on the boats. What killed me was knowing that even if the distress calls weren't received, the *Californian* could see the flares. No wonder its captain was vilified in the press afterward.

With the buzz of passengers, the band playing, and the rocket fire, not to mention the unusually calm sea, the scene was otherworldly, like a theme park version of a disaster—almost too perfectly disastrous. I wondered what such a scene would look like in my time. Would we help each other, or would it be every person for themselves? I hoped we'd never find out.

"Charlie! Look!" Quinn pointed, and I caught a glimpse of fiery red hair coming our way. I ran toward it, dodging people right and left, until I was close. It was Rosalee, carrying a baby in swaddling clothes close to her chest, and Rima, carrying her little brother. I literally sank to my knees, a sob erupting from somewhere deep in my gut, a cry for the *Titanic*, for my friends, for myself and Quinn. They'd made it.

Quinn picked me up as my friends gathered. I hugged them both, along with their precious cargo. They were wearing life jackets but no coats.

"You made it!" I said. "I've never been so glad to see anyone in my whole life." I stripped off my coat, helping Rosalee into it. Quinn was doing the same for Rima.

Rima said, "We have lost my mother and brother. I do not see them anywhere!"

"Listen to me," I said. "Let us get you to a lifeboat. You have just enough time. Quinn and I will go search for Arash and your mom. Okay? Rima—okay?"

Rosalee nodded. "Yes, Rima, we must get to a boat. And, Charlie, I do not know how, but you were right about all of this. I wish we had time for you to explain. But nonetheless, thank you, from the bottom of my heart."

"Rosalee, you will save more people in your lifetime than I could ever hope to. Go, and live your best life." I hugged her again, the baby between us and tears running down my cheeks, stinging them in the cold air.

As I held her, Rosalee added, "I think I misdiagnosed you, Charlie. Your mind and your soul are more connected than I realized."

I smiled at her, grateful for her words, then I hugged Rima. Quinn nodded his goodbyes as the group moved away toward the port side and Lifeboat No. 2.

"So how are we going to find her family?" Quinn asked.

"I have no idea," I said, looking around as if the answer might appear. "Should we go down a deck or two? No matter where we look, it's a shot in the dark." Literally.

Without my coat, I started to shiver in the thirty-two-degree weather. "Charlie," Quinn said, taking off his tuxedo jacket and putting it over my heavy, beaded dress, "we need to think about leaving soon . . . before we risk getting hurt. The ship's starting to list. We're already late to get back to Windline."

"You're right. Let's see if we can find Rima's family. After that, we go home. Deal?"

Quinn half smiled, half frowned. "Stubborn as ever, Charlie Landers. But, yes. Deal."

We went back to the main staircase and down. The scene inside was a mix of gentlemen acting as if a spot of bad weather had cramped their golf game and people running here and there, confused and terrified. The promenade was crowded with people seeking higher ground. Boats were hanging off the sides, lowering like spiders' webs and filled with grateful, stunned people. Some of them were wailing, no doubt having left loved ones on deck.

At first, people didn't believe that the *Titanic* would sink and even refused to get into the lifeboats, feeling safer on the ship than in a small boat on the sea. But now that the *Titanic* was tilting nose down and leaning to port, reality was setting in. Soon the nose would go all the way under and the ship would break between the third and fourth funnels, with the stern rising up in the air and out of the water before doing its own nosedive. We heard shouts and screams.

Then, as we ran, swerving around others on the deck, I spotted Arash, who saw me and Quinn at the same time. We ran to meet each other.

"Charlie, Quinn," he said, breathing hard. "My mother sent me to find Rima. Have you seen her? Or Rosalee?"

"Yes! They should be getting into a lifeboat by now. If we go to the other side of the ship, we can make sure they got in!"

"Lead the way," he said, and we took off for the other side of the Promenade Deck.

We stood at the railing expectantly, much as people had when the *Titanic* left Southampton, except under drastically different circumstances. In what seemed like an instant, Lifeboat No. 2, launched from the davits above, was lowered by ropes, carefully balanced so it wouldn't tip and empty its passengers into the ocean. But something went wrong, and one side began to lower at a faster rate than the other as the boat came into our line of sight. We could see Rima and Rosalee, clutching each other and the children. We screamed to get their attention.

Rima yelled back to her brother in their native language as the boat became more and more lopsided. Something was very wrong with the pulley system on the deck above.

In a flash, Arash was up and over the railing, launching himself to the rope on the high side of the boat. His weight on the stiff ropes pulled the boat down about a foot, steadying it, but not enough. It was still tipping perilously.

Then, in what seemed like slow motion, and before I could stop him, Quinn launched himself at the rope, too. In a second he was gone, no longer by my side but dangling above Rima's brother. I thought I might faint.

As Quinn passed below my eyeline, he called out, "Charlie, go home. I'll be right behind you!"

"Quinn!" was all I could manage.

Rima's brother had lowered himself into the boat and was standing on its back edge to keep his weight there. Quinn held on to the rope, while shouting from above told me that the crewmen were righting the pulley on that side.

As the boat lowered, the *Titanic* moved under my feet, the stem sinking farther into the water. Objects started to slide on the deck.

I realized I had Quinn's coat, and I reached into the pocket, fishing out his pocket watch. It was nearly 2:00 a.m. The last of the boats, Collapsible D, would be lowered soon, and the lights would fail shortly after. *This was it.*

I held the watch close to my chest. With just a thought, I would be back at Windline, safe and warm, and soon after that in my own bed in Malibu, where, no matter the temperature, I'd turn the heated blanket on to its highest setting and roast myself. I'd also shed the well of tears still in me for the loss of life that was to come, or rather, would have already happened.

But as I took one last look around, one last look at this ship of dreams turned ship of nightmares, I saw an object—what looked like a small case—fall in slow motion from the deck above. It fell straight down, down, until it hit Quinn, glancing off him as if his head were made of stone, then changing trajectory and falling into the sea below.

Quinn's body went limp, and he fell, too, a flash of blood visible on his forehead. Like a well-dressed rag doll, his body whizzed past the lifeboat, his ankle grazing the tip of it. He splashed into the freezing water of the Atlantic.

I let out a bloodcurdling scream. Cold air moved in and out of my lungs rapidly. I was on the Promenade Deck, second down from the *Titanic*'s top deck. The ship was sinking more by the second and listing toward the side I was on. The water below appeared to be no higher than a platform diving board. But height didn't matter anyway. Quinn was hurt, perhaps fatally, and if there was the slightest chance he was alive, I was going to find him. If he wasn't conscious, he wouldn't be able to travel home, and he'd drown or freeze in the frigid water, just like so many others would. I couldn't imagine facing my life back home without him. I couldn't imagine facing his mother. *If I die trying to save him, then it will seem right somehow for us to die together with these people. Our families will know where to visit our grave.*

I tucked the watch in the cleavage of my dress and flung off Quinn's jacket. I ran down the railing to get clear of the lowering boat and hiked up my dress over my thighs to climb over the railing.

Then, without hesitation, I jumped.

# nineteen

## 1912
## 370 miles south-southeast of Newfoundland
## North Atlantic Ocean

I took in everything on the way down—the boats paddling away from the ship, figures in white life jackets clinging together, the lights of the *Titanic* reflecting off the dark sea. I felt a momentary freedom, a weightlessness, like a cliff diver who soars in a beautiful arch before landing with the smallest of splashes in the warm waters of some Caribbean cove. Except, for me, the feeling was gone in a blink of an eye, and I hit the water gracelessly, my body crashing feet first into the frigid, sharp water of the Atlantic. It greeted me with a thousand tiny knives on my skin.

The Pacific had always been my happy place—the sight of it, the smell of it, the I-can-never-get-there expanding horizon. To me, it was a stolen beer during a blushing sunset, with a half-peeled-off wet suit and a surfboard. But the Atlantic Ocean was no friend. It was a mad creature swirling in darkness around me with its partner in crime, twenty-eight degrees. This ocean was trying to choke me, to swallow me whole. If it succeeded, my bones, my satin shoes, and the fancy beaded dress that weighed me down would find rest at the bottom of this cold, mean ocean, cradled in sandy hands forever.

The only way to know—really know—what twenty-eight-degree water feels like is to be submerged in it, sinking down into the bitter swirl as water engulfs the body in a 360-degree assault. I twisted and turned in the blackness, not sure which way was up. I tasted the salt in the water as it fought to enter my mouth. The stitches in my head stung for the briefest moment until I didn't feel them at all. My body went numb, my limbs turning to lead, as if the bottom of the ocean had a magnet that pulled them down with an unseen force.

I wasn't alone in the water. I opened my eyes for a second to find the lights above, but when I did, I saw the face of another, like an angel in white dancing and swirling. But the vision was no angel. It was another passenger who'd jumped or fallen, trying to survive just like I was, maybe to swim to a lifeboat. I felt a sharp elbow to my ear and wondered if it had broken off, my first body part sacrificed to the Atlantic.

When I was in junior high school, I'd run cross-country for a season. I hated it. Who wanted to pound on the dirt or the road for hours on end, when surfing was so much more fun? At one of our meets, a girl from the other team had tripped me in the crush of runners at the start, and I'd fallen, dazed by the impact. A teammate had paused and screamed at me, "GET UP!" Like a soldier obeying an order, I'd done as I was told and finished the race.

But no one was going to do that for me as I kicked for the surface of the water. External motivation wasn't coming. I had to find the air on my own. I had to kick, even when my legs wanted to stay still. My mind was going blank, shutting down, the swift numbness in my extremities creeping into my brain.

In twenty-eight-degree water, a human will survive for as little as fifteen minutes. Fifteen minutes of thrashing, of hoping you're the exception to the fifteen-minute rule. They say life flashes before your eyes when you're near death, but there was no Hollywood-style montage of memories of the family huddled around a Christmas tree. No reel of me learning to ride a bike on a sunny Southern California cul-de-sac. No image of my sloppy first kiss in Marcus Schuler's basement.

Then, with one last reflexive kick—or perhaps a convulsion—I finally broke the water's surface and gulped in the stinging night air. Just one simple piece of code, one root command, struggled along the tightrope of my last firing synapse.

*"Save him!"* it screamed.

I came back online, looking around frantically and getting my bearings. The lifeboat—*got it.* The ship—*yes, there it is.* Quinn's trajectory—*that way, I think.* Leveraging my bulky life jacket as a flotation device, I twisted onto my belly, kicking and paddling like a child learning to swim using a mushy raft. It was awkward, and the effort to move was immense, but I was making progress. I tried to keep my breathing steady, since the cold shock response—the reflex to hyperventilate in cold water—could speed up drowning. If I didn't find him soon, I'd lose the ability to maneuver. It seemed like I was swimming through quicksand. The faint voice inside my head started to give me permission to give up.

"Charlie!" It was Rosalee and Rima, screaming in unison from the lifeboat, now rowing furiously away from the *Titanic*. I heard them as if they were far in the distance. "Over THERE!" they were screaming, pointing.

I followed the lines of their fingers and spotted him. It was Quinn, bobbing in the water like a cork, his body upright but his head hanging as if he were sleeping. I pointed my body toward him. Splash. Kick. Stroke. Splash. Stroke. Cough. Kick. Dog paddle. Splash. I was almost there.

My brain mustered the energy to make my legs kick to the finish line. I finally intercepted him.

"Quinn, Quinn!" I yelled, taking his head in my hands, noticeably blue now that they were out of the water. Blood pooled like cherry Popsicle drippings on Quinn's head, matting the hairline on one side. His skin was gray-white where there was no blood.

My face went under as I tried to tread water with my legs while using my hands to examine Quinn. I coughed out the salty ice water. I didn't see any puffs of air coming out of his mouth. I checked for his pulse, which took longer than it should've because the nerve endings in my own fingers weren't to be trusted.

I felt the weak pulse of blood moving in Quinn's veins—but I couldn't be totally sure it wasn't my own. If his heart was beating, there was a chance. He just needed to breathe.

Using my legs to boost me in the water as best as I could, and trying not to push him down in the water, I pinched his nose and put my lips over his, and blew. *Did anything come out of me?* I blew again and coughed at the effort. And blew again. I was doing what I had just worked to overcome—hyperventilating. But I kept going.

Then . . . the most beautiful, tiny cough I'd ever heard came from Quinn and created the most beautiful, tiny puff of visible breath in the cold night air. Quinn was breathing.

"Quinn! Look at me, Quinn!" I rubbed his face with my hands. Shook him a little.

"Quinn!"

His eyelids were nearly purple, but they fluttered open halfway.

"Hey! Quinn, it's me!"

"So cold," he whispered. Even his whisper was raspy.

"Quinn, listen to me NOW! You are a time traveler. We're in 1912 in the ocean. Think about Windline. Go home, Quinn. Go HOME!"

"Cold."

Suddenly the darkness got darker, and I realized the *Titanic*'s lights had just failed. The ship would go under in a matter of minutes, and when it did, we'd be sucked down with it. People were falling all over the place now, filling the water around us. Screams became the soundtrack. This was the end.

I looked up to the heavens for strength. A thousand white stars stood out, bright against a black sky. Those stars would be the *Titanic*'s monument but not Quinn's. Not Quinn's. I took a deep breath.

"Quinn Daniels! You are such an ass! I LOVE YOU. . . . Do you hear me? I LOVE you. So YOU WILL LIVE or else. Go HOME to Windline. Do it NOW!"

Quinn's eyes opened. They connected with mine for a second, then his lids fluttered closed and he vanished. He'd made it out. If I could have cried with relief, I would've.

I looked back at the *Titanic*, a giant shadow in the starlight now, with what sounded like a thousand voices crying out at once. "I'll remember you all," I said to no one and everyone, my voice barely coming out. "Rest in peace, *Titanic*."

And I was gone, too.

# twenty
## present day

I arrived at Windline's gymnasium on my feet but immediately crumpled to the floor beside Quinn. Our only movements came from our breathing until I managed to turn my head to look at him. I was so cold I couldn't feel a temperature difference in the warm room, like an ice cube that stays frozen in an insulated glass.

There are several stages of hypothermia in freezing water. The first involves shivering and loss of circulation. The second progresses to confusion, a weak or slowed pulse, lack of coordination, and sleepiness. In the third stage, respiration and pulse may get weaker or go away entirely. I supposed I was in the second stage. Quinn was definitely stage three.

I felt the solid surface of the gym floor beneath me. I couldn't be sure who was there to greet us, but I heard the thunderous sound of multiple people running, shouting to us and each other.

"Call 911!" yelled one.

"Call Dr. Prakash!" yelled another. "Tell him to call UCLA Medical Center and let them know we're coming."

"Bring scissors and blankets!"

I'd turned my head back to stare straight up at the ceiling. Was I still seeing stars, or were those gym lights? I couldn't seem to blink, and I was okay with that. I wanted to stare at those lights forever. They comforted me, like the stars over the *Titanic*. But a blob with smeared edges soon blocked my view. I didn't care who or what it was, only that I couldn't see those lights anymore. It took a long moment for my eyes to focus.

"Charlie, darling, it's me!" A woman came into perspective, and I could see it was Mom, beautifully familiar with her upturned nose and laugh lines that spread like fans around her eyes.

"Quinn?" I whispered, my throat like concrete that was drying into a hard block.

"Quinn's right next to you, honey. He's here—Connie's with him."

I stopped speaking. I couldn't, and I didn't want to. Ever again. I hadn't wanted to die in the Atlantic. That ocean was getting its share of tribute, despite everything I'd tried, everything Quinn had tried, everything Mr. Andrews and the Marconi guys had tried. But now that I was here—now that I was home—I could pass through this place and just . . . stop . . . being.

My mom screamed, but the sound came from far away. I couldn't see her anymore. I'd closed my eyes.

Voices all around, in the distance with my mother. I

might have felt my dress move, cut from my body and replaced with blankets that weighed me down like gravity.

"There's a pocket watch here," a female voice said.

"She's got the *Rubáiyát*," I heard another voice say. I'd forgotten it was in the bag I'd carried over my shoulder, safely sealed in plastic. At least I'd achieved one small victory.

Then, after a minute, or maybe an hour, I was lifted, the hard surface replaced by a soft one and the feeling of movement. Lights flashed, like the light from the rockets, bright one second and dim the next. Doors closing, opening, closing, opening. New voices.

A long time later, I heard, "Anybody know how the hell I've got two water-immersion hypothermia victims in here? It's not even snowing in the mountains yet."

"Don't know. Family physician called ahead—said it was some kind of prank gone bad."

"Temperature eighty-eight degrees, up from eighty-three when the ambulance picked her up."

"Heated blankets are here, Doctor."

"Thanks. Hang warm saline, wide open. Heated oxygen. I'm going to watch and wait on catheterization. Her mother said she was talking earlier.

"Let's get whirlpool warming for the extremities. We've got some minor frostbite on the distal phalanges, left foot, so page plastics for a consult. The boy is going to need them to take a look anyway, along with ortho. I'll check back in a bit. We'll push meds for pain when we get the temp up to ninety-three degrees. She's gonna have a helluva ride getting back up to ninety-eight-point-six."

Machines beeped in my ears, a pitiful echo of the band playing on the deck of the *Titanic* as the bow of the ship sank lower. Over the sound, I could hear people talking about Quinn. Only a thin curtain separated us.

"Plastics is en route," or "Peritoneal lavage," or "We've got low pressure." Then, "We need to get his temp up before we get a CT, but signs point to a decent head injury here."

If only I could've reached out my arm to touch him on the other side of that curtain, to see him, so I could judge his status for myself. I would've traded places with him gladly, because whatever happened to him, it was my fault. If I'd stuck with my original plan—to stay in my cabin and ignore the tragic drama of the *Titanic* unfolding around me—Quinn and I might never have seen each other on board, and I certainly wouldn't have enlisted him in my plan, the one that had landed him in a hospital bed.

I thought getting Quinn home was all that mattered, that we'd be safe once we were in the arms of our families. But we were far from safe. Quinn, who'd done nothing but support me and try to save a lifeboat full of women and children, was anything but in the clear.

With a mask over my nose and mouth pushing warm air, toasty blankets, and an IV in my arm, I started to thaw. I felt like a white winter snow that gets shoveled into the gutter, mixing with dirt to form a nasty gray mush. As my skin warmed, a thousand pins pricked me, a distant relation to the knives that had slashed at me in the Atlantic. A nurse hurried in and gave me something, and my body relaxed. Before long, I drifted off in a cocoon of warmth.

~

Time crawled by during what turned into a two-night hospital stay, courtesy of low blood pressure. Only, when I was discharged, I didn't want to leave. I wanted to keep vigil over Quinn. My parents and I disagreed on next steps.

"Honey, let's get you home and sorted out, then you can come back and visit Quinn. You need to get your strength up," my mom said.

"You can take my car whenever you want to come visit. Better yet, we'll go pick out a car for you, and you can drive up here on your own," my dad added.

*Why do men always think a car will fix things?*

I refused and shook my head, sore from the replacement of the stitches I'd gotten on the *Titanic.* Actual words were elusive. The doctor had said there was no physical reason I couldn't speak. Whether I couldn't or wouldn't, nothing was coming out of my mouth. "I'd suggest she talk with someone," he'd said. "Sometimes after traumatic situations, we need some help finding our voice again."

*How am I supposed to "talk to someone" when I can't speak? And "we" didn't have a traumatic situation. Quinn and I did. It was our parents and our school that sent us to the Titanic in an effort to turn us into them. To send us on our way to our predetermined genetic destiny. Maybe when I hear Quinn's voice again, I'll be able to use mine.*

Of course my parents failed to mention one key fact to the doctor. I'd been sent on a school assignment, where I'd wound up in the water off Newfoundland while fifteen hundred people faced their deaths in front of my eyes. If my parents had shared the truth, the doctor would've asked Mom and Dad to "talk with someone" instead of me. I'd work through the loss of the *Titanic*, but only when Quinn was on his feet.

The argument about my staying was finally resolved in my favor, and I camped out with Quinn's parents in his hospital room. He was asleep most of the time, despite the nurses' best efforts to poke and prod him every few hours. He had a bandage on his head. One of his feet was wrapped where the frostbite had affected his toes, and the other was immobilized up to the shin from the injury he'd gotten when his ankle hit the boat. One hand was wrapped as well. At first, the doctors had thought he might lose one of his toes.

"His overall prognosis is favorable," his doctor kept saying now, the best five words ever.

Quinn's parents, who were almost like my own, plied me with sandwiches and chips from the cafeteria. I didn't feel like eating. I knew they wanted to know what had happened, but I wasn't much help.

"So I take it you both went down with the ship?" Connie asked.

I nodded and shrugged at the same time.

"Were you together?"

Nod and shrug.

"Do you know how he hurt his head?"

Nod.

I supposed they could've asked me to write down my answers, but I was glad they didn't. If I didn't feel like saying anything, I sure didn't feel like writing anything.

Twenty-four hours after I was discharged, Quinn opened his eyes, and unlike the other brief wake ups, this time he was alert. His father had gone home to change, and his mom was getting coffee. I was staring out the window.

"Charlie?" he said in a croaky, hoarse voice.

I nearly jumped out of my chair and rushed to his bedside. I took the hand that wasn't bandaged, surprised and overjoyed by the warm feeling of his skin on mine. The last time I'd touched him, he was freezing.

I nodded.

"You okay?"

I smiled. *You nearly died, and you're asking if I'm okay?* Now was the time to find my voice, but even though I was reaching for it, it was still lost to 1912.

"What happened?"

Connie walked in, holding coffees. "Quinn! Baby, you're awake!" She practically threw the coffees on the rolling table by Quinn's bed. "We were so scared, but don't you worry, everything's going to be right as rain now!" Despite the dark circles under her eyes, Connie looked five years younger after seeing Quinn awake and alert.

"Mom, is Charlie okay?" He looked at her, then me. I smiled again and nodded.

"She's fine, babe. She's just having a little trouble talking right now, but it'll come back to her. Right, Charlie?"

I nodded. Maybe my voice was lost, like I was. I couldn't be sure. It didn't matter. Everything would be better now. Quinn was back.

# twenty-one

My silver laptop sat open in front of me, the cursor pointed at my Internet browser. I was too afraid to click and had been for days. I knew I'd be opening the Pandora's box of history to find out what happened on the *Titanic*, to find out whether we did anything that had helped at all. Instead, I'd spent my time sleeping, watching reruns of stupid sitcoms, and staring at the ceiling, all interspersed with crying jags.

"Charlie!" Sammy yelled from downstairs on Saturday morning.

*What now?* I thought. I'd been home for a little over a week since Quinn had been discharged, and given that my voice was hanging out on a ship at the bottom of the Atlantic, Sammy had decided to up his annoying factor considerably in an effort to be supportive. When he wasn't at school, he not only talked constantly but also talked loudly, like I couldn't hear. Eventually, I'd locked my door to keep him out.

Guilt was a powerful driver, and my parents were coping by waiting on me as if I'd lost my motor skills instead of my voice, expressing their concern through excessive amounts of food delivered to my room. I became an expert at moving my parents' offerings around the plates, tucking beans under the rice, or cutting the chicken into small pieces that I scattered into the greens, so they'd think I'd eaten more than I had. I did consume all the nachos—even in my state of physical and psychological disarray, I couldn't resist those. My parents also gave me small gifts that arrived at our front door every day, including spirit-lifting treasures like fuzzy slippers with bunny ears and glittery lip gloss. Apparently, they thought the trip had caused me to age in reverse, or maybe they just wanted their little girl back.

Mom spoke to Windline about my situation and secured one more week of freedom for me. One more week until the final report for my Junior Year Test was due. I'd have to know how the *Titanic*'s story ended in order to cover up what I'd changed, if there was anything, but I didn't want to know or to live through the *Titanic* again via the Internet. As it was, I woke up each night in a cold sweat, sure I'd made things worse. Besides, I had no idea yet what I'd learned from my trip. *Maybe—don't sail on a ship you know is gonna sink? Or, don't go to a school that makes you travel on a ship that's gonna sink?*

Sammy yelled again. "Charlie, Quinn's here!"

Quinn's family had pulled in the drawbridge when they'd gotten him home from the hospital. My parents wouldn't have wanted me to visit anyway since they thought I needed "recuperation time." Sure, I could have texted Quinn, but I didn't, except a couple of times to make sure he was okay. And he could've called me, but he knew the conversation would be one-sided, so he didn't. He was healing, and I also figured he might need a break from me. Or worse, he might have started to resent me, to realize I was the root of all his problems. So when I heard his name, I jumped off the bed, threw on some of my sparkly new lip gloss—which tasted disgusting—and hurried out of my room and down the hall to the top of the stairs, limping slightly to keep pressure off the sore toes on my left foot.

Quinn was standing at the bottom of the stairs, propped on crutches, his feet in the kind of hard plastic, velcro-over-the-foot booties to protect his bruised ankle and messed-up toes. The color had returned to his face, so much so that he looked flushed from exertion.

"Hi, Charlie Chicken," he said, almost shyly. He shrugged. "I guess it might be time to come up with a new nickname."

A "yes, finally" almost made its way through my vocal cords, but not quite. I gave two thumbs up and started down the stairs.

"My mom finally caved and agreed to drive me over here. She's in the kitchen with your mom."

Quinn couldn't make the stairs, so we went out on the back patio, where I put him in a lounge chair. I leaned his crutches against the outdoor dining table under the arbor covered in bougainvillea. I grabbed pillows from the chairs to prop up his feet, then stretched out on a lounger next to him. The hazy sun shone down, warming my skin while the breeze cooled it at the same time. We looked out at the blue Pacific in the distance, so perfectly picturesque that it seemed like a green-screen projection. Despite sitting close enough to reach over and touch him, Quinn felt like a stranger. I'd been living in my head for days.

Finally, he broke the silence. "How're you doing?" He looked over at me, and I shrugged. I pointed back at him.

"I'm a lot better. Don't have a lot of energy, though. Obviously my foot and ankle have a ways to go. But I'll be a hundred percent again soon," he said.

More silence.

"Have you researched the *Titanic* yet?" he asked quietly. I shook my head. "Well, I've had plenty of time on my hands, and I had to know. Want me to fill you in?"

Did I? *Better to hear it from him than my laptop, I suppose.* I nodded, bracing myself.

Quinn put his hand on my arm. "Charlie, by most counts, we saved 127 people."

I swung my legs around and sat up, staring at him.

He went on, the emotion causing his voice to break. He cared, too.

"Of that number, forty-two percent were from third class. The number of men surviving went up from the first and second classes, too. I guess men from those classes were asked to fill some of the lifeboats before third-class passengers could get to the Boat Deck.

"Rima and her brother survived, of course. And Rosalee. Rosalee actually went on to invent a 'new birthing technique for improving outcomes of back labor,' whatever that is. Apparently, it was a big deal. She did an interview in 1920 for a newspaper, and the reporter brought up the *Titanic*. There was a picture in the article. She got married to Arash, and they had three kids. She mentioned you, and get this. . . . She named one of her kids Charlotte."

As I watched his mouth move and his words registered, tears welled up in my eyes. I didn't try to stop them. They spilled freely down my face. I jumped up and walked over to grab the patio railing. I looked over at our sloping backyard filled with bushes and flowers, but all I saw was that night on the *Titanic*, looking over the railing as Quinn fell into the Atlantic.

Then I felt it—my lost voice. It flooded back into me, like an empty glass filled to overflowing, until a scream tore from my throat with a ferocity that made up for all of my silence and then some. I screamed, all the stress and the guilt and the uncertainty coming out of me in that sound. The scream was so loud, so desperate, that it filled the canyon, echoing across our neighborhood and reverberating in my head. When it was spent, I sat down cross-legged and held my head in my hands as I sobbed.

Quinn clunked up behind me and crouched down to my level, his hands on my shoulder, and our mothers came running from the kitchen.

"Charlie!" my mother exclaimed.

"She's okay, Mrs. Landers," Quinn said. "I think she'll be better now."

"Honey," Mom said as she approached me on the side opposite from Quinn, "look at me. It's all right. Everything's going to be all right."

"Quinn? C'mon." Connie was close, too, probably trying to get Quinn off his feet and back into a chair.

I turned into my mother's arms, like a little kid, and let out an incoherent string of "so many people" and "tried so hard" and "her child was named after me" and so on. My mother gently rocked me there until I was spent. I'd let the *Titanic* so deep into my heart and soul that it'd taken two weeks for my agony to reach the surface. It was as if I'd been back in the Atlantic all this time, struggling to break the surface of the water again.

~

Two days later, I sat facing Quinn at the end of his bed. His room overlooked the pool and was filled with trophies and books. On the wall above him was a framed jersey from his favorite Manchester United player. He was propped up on a stack of pillows with his feet elevated, wearing gym shorts and a white T-shirt—quite a different look than the debonair first-class transportation mogul on the *Titanic.* I didn't miss my fancy clothes, but I did miss his. He looked ridiculously handsome in a vintage tux.

We'd spent most of the day watching stupid videos online, laughing until tears came out—in my case, anyway—and heckling. But we needed to talk.

"Quinn, I've gotta write my report soon," I started, picking at his navy-blue duvet cover. "I know you can't tell me about yours, but we have to sync our stories."

He scrunched up his face like I'd just given him a spoonful of disgusting cherry cough syrup. "Okay," he said.

"I finally did my research, and I haven't found any reference to you, other than that you were on the passenger manifest and not on the list of survivors."

"Yep, same."

"But my name is all over the place as the mysterious girl who tried to stop the ship from sinking. There's no way the committee won't know I tried to change the timeline."

Quinn nodded.

"So I'm going to fail, and be forced to retake the test or drop out. I'm at peace with all that. What I'm not okay with is you failing, so I'm going to rewrite history—at least the bit of history I *can* control. As far as the committee will know, you weren't involved. I'll even tell them you tried to stop me when you found out, which is true."

"I didn't try very hard or very long."

"Yeah, but they won't know that. I am not letting you fail out. At least I can repeat my test if I want to, but you'd never finish Windline. Your college options would be a lot slimmer." College—a top one even—was an expectation for everyone in our circle. The more the education, the better. "You'd never get your time pin and get to time travel on your own. It'd be a disaster," I added.

The sun had been streaming in through Quinn's windows. A cloud must've floated in front of it because the room suddenly got darker.

"Are you sure, Charlie? I don't want you to fight this alone. I was right beside you on the *Titanic*."

"You've paid a high enough price for helping." I gestured to his foot and ankle.

"They'll heal. It's the scars in my brain I'm a little more worried about."

I put my hand on his knee, the closest body part to me. I hadn't realized he was in mourning as much as I was. I'd lost my voice, screamed, and cried, but he'd always been so stoic and guy-like that I'd thought he was in a better place. Made sense that he wasn't, though. We'd both experienced one of the worst disasters in history, even if we did manage to save some people. Plus, he'd nearly died.

"I know," I said. "But you'll get through this. We both will."

"Together." He opened his arms, and I slipped into them, lying half on top of his chest. His body was warm and solid, and I could hear his heart beating, a sound I'd never take for granted again.

"At least we found each other on the *Titanic*," I murmured. Then, I propped up on my elbow and looked at him, at his bright blue eyes and the stitches visible at his hairline. There was something about his injuries that triggered a kind of weird primal response in me, and I wanted to kiss him and take care of him at the same time. I silently vowed to remember his heroics the next time he annoyed me. He'd been willing to risk his own life for people he barely knew.

"A 1912 penny for your thoughts," he said with a slow smile.

"I was just thinking that if I looked up the definition of 'hero' in the dictionary, I'd find your picture."

"Hah—I doubt that."

"It's true. You saved that lifeboat."

"Maybe I helped, but what about you? You're the real hero."

"I don't think so. . . ." I definitely didn't think of myself that way. Maybe as girls, we were trained to think of ourselves as helpers, to undervalue our own efforts. All I could focus on was what I'd done wrong or at least what I could've done better. *Maybe if this . . . Maybe if that . . .*

"Yes, Charlie, you are. News flash . . . It was your idea to save the ship. You took all the risks. Then you friggin' jumped into the water to save me. YOU were the hero, way more than I was."

"The hero," I said, trying it on for size. It felt heavy on my shoulders. "Wow, that's a lot to own. I just did what I felt like I had to do for the people on the ship, and as for jumping in after you, it was totally selfish." I raised an eyebrow.

"Hmm. Okay, I'll bite. Why's that?"

"'Cause who would drive me to school if you died?"

He laughed. "Well, if you'd ever take your dad up on the car thing, you could drive yourself."

"Maybe I like my chauffeur." I leaned in, getting closer to his face. "And besides, I'd have to find somebody else to kiss, and that'd be a pain. . . ."

"I heard Gustavo might be interested. . . ."

"Who?" I was an inch from his face, his lips pulling me in.

"Shut up and kiss me already, Charlie."

Quinn twined his hand into my hair and our lips met for the first time since the *Titanic*, the heat springing up quickly between us. Something felt different this time. We'd lived our lives in parallel since birth, but in those few days on the *Titanic*, we'd shared a lifetime. So when he rolled over, the weight of his body pushing me down into his memory foam mattress, I didn't just react because he was a beautiful guy and a great kisser. I held Quinn tight because he was my very own life preserver. He was my person, past, present, and future.

# twenty-two

Procrastination wasn't usually my jam, but I put off my JY Test report until the very last minute. With the help of our espresso machine, I stayed up all night writing it the Sunday before I had to go back to Windline. I think it took so long to get started because I resented Windline for sending me to the *Titanic* in the first place, and even more so, I resented the school for making me write about it as if the experience was some ordinary book report. And lessons learned? The *Titanic* wasn't after-school detention, where I could write a hundred times on a blackboard, *I learned that I'm stronger than I thought I was*, or some such crap.

Nothing I could possibly write could capture any of it. Not the ship, with its fresh paint and seventeen-story grandeur, its exquisite craftsmanship and impressive technology, all gained at the expense of eight men who died during the building of it. Not the people either, from Maggie and her folksy wealth and big heart to Rima or Mr. Andrews, who built a coffin and knew it at the end. Not Quinn and his declaration of love or his leap to the rope holding the lifeboat. And certainly not me. Where would I even begin to describe what the *Titanic* did to—and meant to—me?

Thankfully, I was easily able to manage writing the travelogue and even the story of my interventions to save the ship. As history would have it, none of them worked very well. Of course, the captain didn't hear a thing I said until the very end, when he knew I was right. He didn't slow the ship or heed the iceberg warnings, so when Mr. Andrews tried to convince him to slow down, it was hopeless. There were no newspaper or survivor accounts of Mr. Andrews talking to the officers on the Bridge about the preference for ramming an iceberg versus turning away from one to expose the side of the ship.

The Marconi operators hadn't told the *Californian* to get off the line as they had the first time in the *Titanic*'s history. Instead, they'd sent a message, asking her to keep her lines open because the *Titanic* was concerned about ice. The wireless operator on the *Californian* had apparently informed his captain of this message, who disregarded it since all the ships in the area were encountering ice. Given the captain's assurances that the *Titanic* would be fine, the *Californian*'s wireless operator went to sleep as he had before, so the distress calls never made it through. When the ship's captain saw flares in the sky, he eventually put two and two together, realizing they could be related to the *Titanic*'s earlier message. But because he didn't move his ship to action until several flares went up—and the *Californian* was surrounded by ice, making its own movement painfully slow—

he didn't arrive on the scene in time to save the people freezing in the water. I remembered that water—and the fifteen-minute survival threshold. Almost no one stood a chance, though an additional two or three hardy men were rescued from the water thanks to the *Californian*'s arrival.

And as for the lookouts, who had a perfectly functional pair of binoculars thanks to Quinn's steward, they had been talking, probably about the strange passenger they'd just seen, and spotted the iceberg only a matter of seconds sooner than before. The officer manning the Bridge had been dealing with us when the call came in about an "iceberg right ahead." First Officer Murdoch had turned, and the *Titanic*'s side was slashed. It took on water, almost exactly as it had before.

The only thing that made any significant difference was that the captain had ordered the lifeboats to be filled. Scared of the boats buckling, or perhaps just uncertain about lowering them filled with people, some of the crew still sent the boats away half empty, like Maggie's had been. After hearings in New York and London, regulations about ship safety still came out of the tragedy. Maggie still became a famous figure in the aftermath of the *Titanic* and was nicknamed the Unsinkable Molly Brown as before, after arguing with the crewman in charge of her lifeboat to go back and save others.

I tried to track down any mention of Rima. All I could find was a reference to her in the article about the death of the oldest living survivor of the *Titanic*, the baby girl who Rosalee had helped bring into the world. Sadly, the mother hadn't survived the delivery, but Rima and her American husband had raised the baby as their own. When she died in the late 1980s, Rima's adopted daughter had lived a full life as an accountant, mother, and grandmother.

The death of the baby's mother on the *Titanic* had fueled Rosalee's efforts to save more mothers from dying during childbirth. Just what I would've guessed for her future. When I found the article about Rosalee that Quinn had told me about, I printed it out. Windline's yearbooks weren't exactly showstoppers for upperclassmen, since the junior and senior classes were out of school a lot. So Rosalee's article—and the pile of other articles about the *Titanic*—would be my reminders of the time and place, pieces of which would eventually fade, sharp images becoming blurred at the edges.

If the *Titanic*'s monument was the stars, mine would be Rosalee's words, captured in black and white:

*I most certainly would not be the person I am today without having had the privilege of knowing Miss Charlotte Landers on the* Titanic*'s maiden voyage. Somehow, she not only knew the ship would founder but also precisely when the tragedy would occur. I have no knowledge of others whom she might have saved, but she most certainly saved me and my husband, as well as the* *newborn I had just delivered. I watched her, just a young woman, leap into the North Atlantic in an attempt to rescue her beau. I will never forget seeing them in the distance as we rowed away, moments before the Titanic's lights failed.*

Then, later in the article:

*I think of Charlotte when I face obstacles, which means I think of her often. In the very short time I knew her, she taught me to persevere and, above all else, to selflessly demonstrate concern for the lives of others, not as a doctor, but as a human. It was such a simple lesson, yet I have found it a constant challenge to live it properly. My hope is that my contribution to advances in medicine will repay her sacrifice in some small measure.*

She also mentioned her daughter, my namesake. Maybe someday, if I ever managed to get my own time pin, I'd find Rosalee again and sit down for a glass of wine. I'd tell her that her work, and her long and happy life with Rima's brother, were more than enough for me.

Firsthand newspaper and book accounts of my actions on the *Titanic* came from Maggie, Rosalee, and the surviving Marconi operator, Harold Bride, plus a passenger who'd overheard my episode with the captain. In my report to Windline, I confessed to it all. There was no reason not to.

But I never mentioned Quinn, except to say that he'd objected to my plan.

I didn't find anything about Russ Bean in my initial research on the aftermath of the *Titanic*, except that he was among the crew members who survived. After a little more searching in records for the years after the *Titanic*, I found out he went into the Royal Navy during World War I. Turns out he'd escaped death in 1912 only to fall victim to another disaster as a member of the crew of the HMS *Vanguard* in July of 1917, when explosives on the ship exploded in one of the worst military accidents in British naval history, killing 843. I saw photos of pieces of that ship on the sea floor.

I cursed history for catching up to poor Russ, taking his life in another tragedy.

~

The Monday morning I had to go back to Windline came all too soon, and I woke up to my phone's jingling alarm after a less-than-refreshing, thirty-minute catnap from 6:30 to 7:00 a.m. I jumped out of bed thinking I was late, that the sound of my alarm was the first bell at Windline. Just as I realized I was in my room and on time, my mother did the "mom knock" that involved knocking while walking right on in.

"Good morning, sunshine!" she sang as she picked up a stray pair of socks, a coffee cup in her other hand. "Did you finish your report?"

I rubbed my eyes and scratched my belly. I would've done anything to go back to bed. "Yes, Mom. I emailed it in before I went to sleep."

"By the looks of it, that wasn't very long ago." She disappeared into my closet, and I leaned against the door-frame as she pulled out one of my starched school uniform shirts and then a skirt and a blazer from the closet.

"Nope. Couldn't I call in sick? Nobody's back, so I'll just be rattling around the school trying to figure out what 'self-study' means."

Mom's hands went to her hips. "I'm afraid we've already played the sick card, honey. And everyone has to do self-study for the first semester. Pick something you're interested in."

I thought for a second. *Engineering in early twentieth-century ships? Safety on the high seas? The evolution of women's undergarments from corsets to sports bras?* Or, better yet, I could study the various sleep cycles with some primary research sacked out on a couch in the library.

"Sure, Mom" was all I managed.

She dropped my clothes on the bed and sat down in one of my swinging chairs. "Honey, you know you can talk to me about what happened, don't you? I'm always on your side."

"Even if I fail my JY Test?"

"Even if. But you haven't told me why you think you'll fail."

I grabbed a brush and started it down the long length of my bed-head brown hair. "Simple, Mom. I tried to stop the *Titanic* from sinking." I'd been keeping the details from her so she wouldn't worry any more than she already had been. To explain why we were both nearly frozen, I told a half truth: that Quinn was injured when he was knocked overboard, and I had gone in after him. But now that my report had been turned in—to be followed, I was sure, by a beating at my oral report conference—she was going to find out everything. "I literally did everything I could think of," I continued. "I even considered jumping overboard the day we hit the iceberg. To delay us."

Mom's California-suntanned face went as white as my bedroom walls. "Dear God, Charlie. I'm glad you thought better of it."

"I didn't. Quinn did."

"So he knew what you were trying to do?"

*Danger, danger*. I'd said too much. Mom could be trusted, but she was also a card-carrying member of the Windline time travel club. I shouldn't push the limits by sharing too much.

So, I self-corrected. "No," I said. "He got an inkling I was trying to change the timeline when I confronted the captain outside a restaurant in first class. Quinn gave me quite a lecture after that. When I mentioned jumping off the ship in passing at the end of the trip, he figured out why I was considering it . . . and had a meltdown. . . ." Then, for good measure, I added, "I love the guy, but he was a royal—and by royal I mean first-class—pain in the butt as my Minder."

Mom exhaled. "Oh, well, honey, that was his job. I'm glad he tried to do it. And as for you, young lady, you broke the rules and you'll face the consequences, whatever they may be. And your dad and I will stand right behind you."

"Even if I want to switch to a regular high school? I'm not going back to Windline if they make me repeat my test in Nazi Germany or the French Revolution. I couldn't deal, Mom. Seriously." The brush was in my hand, and I waved it around for emphasis. Honestly, I was less worried about another test—though I detested the thought of one—and more worried about staying at Windline if Quinn got kicked out. My getting a time pin and his getting a GED would not bode well for his future or our long-term relationship.

Big gulp from Mom. Suggesting I might not finish Windline was like telling a mob family you wanted to become a police officer. "Let's cross that bridge when we get to it, Charlie," she said, trying but failing to sound open to my idea.

"As long as the bridge doesn't fall and land me back in cold water, I'm good with that," I said, attempting to crack a *Titanic* joke. *Too soon? Definitely.*

~

Mom wouldn't let me take her car to school. She insisted on driving me with my little brother, worried I'd fall asleep at the wheel and careen to my death in the canyons if I was on my own. "I'm not losing you now, when I just got you back!" she said. I tuned the radio to UCLA's station, but the broadcast just made me sad. Quinn was still stuck at home on bed rest, and going to Windline without him being all cocky and annoying in the driver's seat seemed wrong. At least he would be back on his feet in a few more days.

The dark asphalt parking lot at school was almost empty without the juniors and seniors to fill it up. Mom gave my hand a quick "you got this" squeeze, and I jumped out, looking up at the three immense windows I'd seen every day for years. Now it felt like I hadn't seen them in ages. Or maybe I wasn't the same person I was when I saw them last.

The "JV Hallway" housed all the junior-class lockers. They looked like proper wood cabinets—no metal doors with ventilation slats at Windline. I stood in front of mine, staring into its deep, dark corners filled with pens and binders stuffed with loose-leaf paper, tablet and laptop chargers, and a pear that had turned into an unintentional science project.

I walked into homeroom to find a teacher and only one other student there. I didn't know the girl well, but I had the urge to run over and hug her. Her arm was in a sling, and she had scratches on her left cheek. Did they send her to Rome to be a gladiator or something?

"Good morning, Charlie. Nice of you to join us," the teacher said.

The clock showed that I was three minutes late. *Really?*

The teacher went on. "Today is core subject self-paced learning, so pick your poison. You'll also have a self-study research paper due before winter break. You pick the topic, but I'll have to approve it, so don't try to wimp out on something too easy. But first, pick a seat." He swept his hand around the room of empty wooden tables. "Any seat."

I walked to the very back of the room as if the distance would make it harder for the teacher to see me sleeping and drooling on my tablet. Unfortunately, it didn't, despite my clever attempt to take a siesta while propped on my hand and using my hair as a shield. Mr. Roberts busted me each time by "stretching his legs" to walk around the room. After his second "sleeping is for nighttime" comment in the mid-afternoon, I asked to be excused and beelined for the restroom to splash my face with water and grab an espresso from the coffee bar.

The bathroom was empty, and I laughed to myself thinking about hiding in a stall on the *Titanic* with Quinn. *Thank goodness the toilets at Windline don't auto-flush*, I thought. While I was finishing my business in the stall, I heard the sound of the door opening and closing, followed by a gasping cry, the kind you hold in hoping to make it to a safe place to be alone.

Here I was, stuck again. If I left the stall, I'd surprise the poor girl in what was clearly a private moment. If I didn't, Mr. Roberts might come looking, and I desperately needed time to get that espresso. So I flushed, figuring that'd announce my arrival, then ventured out.

I stopped as soon as I took a step. "Tiana?" I wasn't sure if I could believe my eyes. The most gorgeous beaded-haired hippie I'd ever seen was standing there, tears running down her model-perfect cheeks.

"Charlie!"

We threw our arms around each other and hugged so long that we got into awkward territory. But I couldn't seem to let go. When we finally did, we both started talking at once.

"I'm so—"

"—I just—"

"You go."

"No, you."

"Seriously, you're the one crying. What happened? You okay?"

Tiana leaned against the wall as if she needed propping up. "I literally just got here. My mom's waiting outside."

"Was your trip awful?"

"Oh—no . . . You thought?"

"That your trip was awful? Yes. You were totally crying!"

"No, my trip was absolutely amazing. I wish I could tell you everything right now!"

"So why—"

"Why am I crying? 'Cause I met someone," she said, tucking a braid behind her ear. Then, "A girl actually."

My mouth dropped open. "You mean . . . you didn't just meet a girl, you *met* a girl?"

Tiana nodded, biting her lip. She always did that when she was trying not to cry. "How awesome is that? Tiana, that's *huge*! I know it's been ages since you've found someone you were really interested in. I'm super happy for you—I mean, happy and also sorry you're so sad."

"I know—kind of a big life step for me. Really clarifying. What can I say? It was the late sixties. It made me realize a few things about myself—things I'd known but hadn't let myself own yet, ya know?"

I grabbed Tiana in a hug. Maybe we were both a little late to the party in figuring out who we wanted to love. "Must've been devastating to have to leave her. Maybe you can go back when we get our time pins one day?"

"I'm planning on it," she said with newfound strength and clarity. "I've never wanted to graduate more in my life."

"But promise me two things. . . ."

"I'm pretty much afraid of your 'things' . . . but, tell me." She stepped back so we could see each other.

"Well, first, that when your mom isn't waiting in the car, we can really talk about how you're feeling 'cause this is a big friggin' deal we're talking about here. 'Love across time' and all that." She nodded. Of course we would dissect everything, at least the stuff we could talk about before our tests were over.

"And second, that I'll always be your best friend even if you leave me for a hot beatnik?"

"Are you kidding? Of course you will."

"Okay, cool. Then I'm good. Except," I added, "it completely sucks that you can't give me every last detail about your trip and how she became part of it."

"Right? It's *killing* me! Let's make a date after we're done—ice cream, my place. There is so much more to tell you. What about you—I didn't even ask about *your* trip!" She grabbed a tissue off the counter and blew her nose.

Crud. I hadn't figured out what I'd say to her about Quinn and him being my Minder. I thought I'd have plenty of time to figure out how to position the whole bizarre evolution. *Oh well.*

"So I can't tell you anything yet, of course," I started, "but . . . I'm back . . . and, funny enough, Quinn's also back . . . and now we're—I guess—like, together." I knew I was blushing, and even in front of Tiana, it was embarrassing. I hadn't met some cool flower child from the sixties. I was in love with the guy who put a garden snake down my shirt when our parents left us with an inattentive babysitter.

"Together together?" Now her mouth was dropping open.

I smiled. "Like, full out, the words have been said, in love with each other, yes!" I held my hands up and shrugged my shoulders in the universal sign of *what're you gonna do*.

Tiana grabbed my hand. "Get out! You *are* talking about Quinn Daniels, the guy who's been a pain your whole life, right? The hot senior with the hair?"

"That very one, yep."

"Damn, Charlie. I leave you alone for a few weeks, and you're in love with Quinn!"

"And you're in love with a girl from the sixties!"

"Right! What are the odds? Maybe there's something to these JY Tests after all. Kind of creepy to think our committees saw all this coming . . . but how could they possibly know I'd meet Cassandra?"

"Ooooo . . . Casandra, huh?" I got a name!

Now that she'd stopped crying, Tiana's face was starting to glow. "Oops. We'll keep that between us for now."

"No worries. Unless there's a bug in this bathroom, we're good." I held out my pinky. "Cone of silence." She hooked hers through mine, our bestie swear ritual, just like Mom and Connie's.

"Cone of silence," she said.

# twenty-three

The next few days crept by, numbingly boring at school during the day. I spent the evenings hanging out with Quinn or Tiana. Quinn was on his feet, wearing the Velcro boots but with no crutches, so we took short walks around the neighborhood to get his strength back up. Luckily, he had plenty of stamina for kissing, because we couldn't get enough of it. After all, we were making up for years of lost time.

I nearly croaked when Quinn's mom walked in on us making out on his bed. She must've called my mother, because Connie said they were imposing an "open bedroom door" policy. "Until you both are on your own, there should be no expectation of privacy when you have a guest in your room," she said, all lawyer-like, topped off with the classic mom look of shame.

We both nodded and mumbled, "Absolutely," and "Understood," and "Sorry." Once she walked away, we laughed and went right back to kissing. Quinn's room was in a distant corner of their ridiculously large house. Besides, Connie talked a good game, but she loved us both to pieces and loved that we were together even more. She and my mom had been pushing UC Berkeley on us since we were kids, and now they were probably picking out our college dorms—just close enough to keep us together but not too close for their comfort.

Sometimes Quinn and I went outside by the pool in the evening breeze. We'd push two lounge chairs together and hold hands while we lay on our backs and looked at the stars. We'd talk about the *Titanic*, revisiting the details, like the carved wood of the grand staircase, the buttery smoothness of the food we ate, or dancing with our friends in third class, the smell of beer, and the sounds of laughter all around us. What we didn't talk about was the end of the trip—how he got hurt and so many people died a senseless death. Those harsh realities were tucked away in boxes in each of our minds. Unlike the crate we'd stolen the *Rubáiyát* from, we didn't have the tools to open these boxes, at least not often. They contained too much sadness to deal with.

Years after the *Titanic*, newspapers told stories of post-traumatic stress disorder among survivors. Some of them, like Quartermaster Robert Hichens—the one who famously fought with Maggie about turning around their lifeboat to rescue others from the water—had rough lives after the sinking.

Mr. Hichens, for example, lost his wife, became a heavy drinker, and went to jail for shooting a man. He was diagnosed with a nervous condition—what we now know as PTSD—and his sailing career was ruined, the highlight being a stint as the third mate on a World War II cargo ship that took coal to Africa.

Safely on the patio in Malibu, I'd glanced from the stars to Quinn, the warm Santa Ana winds moving across us. I'd sent up a wish that we'd make it through relatively unscathed. Maybe the fact that we knew exactly what would happen—and the whole time thought we would avoid drowning or freezing to death—somehow lessened the impact. Maybe the fact that we'd saved our friends would help us heal. My head hurt thinking about it, and I suspected my looming oral report wasn't doing my psyche any favors.

Finally, the day of my report was revealed.

"So good to see you, Charlie," Ms. Featherwell said when she pulled me out of my oh-so-exhilarating two-person class. "I wanted to let you know that your oral report is scheduled for this Friday at 10:30 a.m."

"Yes, ma'am," I said, my stomach turning flips. "What should I prepare?" Or, not prepare . . . *Why do a bunch of extra work when I'm clearly going to fail for messing with the time stream? I'd rather spend my time with Quinn.*

"No preparation is needed for the oral report. The panel will ask questions, and you simply must answer them honestly and completely. If you want to anticipate the questions, you can certainly take note of the points you'd like to bring out, but that's not necessary."

I nodded.

"Charlie, since I'm on your panel, I've read your written report."

"You have?" I didn't know what else to say. It was crap.

"Yes. I'm sure you know that you didn't quite complete your paper. You failed to include what you learned, which is the whole point of the Junior Year Test."

*There's that f-word, "fail." I'd better get used to it.* "Yes, ma'am," I said. *What did I learn? I learned that my school sent teenagers—or at least me and Quinn—into a tragedy we'd live with the rest of our lives.*

"So I suggest you think about those before Friday."

"Okay."

"And Charlie?"

"Yes?"

"I realize that your assignment was the most difficult task you've ever faced. You didn't choose it, but you have to use it, instead of it using you. Take what you experienced and let it fuel you." Her voice dropped to a whisper. "Think about the *Titanic* in terms of what it's given you—not what it took away." She put her hand on my shoulder and gave me a reassuring smile. "See you Friday," she said.

I watched the woman who'd been everywhere and every-when walk down the hall, her heels clicking on the marble floor, until she turned the corner out of sight.

~

I wanted to tell Quinn about my oral report, but I wasn't supposed to talk about it and he hadn't said anything about his. So, when he showed up in the Jeep that Friday morning for his first day back at school, I didn't mention my test. Instead, I gave him the first kiss of many I planned to give or get that day.

Even though we saw each other almost every night, we had an official date planned for Saturday night, and I was trying to stay focused on that. No matter how bad my report was, or where I might be forced to go for my repeat Junior Year Test, I'd soon be sitting at a dimly lit restaurant, staring into Quinn's baby blues.

Since his foot wasn't healed yet, I drove Quinn's Wrangler to school while he kicked back in the passenger seat. R&B blared from UCLA's station, and we didn't say much. Even my little brother was quiet in the back. Quinn's arm draped lazily over my legs, his hand palm up as if it were waiting for my hand. The sound of the windshield wipers beat in time to the music. The blades were so rarely used where we lived, and the rain was so light, that they were extra squeaky.

The lonely parking lot had a few more cars in it each morning as some juniors and seniors returned from their tests. Thanks to the rain that day, no one was hanging out to greet Quinn, the shining star of the parking lot crowd. No one was there to see us together for real, Quinn's arm around my waist. Surprisingly, I was disappointed.

As we entered the foyer just beyond the entrance doors, Quinn paused.

"Weird to be back here," he said, looking around like he hadn't seen the gothic-library-style stone entry before. "I kinda don't want to be here." He pulled me in close to his chest.

"I know. It's like we were completely on our own, and now we're back in friggin' high school."

"No one has a clue what we've been through," he added.

"Exactly. And we have no idea what others have dealt with. Except Tiana—I don't know much, but I think she had a wonderful time."

"I'm glad for her," Quinn said. "At least you and I had each other."

"We did. And I wouldn't trade that."

"Me neither."

"You sure?" I asked, clasping my hands behind his neck.

"Oh, I'm sure." He bent down to kiss me, first kissing my nose and both cheeks before finally brushing a warm kiss across my lips. "No matter what."

"Quinn?" I murmured.

"Hmm?"

"I'm not going to let you fail your test."

He put his forehead against mine. "If I fail, it's not on you, Charlie. Tell me you know that."

"I can't." If he failed, it was all my fault. I couldn't let that happen.

Quinn frowned and said, "You know you're still the most stubborn human being on the planet."

"I'm starting to realize you might be right," I breathed.

"Finally. And for the record," he said, pulling back to look me in the eyes, "I'm always right."

I rolled my eyes. "If you're always right, then I'm more right."

"Oh yeah? Then I'm the most right." Suddenly, we were our ten-year-old selves again.

"I'm the most, most right." I held the lapels of his school blazer.

Quinn laughed. "We'll take this up later, Charlie Chicken. I'm gonna be late."

We kissed again and hurried off in opposite directions.

~

I left class at 10:15 to walk to the classroom where the panel of robes would be waiting to conduct my oral report, which I feared would be more like an inquisition. I'd been anxious, not so much about the outcome, since it was a foregone conclusion, but about the questions.

I was worried they'd rip the lid off the secured box in my brain, and if they did, I couldn't be sure how I'd react. I told myself to stay calm, then kept repeating over and over in my head, *Don't cuss anybody out. Don't cuss anybody out.*

And so on. If I could manage that, at least my chances of being expelled were low.

I paced back and forth in front of the door, wringing my hands and stretching like I was about to run a track meet. I went through scenarios in my mind, but there was no way to wiggle out of what I'd done. There were too many written eyewitness accounts of a girl trying to avert the disaster. My half-hearted written report omitted a lot, but the school would know. Even if I hadn't used my real name on the ship—they'd know.

At 10:30 sharp, Ms. Featherwell opened the door, waving me in with her mouth set in a straight line, like an usher at a funeral home. She was wearing a black robe. It briefly crossed my mind that the school could've ditched the robes a century ago or at least picked a happier color, like yellow or blue.

I stepped across the threshold to see the panel and a familiar wooden chair in front.

What I didn't expect to see was another chair off to the side. . . .

Quinn was there.

He sat bent over, his arms on his thighs, as if he were recuperating from a run. His head hung down until he heard me come in. Then he looked up at me, our eyes locking. He telegraphed *sorry* with a pained look on his face. He was pale.

I'd mentally prepared for the robes, but I wasn't prepared for Quinn. Why didn't he tell me or at least give me a hint? I knew he couldn't, but I didn't want to be humiliated with Quinn as a bystander while I was trying to protect him.

Was he there to tell the robes if I was being honest? Were they going to play us off each other? If so, would he crack and tell the truth about his involvement?

I only looked away from Quinn when I sat down and swept my eyes across the row of five robes. It looked more or less like the same group who'd sent me off to the *Titanic* in the first place. Their faces weren't unkind, but their actions had been, sending a seventeen-year-old to the *Titanic*. I focused on the feel of my feet on the floor, of my butt on the hard chair. I took a silent, long inhale and counted to seven, then released it to calm myself.

In place of anxiety, butterflies, and a slightly upset stomach, what I found in that calming moment was a burgeoning confidence, rising out of anger and destruction like a phoenix from the ashes. If I could save more than one hundred people from dying on a sinking ship, I could handle this group of "experts" hiding behind the authority of their positions. If I could jump into the ice-cold water to save Quinn, I could do it again here and make a helluva case for my own actions. I didn't save him there to watch him drown here. *Bring it.* I sat straight and faced forward.

The head robe was a man with a dark mustache. He began.

"Miss Landers, welcome back." He introduced the group again.

I didn't move.

"Let's establish a few rules of the road for this meeting. This panel will ask you a series of questions. You may also make remarks at the end if you wish. We'll be here for as long as we need to be."

I didn't move.

"As you can see, your Minder, Quinn Daniels, is in the room with us today. Finally, each member of this panel has reviewed your file, which includes your written report. We also have a dossier of press reports following the sinking of the *Titanic*. We discovered a number of mentions of you in those reports, and they match your written report. Do you have any questions for us before we get started?"

I wanted to scream, *Of course I do! Why would you people send me to the Titanic in the first place?* Instead, I shook my head.

"Very well. Then let's begin."

The female robe on the end sat up straighter. "Charlie, why do you think you were sent to experience the *Titanic*?"

I cleared my throat. "I don't know."

She glanced down the table at the head robe. "Can you guess, then?" she asked.

I shifted in my chair. "Well, first of all," I started, unseen and unspoken anger rising quickly to the surface, "I think it was cruel to send me—to send us"—I motioned to Quinn —"to a place where so many people died a terrible and unnecessary death. You should all be ashamed of yourselves for your part in this, and, worse, for telling me to go there and do nothing to change it, to sit by, knowing the people on that ship were doomed. I think you should all be fired and your time pins taken away, honestly." I should have added *don't suggest they be fired* to my *don't cuss them out* mantra. Not an auspicious start.

The panel took my accusations pretty calmly. Perhaps they'd gotten them before. The same robe continued. "You didn't follow the rules, though, did you?"

"Nope. Actually, that's not true. I did for a few hours. But I decided that fifteen hundred lives were more important than some set of high school rules in the twenty-first century."

"But the rules aren't high school rules. They're the rules for all licensed time travelers. Don't you think there are good reasons for those rules?"

"Maybe in some cases, but not for the *Titanic*."

"How successful was your attempt to subvert history?" asked another.

"You say 'subvert' like what I did was some awful thing. I tried to change history, not subvert it," I said.

"And how did that go—changing history?"

"Not great. It was like nothing I did really mattered. The story was written, and all I could do was push around the edges of it. It's like history is almost human."

"Human?"

"Well, like, alive. Like it has a will of its own."

"Could it be like the wind?"

I thought for a second. "I suppose. Like a wind blowing so hard you're swept along with it no matter how hard you try to go a different way."

"So 'the winds of time' might mean something."

It was a statement, not a question, but I answered anyway. "I guess it's as good of a description as any. But what I was able to do was save my friends."

"Only your friends?"

"And about a hundred and twenty other people. That's not insignificant."

"No, no it's not. And how do you feel about having saved that many people?"

*This guy must be a shrink. How do I feel? I feel like ten times that many died.*

I answered,"I wanted to save more. But saving 127 human beings is the most significant thing I've ever done. I'm proud of it. That's 127 who lived to see their loved ones again. Who watched their children grow up. It mattered."

Another robe. "But I thought you didn't think too highly of the human race?"

"I don't. It's the human race that created the *Titanic* in the first place. It's the arrogance of men that caused the tragedy, not the iceberg. But I realize now that the human race I dislike so much is made up of more than eight billion stories. That's more than eight billion people with dreams, with friends, with families. People who have bodies that will freeze in twenty-eight-degree water in fifteen minutes. I wasn't going to let a single one die if I could help it."

"Including Mr. Daniels?"

Quinn looked up as if he'd been asleep.

"Especially Mr. Daniels," I said, looking at him. "I've known him my entire life. He's my family."

"So he helped you in your quest to save the ship?"

I glanced over at him again, then faced the panel, confident in what I was about to say. "Not at all. He was against it when he figured out what I was doing—well, when I made a spectacle of myself confronting the captain."

"You're sure of that."

"Totally sure, yes." I nodded.

Ms. Featherwell spoke up. "Charlie, you should know that Quinn was required to give his report this morning before yours. He confessed to us that he helped you."

I looked from her to Quinn.

Quinn sat up straight. "I couldn't let you lie for me, Charlie. Trying to save the ship was the right thing to do—"

"Mr. Daniels," said the main robe, "I'll remind you that you are not to speak during your friend's report unless you are asked a question by this panel."

Quinn went back to looking at this hands. I knew he was being selfless, but I wanted to scream at him. He'd thrown his whole life away just to spare me from lying. Not an equal trade-off!

Ms. Featherwell spoke up again. "Charlie, would you like to change your statement?"

"What I said—that Quinn was against it from the beginning—is completely true. He tried to stop me. It's just that somewhere along the way, he realized . . . well, he realized what he just said. It was the right thing to do."

"Charlie, could it be possible that you were sent to the *Titanic* to fight the time stream?"

I furrowed my eyebrows and frowned. "So, what . . . you're saying is that the panel thought I might choose to save the *Titanic*?"

Ms. Featherwell looked at me with so much sympathy that I felt tears stinging my eyes. I took a page out of Tiana's book and bit my lip, hard, to stop them. "I'm saying that we hoped you would."

I sat without speaking, replaying that line in my head to make sure I'd heard it right. I glanced at Quinn, meeting his wide eyes, then looked back at Ms. Featherwell. "So you sent me into a hopeless situation with strict instructions not to change it—and a Minder who had the same instructions—actually hoping I would break the rules?" *These people must be insane.*

"I'm saying the true test of a person's character is how they balance right and wrong in the face of rules that lead to human tragedy. Imagine Germany before World War II. How many good people in that country followed the rules while Hitler rose to power? He didn't kill fifteen hundred people. He killed millions."

After a few moments of silence, the idea soaking into my pores, another panel member spoke up. "Miss Landers, you said Mr. Daniels is your family, correct?"

I nodded.

"Were you not worried about him failing his Senior Year Test because of your actions? Failing out of Windline?"

"I was—I am. And I felt . . . no, I feel terrible about it. But I couldn't let the ship sink, and let all those people die, just because one guy would lose the chance for a time pin, no matter how special he is. Thankfully, Quinn agreed with my decision eventually. He nearly died saving a boat full of people."

"Tell us about that."

"We'd been on the deck trying to find my friend's brother. When we found him, we went to locate the lifeboat carrying his sister, little brother, my doctor friend, and a newborn baby. The lifeboat was tipping over while it was being lowered. Something was wrong with the pulleys, or the rope was stuck or something. Quinn jumped on the rope to help level the lifeboat. Something flew off the ship and hit him in the head. He was knocked out and fell into the water—unconscious in that ice-cold water."

"And what did you do?"

"I jumped in after him."

"What happened then?"

"I swam over to him," I said, a chill spreading through my body. "His heart was beating, but he'd stopped breathing. I resuscitated him."

"You did all that in freezing water?"

"Yes. It was hard, but I'm a good swimmer. And I was motivated. He would've died there."

"And that's how you both got hypothermia." Again, a statement, not a question.

"Yes, didn't Quinn tell you?"

"He didn't quite tell us the whole story, I'm afraid."

Quinn had been watching me but started looking at his hands again.

"He was a hero," I added.

"Sounds like you were, too," the robe said.

"I just did what anybody would've. Plus I always knew I could come home."

"Do you really believe that, or are you minimizing your accomplishments?"

Heat rose to my cheeks. "Uh—maybe." *The perfect non-answer*, I thought.

Ms. Featherwell spoke again. "Charlie, did you learn that you could do extraordinary things—that in fact the hesitant girl who didn't even care about time travel or people could go down in history as the hero of the *Titanic*, in more ways than one?"

Quinn's mom, the lawyer, would've said that Ms. Featherwell was leading the witness. I wondered if she was pressing levers, like Oz behind the curtain, guiding me to a preordained conclusion. *Is free will even a thing?*

"I've never thought of myself as a hero," I answered, crossing and uncrossing my legs, "but I guess I tried to do something that could be considered heroic. But so did Rosalee, who stayed in third class to help a passenger give birth, even though I'd told her the *Titanic* would sink. Rima's brother, Arash, was a hero—he jumped on the ropes, too. The wireless operators were heroes. They kept trying to get help until the very end. And the band—they played on the deck without even trying to save themselves. I think anyone can be a hero."

I paused to collect my thoughts. Then I added, "I guess it's just a matter of giving a damn and putting the well-being of others ahead of your own."

"So if I were to offer you a pill," said the head robe, "and that pill would turn off your ability to time travel forever, would you take it now?"

I thought about visiting Rosalee again or going with Tiana to meet her Cassandra in the 1960s. I thought of all the horrific events time travelers might not be able to stop but could improve around the edges. Then I looked at Quinn.

"No, I wouldn't."

"So you see the value in time travel now?"

"In some ways," I answered, "I was kind of right before when I said there was no point in time travel. The time stream is tougher to impact than I ever thought. But now I know the past holds possibilities just like the future does. I do think the *Titanic* taught me that. So, no. I wouldn't take your pill. I want my time pin." I hadn't known how much until that moment.

The members of the panel nodded and fell silent. Then the head robe asked, "Is there anything else you'd like to share before we deliberate, Miss Landers?"

"Only that Quinn deserves to pass. If someone should fail, it's me. Please let him graduate. He really did try to stop me at first, and I dragged him into my plan anyway."

"Is that all?"

"And . . . I think I understand better now why you sent us to the *Titanic*," I added as the realization was coming together in my head. I hated to admit it, but it was true.

Ms. Featherwell nodded. "Thank you, Charlie. Remember what I said to you the other day?"

"That we have to take the good with us from the *Titanic*," I said, echoing her words from before.

"What will you take with you?"

I couldn't list all the good—my friends, my love for Quinn, my courage. The realization that changing just one thing might never be enough to alter the past or possibly even the future, which meant there was no reason to beat yourself up for every little thing. Life was a whole fabric, not just a thread.

"A lot," I managed to say as tears welled up in my eyes. This time, I couldn't stop them. The box in my brain had been opened, and memories were spilling over and out, cascading through my consciousness.

"You know," I said, almost to myself as I wiped my face with the sleeve of my blazer, "when I was in the water right before Quinn went home, I saw the *Titanic*'s lights go out and I looked up at the stars. They were so bright that night. They're the gravestones for the people who died there. But maybe all the people who lived, like Rosalee Dunner and Maggie Brown, were meant to be the *Titanic*'s legacy. Now Quinn and I are the ship's only living survivors. We have to carry it on."

"And what does that look like for you, Charlie?" Ms. Featherwell asked softly.

"I don't know. But I'll spend a lifetime figuring it out."

"Same here," Quinn said, standing up and closing the distance between us in a few quick strides. I stood to meet him, and we threw our arms around each other, clinging as I cried, ignoring the robes.

# twenty-four

The sand crunched under my neoprene boots as I shifted my weight back and forth, just inches from where the water could reach me. A black wet suit was pulled up to my waist, the top half hanging down over my hips to my knees. I wore a bikini top, its bright yellow standing out against a gray late afternoon, like the only pop of color in a black-and-white photo. My hair blew in the salty wind and fell heavy on my back.

Just two days ago, the robes had given both me and Quinn passing grades, along with the slap-on-the-wrist punishment of cataloging items in the archives after school for the rest of the semester. Another huge surprise—the robes had also asked us to join an elite group of upper-level students. We'd train to become Time Guardians, the Windline leadership group that policed the time stream and basically managed time travel with graduates of the other two schools. I had a slight case of whiplash. I'd been sure I'd failed and that Quinn's future was ruined. Now, not only would Quinn graduate, but the future and the past would be his for the taking.

When the robes had offered their unexpected invitation, apparently a coveted one, I hadn't known how to answer.

After all, I'd known some kind of SWAT team existed, but I had no idea the elite training for it started at Windline. I hadn't given them an answer. Quinn and I would both take the weekend to think it through, to talk with each other and our parents.

Neither of us had mentioned Windline drama at dinner during our big Saturday-night date. Since our evenings together on the *Titanic* didn't really count, the date was technically our first one, and we'd wanted it to be special in that it would just be . . . normal. No Guggenheims. No Louis XV furniture or pickled herring. No kisses on Quinn's bed with the laptop open.

Quinn and I had eaten way too much bread and pasta, talked way too much about the fact that we were on a *real* date, and stayed out way too late. We'd clinked glasses to celebrate the fact that Quinn's body was healing, with his fingers, toes, and brain all intact. He wouldn't suffer any lasting effects, except maybe a little bit of numbness along the top of one of his feet. He still had stitches in his head, but his hair had grown enough to hide them.

We'd lingered at the table, gazing out at the ocean view from the restaurant on the outskirts of Laguna Beach. Then we'd drifted down the Pacific Coast Highway to find ice cream cones and browse through the art galleries. Over my protests, Quinn had bought me a cheap necklace on a leather cord from a brightly lit, tacky tourist shop.

The necklace had white beads that spelled *I LUV CALI.* He'd tied it around my neck, then took an off-angle selfie cheek to cheek with me in my black sundress, pointing at the necklace. I'd rolled my eyes, but what his gift said was true—I did love California. I could love other places, too, after the *Titanic*. My world felt bigger.

Underneath it all, necklace-buying Quinn was clearly still a big dork of the he's-so-hot-no-one-notices, everyone-loves-him variety. But the *Titanic* had changed him, too. He was deeper—wiser beneath his occasional goofiness, maybe. And more of a gentleman. Even with his sore ankle, he'd picked me up and carried me the short distance from Main Beach's wood plank walkway over the sand to the shore. I guess hanging out with all those stuffy, well-bred, first-class men did him some good after all.

Quinn had driven me home at the end of our date, a long ride with the coastal breeze coming through the cracked windows. We'd held hands, not feeling the need to say anything.

When we'd pulled up to my house, he'd opened the passenger-side door to help me out of the Jeep. He'd actually escorted me up the walkway to my front door, which was kind of weird since we practically lived at each other's houses. We'd stood under the warm glow cast by the porch light, and he'd looked down at me, his fingers weaving into my hair.

I'd put my arms around him. "I had a lovely time this evening, Mr. Daniels. Thank you for a most enjoyable outing," I'd said, reverting back to my best stilted 1912.

"As did I, Miss Landers. I hope there will be many more to come." He'd kissed me then, a proper feel-it-down-to-your-toes goodnight kiss that reminded me of our first kiss on the *Titanic*.

~

On the Sunday afternoon after our big date, I stood on the beach alone, visiting my old friend the Pacific Ocean. My surfboard was standing in the sand beside me, tethered to my ankle and ready to hit the waves. But I couldn't bring myself to get in the water or even finish putting on my wet suit. Even though the Pacific had always been my happy place, it was related to the Atlantic after all—two powerful daughters of Mother Nature. They met at the tip of South America, swapping bits of each other at the edges in a watery embrace.

The *Titanic* had been a man-made wonder, a seventeen-story-tall marvel of metal and wood and hard work. Nonetheless, it had been a small pebble in a big ocean, just as the *Titanic*'s tragedy was a blip in the span of time. But I'd come to realize the importance of small pebbles. The Pacific might've carried a piece of her sister, the Atlantic, all the way to the shallow water in front of me. If so, when I stepped into the Pacific, I might feel the *Titanic* in my bones. I might be transported back to that night when screams pierced the veil of the dark. I might hear the musical notes of the band in the movement of the water contributed to the Pacific by her wicked sister. I'd come to realize that all things are connected in nature, space, and most definitely, time.

The afternoon crept into early evening, the lights of the houses around the curve of the shoreline coming on, and still, I stayed on the beach. I looked at the horizon, where the water appeared to end and the last muted rays of the sun were lingering. I used to see endless possibilities in that horizon, and honestly, I still did. But now I would always think of the *Titanic* just past it, beyond my reach. I'd think of Rima and Arash, Rosalee, Maggie, Russ, Harold, Mr. Andrews, and even the captain. Of course I'd think of Quinn, the dashing "transportation mogul" who wore 1912 like an old, familiar sweater.

Out of the corner of my eye, I caught movement down the beach and turned to see Quinn walking my way. I knew it was him. I'd recognize the shape of him anywhere.

"Hey," he said as he got closer.

"Hey, yourself," I replied. "How'd you know I was here?"

"I have my ways," he said, raking his hand through his hair.

I smiled. "You mean Connie called my mom."

"Exactly." He laughed. "Like our own spy network. So whatcha doin'? Getting a little late for surfing, don't you think?" He slipped his arm around me, the warmth of his hand pleasant on the cool, bare skin above my waist.

I looked back out at the ocean. "I'm tryin' to get in the water, but I can't seem to do it."

We stood quietly together for a moment. Then he said, "Because of the *Titanic*. I get it."

"Yeah. I used to think of the ocean as so alive," I said. "Now it's a graveyard."

"Maybe it's both."

More silence between us, the gentle lapping of the waves the only sound.

"What if we went back—to say goodbye?" Quinn said.

"That would be nice," I said, "but we can't go back."

"Sure we can." Quinn reached into his pocket, pulling out his family's time pin and holding it in front of us.

I looked from the time pin to Quinn's face.

"Do you trust me?" he asked.

"With my life."

"Then come with me."

I leaned down to untether my surfboard, then stood, putting my hand in Quinn's. We held the time pin between us, palm to time pin to palm. In a blink, we were on another beach in broad daylight, the ocean spread wide in front of us. The temperature was cool, a bit of chill in the whipping wind. Gulls cried overhead.

I looked around to get my bearings, noting the rock formations of the rugged coastline that surrounded us. I spotted a few people, barely visible down the beach. "Quinn, where are we?"

"You'll see." He took my hand and pulled me toward some craggy rocks. Steadying each other, we picked our way carefully over them until we stood on a point with a panoramic view of the ocean.

After a few minutes of watching the ocean move in front of us, the *Titanic* came into view in all her glory, her three functioning funnels blowing dark smoke into the air as she slid through the water. She was postcard perfect, with her dark gray lower hull, white upper hull, and black-tipped smokestacks rising high in the air. I sucked in my breath as if I'd been punched in the stomach and clapped my hand over my open mouth.

"We're on the coast outside of Queenstown, in County Cork, Ireland," Quinn said, his hand shading his eyes as he looked out to sea. "The *Titanic* is making her way to open water for the crossing."

"And we're on that ship."

"Yep."

"She's amazing, isn't she?"

"Definitely."

"You're amazing, too," I said to Quinn, not taking my eyes off the *Titanic*, "for bringing me here."

We watched the ship until she was a speck on the horizon and then disappeared altogether. I whispered, "Goodbye, *Titanic*. We'll never forget you."

I wound my way down a worn path between the rocks to the water's edge. Quinn followed. I stood on the sand and wiggled into the top half of my wet suit. I looked at him with a question in my eyes. He couldn't go in the water because of his injuries—not yet, anyway. He stepped toward me and slowly zipped the back of my suit.

"I love you, Quinn," I said. "Thank you for this." Our relationship had started seventeen years earlier, on the day I was born. It just took the *Titanic* to make me realize that the person I wanted had been there all along.

"I love you, too, Charlie. Even if you were a chicken when you were six." He smiled, then kissed me, our lips cool from the wind, but the heat always there between us.

When we separated, I turned to face the monster that was the North Atlantic, the one that had devoured the *Titanic* and so many lives in the early morning hours of April 15, 1912. I breathed in the salty, seaweed smell of the water and walked into the surf, the cold water penetrating my wet suit, shocking my skin, then warming. No beaded dress this time, no *Rubáiyát*, no screams in my ears. And Quinn was safe.

The Atlantic's waves pounded on me, trying to push me back toward the shore, but I moved forward. Soon my feet no longer touched the bottom. I dove under and swam out until my lungs were empty, and I broke the surface again, treading water. I looked up at the sky, and this time it was filled with low, puffy gray clouds against an expanse of muted blue with a hazy yellow sun.

This time I was a different person, shaped by my genes, my parents, my school, my own choices. None of that mattered. I'd done my best and saved my friends, plus more than a hundred others. I was exactly who I wanted to be, with the person I couldn't imagine living without.

The box I'd constructed in my mind to lock away the Junior Year Test—my *Titanic* test—was permanently open, and the memories roamed free, lacing around my veins like ribbons. The ship and its colorful ghosts were part of my history now. They'd go on as part of my future, too, alive in the rhythm of the sea, the blue of Quinn's eyes, the sweet melancholy of a violin . . . and the steady beating of my heart.

⚓

Dear Reader,

I hope you enjoyed Charlie's high-stakes quest as much as I enjoyed writing it and that the *Titanic* lives on in *your* heart, as it does in mine.

While *The Titanic Test: A Love Story* includes many authentic historical details, I should note that since it is a work of fiction, I took the liberty of modifying some of the non-essential facts of the *Titanic*'s maiden voyage. For example, Margaret Brown, later known as the "Unsinkable Molly Brown," boarded the ship at Cherbourg, France, rather than Southampton, England. And where sources differed or were silent on the ship's decks, stairways, boarding procedures, etc., I opted to take the approach most expeditious for the story.

If you would like to learn more about the ship and its passengers, check out the list of resources on my website, annksimpson.com. You can sign up for my email list there too.

Thank you so much for reading, and please stay in touch!

Yours truly,
Ann

P.S. If you enjoyed *The Titanic Test: A Love Story*, please post a review and spread the word.

## Acknowledgments

My thanks to Natalie, Southern, Sandra, James, Chelika, Rachel, and so many others for their support on this journey.

Here's to love, friendship, and many more adventures.

An incurable romantic, Ann K. Simpson was raised with big dreams in the deep South and collected degrees from the University of California, Berkeley (law), the University of Texas at Austin (journalism), and the University of Alabama (Spanish). Her contest-winning fiction has appeared in *Say Good Night to Illiteracy*, *Transformation*, and the *Texas Bar Journal*, and her nonfiction has appeared in various magazines and newspapers. The mother of two currently lives in Washington, DC.

*The Titanic Test: A Love Story* is her debut novel and reflects her deep passion for personal growth, humanity, and—most of all—love.

Find out more at annksimpson.com.

Made in the USA
Columbia, SC
29 November 2024